A RIDDLE IN RUBY

RUBY

THE GREAT UNRAVEL

KENT DAVIS

A RIDDLE IN RUBY

THE GREAT UNRAVEL

BOOK
THREE

GREENWILLOW BOOKS

An Imprint of HarperCollins*Publishers*

A Riddle in Ruby: The Great Unravel
Copyright © 2017 by Kent Davis

The text of this book is set in 11.5-point Sabon MT.
Book design by Sylvie Le Floc'h
Library of Congress Cataloging-in-Publication Data is available.
ISBN 978-0-06-236840-9 (hardcover)
17 18 19 20 21 CG/LSCH 10 9 8 7 6 5 4 3 2 1
First Edition

 Greenwillow Books

To Chris,
the best storyteller I know

To Bobo,
sire of Sleipnirs, grandsire of ottermatons

CHAPTER I

A deep, burning desire for what is Fair.
This is the crucible in which we forge Revolution.
—Thandie Paine, *Simplicity*

Never put your faith in your dreams.

Long months of imprisonment to the most ruthless servants of the crown had taught Ruby Teach to expect little from her fantasies. The Reeve squashed dreams like ailing horseflies.

Sometimes, though, when you least expect it, dreams come true.

Ruby and her companions tumbled out of the cave

like an avalanche of ninepins, skidding to a halt, teetering above the storm-swept valley below. They crouched against the cliff face, lashed by wind and rain. Ahead lay a steep, winding track down the side of the mountain. Above and behind loomed Fort Scoria, prison fortress of the Reeve of England.

"Ruby Teach." Ruby's father helped her to her feet, a glint of mischief in his eye. He pitched his voice over the crashing rain. "Tell me, Daughter. What do we do when the devil himself is coming for us?"

The motto of their ship, the *Thrift*, filled Ruby with a joy she thought she had lost. She grinned so hard she thought her face might crack. "Why, Captain Teach, when Old Scratch is hot on our stern, we run till the devil himself cries, 'Mercy.'"

They lit out down the trail, and the old saying hung in Ruby's mind like a promise of better days.

She hauled herself around a tree to launch down a switchback, her fingers scraping over the bark. Only a few moments ago a brass spike had stuck out of both forefingers. She had *grown* the spikes there, bit by excruciating bit. Ruby still had only the faintest inkling of how to use this power called changing, but the little spikes had been just enough to allow her to pick the lock on the cage in the heart of the fortress and escape—only to find that her crew had finally come to rescue her.

She hoped they could keep up.

Ruby *had* changed, but not just physically. Yes, her reeve-honed balance on the steep path was sure, and her reeve-strengthened feet struck true on the muddy ground; but in her time at Fort Scoria Ruby had stripped her insides down to the core, toiling through torturous training and then blinded and locked in Emmanuel Swedenborg's cage, her blood harvested for his fiendish experiments. She drove her legs ever faster, feet splashing on the muddy path, straining to put distance between her and the delicate tightrope of deception she had walked—bowstring taut—between the Swede and the cunning reeve lord captain, Wisdom Rool.

Her foot caught a root.

She careened forward, struggling for control. The ravine yawned dark and deep below.

A brown hand, calloused and burned from a life of chemystry, shot out of the dark. Ruby grabbed it and was hauled back onto the path with surprising strength. She looked up, way up, and Henry Collins smiled down at her, lit by the cool blue glow of a tinker's lamp. Even more mysteries danced in that face than when last she had seen it.

A flailing windmill of arms and legs skidded up behind them, just avoiding pitching the lot of them over the edge. Even in the light of the tinker's lamp Ruby could see that Cram's pasty complexion had weathered. His jaw, once weak, sat firm under questing eyes. The rat-faced boy had somehow become a wolf. He grinned, chest heaving.

Henry shared the grin for a moment. "Careful, Ruby. No use saving you if we all die smashed upon the rocks." He gave her arm a quick squeeze and then turned and launched himself down the precarious path.

Questions flashed through Ruby's head as she followed. How had her father and friends gotten here? What had they been through on their journey to rescue her? How had they found a way into the fortress? How was she suddenly, impossibly *out* of it? At that the questions dissolved, and joy coursed through her body like surf crashing on the shore because she was gone, she was running, she was free.

They pounded around another switchback, and her father caught her eye in triumph. She looked away, suddenly uncertain. No matter how far she ran, could she outdistance the past? What did Captain Teach see when he looked at her, his eyes welling with pride? The joy of escape? The thrill of victory? Or the terrible things that had happened to her? The terrible things she had done?

She tried to let the rain wash away the two friends she had betrayed, but the fates of Evram, her fellow reeve in training, and Sleipnir, his magnificent automaton horse, clung to her like melted tar. Both destroyed. Trying to help her. She kept her eyes on the path. She reached back to touch her pack, to reassure herself that the artifice otter was still there. Evram had made it out of the remains of Sleipnir; she could not contemplate losing it.

Athena Boyle waited for them at the bottom of the

trail, her dark braid hanging somehow looser than when Ruby had last seen her. Where Cram's skin had leathered, hers had reddened, freckles dancing across her aristocratic nose. Fear and worry warred across the other girl's features for a moment, but then the old mask of distant amusement slammed down over all of it. "Here we are again, Ruby Teach. Three breaths ahead of peril." She flourished a hand to the two girls waiting beside her, one long and dark, the other fierce and fair. "Allow me to introduce Vera Medina"—the tall girl nodded gravely—"she is the smart one, and Alaia Calderon"—the shorter girl looked Ruby up and down and sniffed—"she is the mean one."

Alaia punched Athena in the shoulder. To Ruby's shock, Athena grinned. "I hope you're worth it, Ruby Teach," said Alaia.

A year ago Ruby would have rolled her eyes and risen to the bait. Instead she just said, "I hope so, too."

Athena lifted an eyebrow. "Well then. Quick and silent. Our companions await through the trees. Unless you wish to return to your jailors' stony embrace, we must fly!"

As if on cue, a horn rang from the heights above.

They tore into the trees like a litter of spooked rabbits.

It was a mad dash: through brush, around tree trunks, and once through a crowd of grouse. Through it all Alaia flitted back and forth like an angry finch, keeping them moving, pointing the way ahead, her boots making no sound save the softest of rustles, scanning the trees behind, and distractedly flipping a little pipe through her fingers.

"You going to whistle the Reeve away for us?" Ruby panted.

Alaia ignored the question. "Come! Come! We must hurry, you laggards!"

The rest of the pack spread out through the trees, fast as they could but quiet as they might. It was something from a dream. They flew through fern-dappled mists, racing into the unknown.

Behind them, the forest sounded . . . quiet. Scared. Ruby's mouth was a salt bed, her forehead an anvil. She pumped her legs harder though, the months of reeve training serving her well.

Some were not so hearty.

Bit by bit, thorn brake by hillside, Cram lagged behind.

Cram's bag had only gotten larger since Ruby had last seen it; he hauled it as good as he could, but the thing was straining at the seams. It kept knocking and catching on logs and rocks and roots. A sharp branch tore into it, hauling him to a stop. He turned to unhook it.

Alaia whirled about in disbelief. "Leave it! We have no time."

"I ain't leaving it! It's Heroes' Gear!"

Ruby knelt to help him, but they lost precious moments pulling it loose. She glanced down at the bag with a ghost of a smile. "At least some things haven't changed."

Cram nodded, wheezing.

The two of them and Alaia burst last out of the forest into a long clearing before a deep gorge. The sun rose through rain clouds across the canyon, lighting up the longest, ricketiest, skinniest rope bridge Ruby had ever seen. On the other side, a group of men and women crouched, hazy in the distance.

Henry, Athena, and Ruby's father were mid crossing, bobbing up and down on the wobbly cables.

Out of the trees behind Ruby flew a woman, her uniform blacks flapping in mid leap, red hair streaming, cool rage lighting her face.

It was doom that flew toward them.

"Edwina Corson," Ruby whispered. Ward Corson was an avalanche in human form, and Ruby's old teacher was about to smash down upon them. They were truly done and dusted.

Alaia cursed and raised the pipe to her lips. Her cheeks bulged. There was a little *pfft*, like a robin taking off from a branch.

The reeve twisted in midair; but the dart hit her in the neck, and she flew off course, slamming into the ground in a tangle of arms and legs only feet from the three of them. A palsy gripped her. She quivered and shook like a dying fish. She tried to pull the dart out, but her arm would not stop shaking. "Poi . . . son." She fought the word out through gritted teeth.

Ruby turned to Alaia. The girl winked. "This is not

the first time we have fought reeves. She will not die. Hurry. More will be coming."

And indeed, when Ruby looked over her shoulder, a wave of gray and black tunics rolled out of the woods up the slope, racing toward them.

She looked down at the quivering red-haired woman. "Apologies, Ward Corson," she said. "I won't be able to make assembly this morning."

The edge of the gorge lay before them. Her belly jumped up into her gullet. Far below, body breakingly, eye poppingly far below, lay a roiling river, the shores on both sides studded with rocks.

In front of Ruby, Cram edged forward, muttering under his breath, "There ain't no tonic like perilous danger. There ain't no tonic like perilous danger . . ."

Alaia brought up the rear.

Cram shuffled forward quickly, but not quickly enough, alternating death grips along the guide ropes. The "walls" of the bridge were nothing but a cat's cradle of frayed cord holding up a floor of two thick parallel cables, each about as wide as Ruby's waist. The very long, very scary structure bowed across the river like an upside-down rainbow to the far side of the gorge. The white water rushed hungrily below, daring her to fall. Behind her Alaia muttered, "Faster, faster," like some kind of prayer. And Cram did go faster. They were at the bottom of the curve now, halfway across. The company came into focus as they scrambled closer: a cluster of hunters, hard, lean women and men poised on the rocks, bristling with weapons and steely of eye. Ruby could see their faces more clearly now, a mix of tension and anticipation. Athena stood among them, but she was pointing back across the gorge, behind them. Ruby risked a look back, and her blood went cold.

One of the fastest reeves, a lanky girl in gray with curly brown hair, had made it to the bridge and was running toward them at an impossible speed, her hands not even holding on to the guide ropes. Ruby's pulse skipped a beat. Avid Wake.

Alaia's blowpipe hissed again, but whether it was too far or Avid was just more prepared for it, the reeve cadet threw herself to the side, and the dart sailed past. The bridge wobbled back and forth now, but the girl righted herself and kept coming. "Run, run!" Alaia waved them forward. "If she gets to us, we are lost!"

A clunk echoed out across the bridge, followed by several more.

Axes flashing, four burly hunters were chopping at the ropes.

Cram ran, a shuffling, jerking, wobbling run, holding on to the guide ropes as much as he dared, but he ran. Ruby scrambled after him, and she forced her eyes forward. No use watching Avid gain on them. The bridge shuddered with every axe blow, and the wobbling got worse and worse. Would they cut it with the three of them still on the bridge, even Alaia, who was one of their own? Cram's breath was reduced to a tortured whistle; but he kept scuttling, and the back of Ruby's neck tingled with expectation. It might have been half a minute, but it felt like the longest moment of her life.

When they clambered onto stone on the other side, Ruby had never been so happy to bang her shins on a rock. The three of them threw themselves down in relief onto the solid ground.

"Now, now!" someone yelled. The axes doubled in speed, raining down upon the ropes. And then all at once, with a *pock pock pock pock* like distant gunfire, they broke.

The bridge lurched and snapped like a flinching snake, cords trailing into the mist like spiderwebs. Avid was halfway across.

She fell.

Ruby's heart leapt into her mouth.

Then, somehow, Avid did something with her feet in midair and, by Providence, caught herself up in the ropes. She hung, bum over head, as the bridge tumbled away into the gorge. No one spoke.

Across the gorge the full weight of the bridge hit the remaining supports, and they groaned in protest. Somehow, Avid twisted her body *just so* to get the mass of cables between her and the rock face before the bridge slammed into it. She hung there, stunned, but still moving.

Against her will, in spite of the pain and desperation

of the past months, Ruby's heart swelled with pride. Her rival was a truly gifted reeve.

A crossbowman took aim at Avid, but Ruby lunged, quick as lightning, jostling the man's elbow into the stock. The bolt sailed to the right, skittering off the rocks. The man turned to her, enraged. "Stupid girl! If one of them gets to us, just one, who knows what evil might come to pass?"

"*I* know what evil might come to pass. Believe me." Ruby rode the sudden wave of her own anger to move nose to nose with him. "And that reeve, hanging by her ankles on the other side of a by-Science *canyon*, is no immediate threat to you."

"Listen to the girl, Nic." A wolf of a woman flowed up, the silver streak in her hair matted with wet and mud. "We are clear. No need to poke the jaguar any further."

The hunter blew out a long breath and then lowered the weapon. "Yes, Captain."

The woman inclined her head to Ruby. "I am Petra alla Ferra. These"—her wave took in the pack of hunters— "are my people, Los Jabalís. You have us to thank for your rescue. I hope you will not interfere any further with their attempts to keep you safe." Her stare nailed Ruby to the rock underneath her.

Before Ruby could respond, Petra alla Ferra turned away. She ran her eyes over her company, and a tense silence fell on the lip of the gorge.

Then, with a huge grin, she thrust her hands in the air.

The hunters exploded with hoots and hollers into what Ruby could only describe as a carnival, with the Jabalís swapping jokes and pounding one another on the back. From somewhere instruments were produced, and an impromptu jug band sprang up.

She looked about in disbelief. "Cram, what is happening?"

Head cocked like a puzzled terrier, he watched the cold killers kicking up their heels in a jig for a moment. "The Jabalís are, well—hmm. You see—"

Petra alla Ferra appeared behind him. "We are triumphant, young Sam."

"Cram."

"Yes. We are triumphant, and we celebrate our victories. This is a victory, yes?" She ruffed his hair.

"But we need to go," Ruby said. "We need to keep running. If they catch us, we all will die."

The woman lifted an eyebrow. "All the more reason to celebrate now, is it not? Even if only for a few moments." She chuckled. "As you so eloquently pointed out, the reeves are on the other side of a canyon so wide not even their finest could leap across. It will take them days to find another way around. By then we will be gone. So now? We celebrate. We have a reputation to uphold. The world needs to *know* what hearty band of mercenaries came right into the den of the reeves and tweaked their noses. And they need to know that in the face of fear, when others cower, we laugh." The smile disappeared. "Have no fear, Ruby Teach. I will protect you and yours. After all, you are very, very valuable to me." She snagged a wineskin from a passing hunter and was gone.

Ruby looked at Cram.

He shrugged.

The spectacle of the moment was Avid, and wagers

began flying fast and furious over whether she would get back to the top of the bridge. The growing crowd of reeves on the other edge began to organize to get down to her, but in the end she did not really need the help. Hanging ipsy-dipsy, she swung herself back and forth with her arms in ever-wider swings. Then, at the top of a swing—and Ruby had to give her credit—the girl hinged at her belly and then grabbed on with her hands above her feet. The mercenaries cheered good-naturedly. Cram whistled low.

Ruby and Cram crouched in the rain on a rock like two grasshoppers, and Captain Teach, Athena, and Henry drifted over until they all were watching the show. Seeing Avid—her bully, her rival, her companion, on the brink of attacking them, then in grave danger, and then escaping in such brilliant style . . . it stretched Ruby's insides. She didn't know whether she was sad, or glad, or just plain addled. "I know that girl."

Cram looked at her for a bit, perplexed. "She your friend?"

"My friend?" Ruby sighed out a long sigh. "Honestly, Cram? I have no idea."

He cracked a grin. "Well, at least you got us to protect you."

She wiped the rain from her eyes, and she took in her rescuers for a moment. "But who's going to protect *you*?"

Avid had finally reached the top guide rope, and she pulled herself hand over hand back to the crowd of waiting reeves. The press parted in a wave for Wisdom Rool. The reeve lord captain hauled Avid up to the lip of the canyon. The mercenaries gave a rousing cheer, and Avid curtsied in response. She was tall, but the lord captain of the king's Reeve topped her by more than a head, and he seemed twice as wide. Rool clapped Avid on the shoulder with encouragement, and they had a word, after which she nodded. She turned back and gazed across the gorge. Her eyes met Ruby's, and for a breathtaking moment Ruby thought the girl might try a Work to jump across. It was too far. A hundred yards, at least. Even Wisdom Rool couldn't make a jump like that. Could he?

Still, excitement fluttered in Ruby's chest. When the young reeve cadet turned about and made her way back into the crowd, Ruby couldn't help feeling just a bit disappointed. A pang of . . . was it loneliness?—struck her. The Jabalís clustered about them, faintly ridiculous in their strange carnival, and none of them knew what Ruby had gone through in the past year. Nor did her friends. One of the only ones who truly might understand had just disappeared into the press of reeves standing united behind their leader.

The rain hammered down on Wisdom Rool. It was too far across to see the ropy scars that twisted all around his body, but they burned in Ruby's mind's eye as the man lifted his hand to his mouth. "Ahoy, the gorge!" His voice rang out raspy clear over the wind and rushing water.

Petra alla Ferra stepped forward, leaning forward carelessly over the edge, one hand grasping a stump of guide rope. "Ahoy, the Reeve!" she called. Los Jabalís snickered among themselves. Like the crew of the *Thrift* loved Ruby's father, they loved this woman, this woman who had led a band of unruly outlaws against the Reeve and *won*.

"I am Wisdom Rool, lord captain of the king's Reeve! To whom do I have the pleasure of speaking?"

Alla Ferra tucked a stripe of silver hair back behind her ear and hesitated. Ruby sympathized. The smart move here would be to make up a name, a false identity to throw the Reeve off the scent. Buy some time.

"Captain Petra alla Ferra at your service! My stouthearted companions here are Los Jabalís!" Another murmur rose up around Ruby: one part fear but two parts approval. Ruby ground her teeth. Didn't they know they were giving away their advantage? Heedless. Careless.

"A brave company indeed to steal from the house of His Majesty, especially in times like these!" Rool called.

"Tell your friends! We are always looking for work!" Los Jabalís laughed in appreciation. "Besides, this massive gorge between us bolsters my bravery! And I am not certain I understand. What is it we have stolen from you? A bangle? A set of solemn churchman's garb?"

Rool smoothed down his reeve blacks theatrically in response and then pointed at Ruby, sitting exposed on her rock perch. "That girl. She is a prisoner of England, and we would have her back!"

Ruby's head spun like a top. He was putting on a sharp,

a show for the other reeves. He didn't want her back. In fact, Wisdom Rool was the one who had let her go. He had given her a rope to climb down the cliff, for Providence's sake. The lord captain and Ruby had made a deal to steal the notes of the tinker they called the Swede. Ruby had lived up to her part, and Rool had helped her escape to her friends. The rest of the Reeve didn't know that, though. The crowd of black and gray teachers and students loomed behind Rool: a storm waiting to be unleashed.

Petra alla Ferra swung her head about to peer exaggeratedly at Ruby, as if she were some strange bird. She projected relaxation, amusement even. She pointed at Ruby. "This girl, eh?" She held up her hands in an elegant shrug. "Alas, sir. This is not English soil. The bears and wolves are constables here, and it is their law we obey. Besides, even if this"—she tapped her foot on the rock—"were your land, it is currently on the other side of a canyon from you!" At this, Los Jabalís erupted in cheering and jeers. A few of them had gathered some flowers and began tossing them into the gorge like pining lovers. Ruby shook her head. These people were mad. The Reeve would pursue them to the ends of the earth. Ward Corson and Avid were already leading a detachment scaling down the remains of the bridge. Ruby guessed they could cross the river and get up the sheer face of the canyon before nightfall.

Wisdom Rool stood motionless on the other side. He waited until the cheering subsided.

"Very well then! Please remember that I did ask nicely! When next we meet, perhaps it will be within arm's reach!"

Petra alla Ferra laughed. "Come if you will, Sir Wisdom! If you catch me, I will give you a kiss!" She blew him one then and stepped back onto the firm ground, igniting a new round of cheers from the Jabalís.

Wayland Teach was waiting for her. The moment of sun was gone, and the rain had taken up again in earnest. Distant thunder rumbled in the distance. He leaned in and muttered something in the huntress's ear. Alla Ferra's gaze flitted over to Ruby and then back to her father. She nodded once.

Teach walked over to Ruby and said simply, "Come with me."

What was he about? As the hunters burst into action, finally making ready for their escape, her father led her farther into the little clearing on the other side of the bridge. A small woman stood motionless amid the jumble, her features completely hidden in a metal mask. Ruby's friends had followed behind, all their mirth suddenly gone. As one they looked to Ruby's father.

He stared at Ruby, beard dripping in the rain, mouth open as if he were trying to catch the words of a once-remembered song. A kind of fear took her. Her pulse thundered in her ears. Teach offered Ruby his hand, and she took it. He walked her down into the clearing until she stood opposite the woman in the mask.

"Ruby—" said the captain.

She looked up at him, but he said no more.

Petra alla Ferra had followed them. "Only for a moment," she said to Teach, "and then we must be on our way."

He looked at Ruby, then nodded.

Alla Ferra cast her eyes about the clearing at her

people. Her voice cut through the downpour. "Ready your weapons!"

Muskets, axes, bows, and swords flew into hands. Three hunters took positions just behind the woman in the mask, weapons ready. The one in the middle was a huge brute, and the edge of a wicked carving knife lay between the masked woman's shoulder blades.

Ruby scanned the faces of her father and her companions for some hint of information. "What is this?"

No one answered.

What was this grand opera about? Who was this masked woman who struck fear into a company of hardened hunters? Why, in the name of Science, stop their flight from the full might of the Reeve for some sort of overblown mummer's show? Petra alla Ferra drew a chain from around her neck. At the end of the chain was a green metal key. She held it out to Ruby.

"I don't understand," said Ruby. A creeping dread scrabbled up her spine. "I say again, 'What is this?'"

The masked woman had not moved this whole while, hands clasped up under her chin, as if in prayer. Short chains ran down from just below the engraved ears, binding both her wrists in place. The mask itself encased the woman's entire head. Its weight rested on two broad shoulder supports. The face was that of an Athenian statue, classic and grave. The eyes were plugged, and a tiny hole opened at the mouth. Twisting across the features, engraved chemystral demons warred with scaled and winged angels.

The rain pounded down. It coursed around the iron eyebrows, rushing across the sculpted, empty eyes and down the cheeks, spattering on the rocks at the woman's feet.

The wearer of the mask waited, the wrist manacles carved with equations that skittered from the eye. Ruby looked about at the circle of staring faces, witnesses half lit in the rain-swept morning.

The huntress handed her the key. "This is for you to do."

Ruby almost dropped it, slick in the downpour, but caught herself and willed her hand to stop shaking. It wouldn't. Using both hands, Ruby managed to get the key into the keyhole, just below the right ear of the mask.

She turned it.

Click.

A small handle popped out of the mask at the right temple, and Ruby pulled it across, the metal face opening like a door on hidden hinges. Time slowed as the pieces of the puzzle fell into place. A woman who could terrify an entire clearing of hard cases. The deep concern for Ruby writ large on everyone's faces. The way the woman stood, like a mirror to Ruby's own body. It could be only one person. Ruby put her hands down at her sides, clenched tight, and willed herself to look.

Inside the mask, shadowed but dry, lay a face that almost matched Ruby's, tangled hair yellow instead of black, tiny bird's tracks at the eyes where Ruby's were smooth.

"Hello, Ruby," said her mother.

Ruby Teach quieted her shaking hand, and then she punched her mother square in the face.

CHAPTER 2

CATHERINE: *A slavering horde? A devouring plague, the likes of which our world has never known?*
FARNSWORTH: *(Shudders) Worse.*
CATHERINE: *You and I, Farnsworth, we have faced down thieves and villains, pirates and scoundrels. What pack of devils awaits outside that sets you cringing, so?*
FARNSWORTH: *It is your family, my lady.*
CATHERINE: *Egad. Bar the door. And fetch my musket.*

—Marion Coatesworth-Hay,
A Most Tenacious Flame, Act I, Sc. iii

The whole clearing gasped. Someone said, "Ooooooo."

Fair being fair, Cram had said it himself, but he couldn't keep it in. Somewhere in the past months the Ferret had learned to throw a punch, and she had whupped out a good one.

Ruby's mam stumbled back. The big cook propped her up.

Cram cleared his throat. "Good to have you back,

Ferret!" Well, someone had to say something. Ruby turned to him, a painful stew of feelings warring on her face. Poor girl. Not the finest way to meet your mam.

Petra alla Ferra stepped into the silence. She slid past the Ferret and in one motion clapped closed the little door on the iron mask and removed the key. She whirled about, and her voice rang out in the still, wet clearing.

"Come, my boars," she said, fierce and urgent. "The carnival is over. We have made our presence known, families have been reunited, we have these fine people to deliver to our employer, who has promised us many piles of money, and then we can take ship and sail far from this hostile land!" They hollered and cheered. "I tire of these colonies and yearn for fair Barcelona. The hunt is on, *meva familia*. Split up and lay many trails. We must confuse them as much as possible. May San Huberto, patron saint of hunters, walk across your tracks. We rendezvous at our special hideaway. Quick and quiet as you can. Go!"

And just like that Los Jabalís were on the move. Little flocks of men and women started peeling off from the clearing like pigeons from an angry tomcat. Ferret and the crew were buckling their rucksacks and checking the straps at the far end of the clearing, so Cram hurried over their way past a chokeberry bush.

The bush hissed at him.

He stopped in his tracks. The wee white flowers were quite pretty, but the wild was tricksy and dangerous. The dense, dripping leaves might hide anything. "Could be reeves, could be a mess of ball-tail cats," he muttered. "Some fella might need to suss this out." He looked about. Nobody else was paying any attention. He unfastened his butter churn from its strap across his back and crept closer.

The shrub hissed again.

Cram started back a step but then got a halter on his fear. "That ain't going to get you anywheres, chokeberry. Name yourself 'friend' or 'foe' this second, or I call out—"

A gnarled knot of a hand shot out of the bush and yanked him forward. He barely had time to squawk. Before he knew it, he was lying on the ground in the middle of a little ring of chokeberry bushes. He scrabbled around, trying to get his legs under him, ready for the next charge. His attacker moved forward into the shady light.

Winnifred Pleasant Black.

Cram sighed a sigh of relief. "Miss Winnie, you scared me right to death!"

The woodswoman hissed again, then whispered, "Quiet, Cram. I need to speak at you."

Cram blinked at his teacher. "What is it?"

Winnie Black's six-year-old son dropped soundlessly out of a tree to the ground and pushed his beaver-head hood back from his eyes. "We's skarperin'."

Winnie Black knelt a buskin-clad knee on the mud without hesitation and leaned in close, nodding to the boy. "Cubbins and me are making a break for it."

Cram's heart sank. "What? Why? Now that we got the Ferret back, things are looking up."

"For you perhaps." The woodswoman's eyes darted back and forth, searching the foliage. She absently scratched the cheek of her hood, the head of a white wolf. "For us, this journey is turning into a mess of hardscrabble pie."

Cram's head reeled inside as if someone had hit him with a frypan. "But Miss Winnie, you—you guided us through the wild. You and the captain got yourselves captivated for us! Without you we would have never saved the Ferret."

The woodswoman nodded, her flat face still. "That's right, and my bargain to Wayland Teach and the rest of your people is done. Cubbins and me did what we said we was going to do, and now it's time to go. Alla Ferra don't want us or need us anyhow. We were just extra critters she got in her trap when she closed it on Captain Teach."

Cram's heart beat faster. "But you've been teaching me the ways of the woods and moss and beasts and such—"

"And that's why I grabbed you."

Miss Winnie's mount, the great black goat Peaches, pushed her head through the chokeberry branches as if they were lace curtains and butted up against Cram's elbow. He pulled some corn out of his pocket and fed her. "Why then?"

Black watched him feed Peaches for a moment. "'Cause we want you to come with us."

Shock lanced through Cram, with joy on the heels of it, but then overtaken just as quickly by sorrow. "I—"

"Before you answer, hear me out. Alla Ferra and Los Jabalís, they're after your girl Ruby, and they also want Henry and Athena. The captain, too. Sounds like whoever they're hired out to will offer a pretty penny for their safe return. Now"—her lips quirked—"whose name didn't I call out?"

Cram licked his lips. She had a point, but these were his people she was talking about. "Mine, but—"

"No buts about it, boy. You are serving them well, but you are traveling back into a world at war. Talk around the campfires is that the French and English are at each other hammer and tongs." She spat. "And in times like this people like us"—she held his gaze—"like you and me and Cubbins, people like us tend to get smashed on the forge."

"What do you say? Lady Athena would never—"

"She would never sacrifice you? Never pay your life in exchange for her own?"

"Never."

"What about for someone she had a duty to? Like this Ruby? Or someone she loved? Like her pa?"

Cram thought for a moment about that. Little vines of doubt started creeping across his shoulders.

Somewhere on the other side of the bushes, someone called, "Last groups, move out!"

Winnie Black stood and wiped her muddy hands on her leathers. "Time's run out. If we go now, they won't miss us until it's too late, and with reeves on their tails, I wager they won't try to get us back." She held out her hand, equal like. "You'd be a full partner with us."

Peaches worbled low in her throat, and Cubbins's tiny fingers wrapped around his own.

It pulled at him like taffy. Winnie Black had opened his eyes to woodcraft, to the glory of the forests. She had taught him the ways of beast and fowl and, more to the point, how to be his own man. With Lady A. and the Ferret and the rest headed for the cities, he was going back to a place where the measure of him, if anyone noticed him at all, was the measure of his Lady. His belly twisted something fierce.

He looked down at Cubbins, who stared up at him, unblinking. "Brothers?" the little boy said.

You could have knocked him over with a feather.

Cram took a deep breath, and then he carefully unwound the little fingers. He knelt and looked Cubbins in the eye. "I can't, little beaver," he said. "Lady Athena and the professor and Ruby . . . I have to stand by them. They're my people, just as much as you are."

Cubbins held his gaze. Then he nodded once, gravely. "Don't get et."

Cram smiled, but he couldn't say nothing. He was flat out of words. He stood back up and looked Winnie Black in the eye, like she had taught him, and then took her hand.

Winnifred Black pulled him in and hugged him fierce, and up against her shoulder he breathed in deep her smell of leather and earth and blood. She held him out at arm's length. "We're headed back to Harris's Ferry. If you need me, find me there."

Cram nodded and forced a smile.

They loaded up onto Peaches, Cubbins up on the ram's horns. Cram held up his hand in farewell. Winnie Black gave him a grim smile and a nod.

Cubbins held up his hand in return. "Bye, brother."

Cram smiled against the sadness, because that's what you did with little ones. "Bye now."

The woodswoman clucked once, softly, to Peaches, and then the branches shook and they were gone.

Cram sighed, hauled his bag onto his shoulder, and then ran off to catch up with the others.

CHAPTER 3

Birds in the air, flowers in bloom, the earth beneath yer feet. A ramble in them woods? Ain't nothin' finer.

'Cept for maybe a pigeon pie.

—Jimmy Two Hands, *hunter extraordinaire*

Los Jabalís knew their business. Ruby and her crew's mercenary escorts tore through the forest with a quiet and speed that recalled Ruby once again to the crew of her father's ship, the *Thrift*. She could keep up; the Reeve's training had at least been good for something. But there was nothing quiet about it. When Ruby moved soft, she had to move slow. The pace Los Jabalís set was a headlong dash, and the only way she could match it was to snap limbs and galumph through leaves like the rawest apprentice. Somewhere her old stealth master Gwath was shaking his head.

They ran, walked, stumbled, and then ran again in gasping silence, with no extra breath for words. Cram with his bag, Athena and Henry, and her father behind, whistling like a chem engine. Ahead, ever in front of them, trotted the big mercenary carrying Ruby's mother. Her mother! Ruby's hand ached. She tried to find the emptiness the Reeve taught, to stay calm, but too many thoughts banged through her head, threatening to spill out of her ears and onto the forest floor. The woman had abandoned her when she was a baby, but not before coding Ruby's blood with a set of plans for a horrific machine. While Ruby was prisoner of the Reeve, Dr. Emmanuel Swedenborg had harvested her blood daily and experimented upon it until he had solved the puzzle and assembled the plans. He had built the machine, which he had promptly used to drain the arcane essence from his apprentice, Ruby's friend Evram Hale, rendering him a terrible husk in the process. All of it the fault of Ruby's mother. What kind of monster creates a thing to suck the life out of others to begin with? And then hides the plans in her own daughter?

But *was* it her mother's fault? The thoughts ravaged Ruby. She, not her mother, had convinced Evram to help her. Ruby, not Marise, had commanded the brilliant gearhorse Sleipnir to defend her to the death.

That guilt burned: a pain far worse than the simple ache of running.

They passed in and out of the forest, winding through abandoned farmsteads and burned-out villages. The war Rool had warned her about had finally come: the French the anvil, the English the hammer, and the colonists ground to flinders in between. Human shapes appeared a few times on far hillsides, watching them pass, but quickly ducking for cover, taking care of their own skins. Every so often Ruby caught a glimpse of Jabalís trailing behind, working to obscure the companions' clumsy tracks. Mostly, though, it seemed as if their little pack were running across the ruined landscape utterly alone. These Jabalís knew their work.

But—Ruby knew too well—so did the Reeve.

And worse, pecking at the back of her mind, were Wisdom Rool's last words to her: *You are a wild wind, a fire in the field. Destruction follows you wherever you go.* Was it following her now? She glanced about at the struggling troupe. Cram, wrestling with his huge bag, seemed terribly exposed. Would a reeve arrow pick him off in an ambush designed for Ruby? Henry, limping, caught her eye and gave her a game smile. She tried to smile back. Now that she had found her friends, would destruction come for them as well?

Daylight slipped away and burned up the worry with it, leaving only the need to stay upright and take one more step. Ruby, Cram, Henry, Athena, and Ruby's father formed themselves into a stumbling, gasping many-legged beast, taking turns holding one another up.

Finally the big Jabalí carrying Ruby's mother followed the hunters down a slope into a deep dead-end thicket. They followed after, too tired to speak. A small passage wound into the brake. On the other side, one of Alla Ferra's lieutenants, the taller of the two, Vera, stood at the foot of a small cliff, next to a high waterfall that drained into a pool filled with water lilies. The thorns ran in a circle from the rock all the way around the pond like a high garden wall. One by one they ducked stumbling past the girl through the curtain of water.

When Ruby's turn came, the girl bowed to her. "Hello again, Ruby Teach. Welcome to our little hunting lodge."

Ruby nodded her thanks and ducked her head through the falls. On the other side lay a large, high cave smelling of sweat and warm leather. Most of Los Jabalís were already there, sleeping or sitting exhausted, drying themselves around hand-size chemystral furnaces.

Alaia led the entire group into an empty side cavern, lit and heated by another of the little tinker stoves. Skins of fresh spring water lay beside a small pile of pemmican. The lumbering cook followed Ruby in, still sweating and breathing like a bellows. Such a feat of strength. That man had carried Marise Fermat the day long. He held Ruby's gaze for a moment and smiled, as if he somehow knew her. He turned away to guide Ruby's mother to a seat on the stone and then disappeared into the darkness, presumably to pass out. Alaia turned to Henry, of all people. "The captain thought you might want some privacy."

"Thank you, Alaia," Henry said.

The girl disappeared, and suddenly, strangely, terrifyingly, they were truly alone.

Her father came first, enveloping her in a suffocating hug, then, Cram, and Athena, and Henry. They all came together, holding on to arms, legs, whatever they could reach. No laughter, no joyful howls, just still, quiet breaths.

After a moment, when she could trust herself to speak, Ruby said, "Well, I like all of you, too."

They untangled themselves and sat around the wee furnace. They all were staring at her, full of gentle smiles and patient nods. Ruby didn't know where to look or what to say.

"You saved me." She tried. "You came for me." There was nothing past that.

Ruby's mother leaned forward. Her voice rang hollow from inside the mask. "I hope this is a better time to introduce myself. I— It's a pleasure to meet you."

Then there was that. Ruby's belly tightened. How to speak to this woman? What to say? How to begin? Did she even want to? She couldn't. The words would not come.

Athena was watching her, concern plain on her face. She jumped into the silence and glanced innocently at Henry. "Ruby, did you know that since you last saw him, someone in this room set a forest on fire?"

And then the dam broke, and the stories tumbled out fast and furious, each more amazing than the last.

"A *giant* beaver dam, I tell you!"

"He climbed up into the balloon, of the *flying house*!"

"She fought two of the beasts at once—"

And the stories stretched out deep into the night, like a glittering river, until Ruby found herself offering her own as well: Swedenborg, and Corson, and the changing, how she had grown picks out of her own two hands and picked the lock of the Swede's cage. She even told them about Sleipnir. And Evram. These were her people. They were the ones who should know. She was deathly tired of secrets.

They talked and talked until one by one they fell into the deep, sweet sleep of friendship renewed.

It was only after she was certain everyone was dead to the world that Ruby slipped away.

Ruby found a shoulder-high rock shelf at the end of a small passage at the back of the cave, past sleeping Jabalís strewn across the floor like piles of wolf cubs. The drawn-down light of the furnaces cast a wavering blue glow across the rough stone of the passage. She hauled herself up onto the shelf with aching shoulders and quivering legs. It reminded her of her windowsill at Fort Scoria. She didn't know whether to be comforted or horrified. She had crawled into that window night after night, huddled against the bars, staring down at freedom coursing through the river valley far below.

She pulled the otter out of her rucksack. It was brass, a gift from Evram, made before the Swede had sucked him dry of tinker's energy and so much more. She had found it, neglected, on a table in front of him, where he sat wizened and drained by Swedenborg's infernal machine. Its eyes were closed, and it did not move, lifeless as the beautiful gearhorse from which its parts had been salvaged. She held it to her chest as a toddler would a toy. What should she do? Where should she go?

A rock crunched in the passage, and a bearlike shape lurked below her perch.

"Permission to come aboard?" her father murmured.

She sighed. "Granted."

She tucked the otter back into her pack. She didn't know why, but she wanted it to be hers and hers alone, at least just now.

Wayland Teach climbed up next to her. He, too, had changed. He was rangier and quieter. The oakum and salt smell of him was gone, and instead, there was . . . what?

"You smell like a pine forest," she said. "Everything is different."

He nodded. "Always." He reached for her tentatively, and she snuggled in.

She wished it could have lasted forever.

"You know, your mother—"

"No. No." Her mother had left her with her father when Ruby was barely a year old. Why was she here? Ruby did not know, and she tried to tell herself she did not care.

Thankfully he said nothing more. They sat for a bit. The quiet of the cave was deafening.

"We're running tomorrow," she said. It was obvious and stupid, but it was a safe thing to say, a certain thing in a sea of chaos.

"Yes," he murmured.

"And then the day after that and the day after that."

He paused. "Probably."

Ruby levered herself up to look at him. "What happens when they find us?"

"They won't."

"You can't know that. I've spent months with these people. They will never stop—"

"But Rool *helped* you escape, didn't he? And this Swede"—his mouth twisted with anger—"he has what he wanted from you, doesn't he? Would he really—"

"It's not just them. It's me. Rool said—"

"We've gotten away from him."

"Let me finish. He said that I was a spark, a spur, that I created mayhem." She took in a shuddering breath. "I think he is right. Even if Rool and the others are not coming for me, someone else will, and—" And then who would be the next person to get hurt?

"Aruba"—her father took her hand and squeezed it so hard that it hurt a bit—"I—I want to tell you that I can make it better again. That we are only a stone's throw from happiness. That all we need to do is push through one more day, and that we'll find sweet fairies and Captain Faustus's treasure and a secret port with gentle tides and the ripest of breadfruit and, and a cute little cottage with a proper family." He touched her finger, right above the spot where the spike had come out. "But I can't. What I can promise you is that, by Providence, I will stand against wave and thunder, against reeve and beast, so that we may never be parted again. If you want to talk, talk. If you do not, do not. You know what you have been through, and it is enough for me that you are here."

Ruby tucked back into her father's shoulder and closed her eyes.

For the first time in many months she could go to sleep feeling safe. Her father's arms were the definition of it, a warm castle wall against the threatening world. But it was a lie, wasn't it? It wasn't that she wasn't happy they had found her. She was. It wasn't that she didn't feel safe with him and even somewhat whole again. She did. But her father and her friends didn't understand that monsters—forces of nature, demons in human form— were coming after her. Even if Rool was happy letting her go, Edwina Corson would never rest until she found Ruby. Nor would Avid or the other cadets: Gideon Stump and the Curtsie twins. In their eyes and—she had to be honest—in her own she had betrayed them. Betrayed their order. Betrayed their trust.

And what of Emmanuel Swedenborg? The very thought of him had her stomach twisting in fear. He was a true monster. Worse by far than the reeves, who at least were loyal to their country. The Swede had relished Ruby's pain, but more, he had been willing to spend her life like pocket shillings in exchange for knowledge and power. He had done worse to Evram. Ruby had stolen the Swede's prized journal for Rool, and she was certain his pride could not bear her escape and her defiance. He would be coming for her.

She breathed in her father's piney, earthy musk. Felt the rough leather of his buckskins on her cheek. She took care to catalog it all, so she could think back on it when she no longer had it. What Ruby understood, now more than ever, was that this was her family. And she couldn't let anything else happen to them.

The best thing in the world for them? Was to be nowhere near her.

After Teach's breathing had settled into deep sleep, she counted to fifty and then slowly, ever so slowly, eased herself out of his arms.

Ruby cleaved to the bouldered shadows on the wall. The crash of the waterfall at the cave mouth masked the sound of her slipping into the pool, and her reeve training made it a simple matter to hold her breath long enough to dart among the rocks in the darkness of the lake bottom until she surfaced at the other end of the grove, far from the view of the sentries.

She pulled herself, dripping, out into a bank of reeds in the shallows. Once she was through the thorn brake, any direction would do. But where would she go? She had to put enough distance between her and the Jabalís that they would cut her loose and keep running from the Reeve. Ruby was fairly certain she could keep ahead of her own crew. As soon as she was out of hearing, she could start running. The half-moon filled the clearing with mad shadows. Rocks and gnarled trees hunkered down like elderly giants, and she wove her way between them until she reached the edge of the thorn brake.

"Going somewhere?"

The voice stopped her short. There in the moonlight, back up against an ancient oak, sat the huge man who had carried her mother.

Ruby brushed her palms on her pants, playing for time. "I might be."

"Looking for a companion?"

"Not particularly." Careful. Had this man suspected

she would try to escape? But how? She had barely decided it for herself! "What are you doing here?"

"I followed you."

Ruby took a step back. "You followed me? But you're in front of me."

He grinned, teeth flashing in the shadows.

Ruby cast her eyes about. There had to be other ways out of the clearing.

He rose, slowly, arms out to reassure her. They were huge and muscled, and did nothing of the kind. "Looks like you might be stuck. You're not big enough to kill me, and if you run, I call for the guard, and the Jabalís will be on your trail in moments."

"You think those are my only options?" She was bluffing. They *were* her only options. She shifted her weight to the balls of her feet, just in case he thought to grab her.

"Use the world as it is, not as it should be."

The words rattled her down to her toes. "What did you say?"

"I won't, though. I won't try to grab you." He was

messing about with something in his hands.

Ruby tensed. Was it a weapon? She took a step back.

"In fact, I promise I will not say a word if you decide to leave, just so long as you take a look at this first." It was a tiny tinker's furnace he was holding.

What did she have to lose? "All right. What is it?"

Light bloomed upward, casting shadows across the rough planes of his face.

But not the mercenary's face.

It was Gwath.

CHAPTER 4

Friendship is like salt pork. If you find a wizened old piece in your
pocket, count yourself lucky.
—Precious Nel, Scourge of the Seven Seas

"Gwaaaaaath!"

That joyful noise might have echoed back to Fort
Scoria if her old mentor's hands, quick as ever, hadn't
covered Ruby's mouth.

Instead, what came out a muffled kind of
grrrrrfffff!

He inched his hand away, wary, ready to quiet her
again.

She threw herself at him. It was a silent dance of pure animal joy, and for the next few moments she rotated back and forth between pummeling, hugging, pounding on the back, and more pummeling. The last she had seen him, he had been stabbed in the gut in a desperate midnight fight on the deck of the *Thrift*, guarding their retreat from Wisdom Rool. He was her teacher, her ally, her dearest friend, and Ruby had feared him slain.

She finally beat herself out, and then flopped down in a heaving mass in front of him.

The big man rubbed his shoulder appreciatively as he looked her up and down. "You're stronger."

"And faster, too. And—" What? More . . . *brutal*? She filed that away for later and moved on. If anyone from the cave were looking for them, the stupid, sparkling grin on her face would have led the guards like a lantern, but she couldn't get it to go away. "What happened? Where have you been? How did you escape? How did you find us? How did you get with Los Jabalís?" She clenched her fists. "Does anyone else know?"

"Athena does."

"What? And she didn't tell me?"

"I told her to keep it a secret. She has apparently been excellent at that for a long time."

She waved away the distraction. "Doesn't matter. What *happened*?"

He crouched down next to her on the balls of his feet. "I kept Rool as busy as I could until you three had cast off from the ship." He grimaced. "That man is . . . strong. I have never seen his like. At the end I had to fall over the side before he took me apart for true."

"But the water? You were wounded unto death *before* I ran—" Ruby blinked. The memory of that night grabbed her by the neck.

Gwath shook his head. "I *told* you to go, Ruby. There is no shame in that." He blew out his breath. "I swam."

"Across the bay? With a gut wound?!"

He shrugged. "I couldn't go back to the ship. I went to ground with the Da Rocha sisters at their fish shack on the docks. By the time I was healed you were gone"—he snapped his fingers—"spirited away by the Reeve. Dores Da Rocha heard about someone asking after you in the

Shambles, and I tracked them down." He waved his hands as if finishing a magic trick. "Los Jabalís. From there it was the matter of a quiet conversation (and a small mountain of coin) with Rafa, and Los Jabalís were eating better than they ever had." His smile warmed her to her toes.

But Ruby had run enough sharps with him. The smile was a diversion, a distraction. Anger stirred in her belly. She pulled at his cheek. "This disguise must take a long time to prepare. Do you use powder? Greasepaint?" She looked about. "And out in the woods, with no privacy to change—"

The faintest flicker in his smile was the only giveaway. "We all must have our secrets, pirate queen." And he reached out to ruff her hair.

He reached out to ruff her hair?

She jerked her head out of the way, and his eyes widened in surprise.

"You must have your secrets?" said Ruby.

"Well, yes." He cocked his head. "That's the way it works."

"The way how works?"

"I'm your teacher. I am, you know, mysterious." He shrugged. "It's part of the—"

"You parcel out your wisdom like breadcrumbs, leading me placid as a well-fed cow through your training."

He frowned. "Well, *cow* might not be how I would—"

Ruby stood. She could not sit any longer. Her heart hammered at her chest. She had to know. "Tell me the truth."

Gwath looked up at her. "I'm sorry?"

Her hand burned, and she thought of her friends and father, of her inability to protect them because of what this man had withheld from her. A thumb's width of brass spike emerged from her finger. "This." She poked him in the chest, and she didn't care that the point pierced the flesh. "Why don't you tell me about *changing*?"

"Oh." His mouth quirked up at the side in a larger grin. Ruby hadn't thought she could get any more angry.

"Yes. Oh." She couldn't yell, so she whispered so hard it tore at her throat. "You can do it. And I thought you were just a master of disguise."

"I'm terrible at disguises."

"Stop trying to distract me. You knew I had it in me, didn't you?"

Gwath blinked. "I knew that you *could* have."

"So why didn't you teach me?"

"It was too early."

"Why?"

"It's dangerous."

"*Dangerous*? Do you know where I have just been? What I have been doing? Are you saying that changing is more dangerous than secret missions with deadly explosive salt metal, huge men with pickaxes that want to skewer you, drawing the ire of a mad tinker, being the target of, I imagine, every reeve on this continent?"

"Well, when you put it that way . . ."

"Well?"

Gwath looked her dead in the eye. "Yes."

It took Ruby a moment to get the word straight in her head. "Yes?"

"Yes."

"Yes, it is more dangerous?"

Gwath stood, serious as stone. "It is more dangerous than all of those things. Changing can erase who you are forever. I had to be careful. You were not ready."

"But you took me on all manner of dangerous assignments. You routinely exposed me to fire, guards, acid, blades, and once even a rabid ocelot."

He took her hand. Hers was a miniature of his. She had never noticed. "Those were dangers to the body. Changing is a danger to the very heart of you. You can forget who you are. And not just for a little while. For good."

"Fermat told me that it, changing, was a family thing."

"Fermat? The chemyst?"

Ruby looked down at his hand. "Are you my father?"

He swayed, just a little. His hand twitched around hers. "I am."

A faint ringing filled her ears. So many questions, like a song just on the edge of hearing. "Does Fa—Captain Teach know?"

"I—I am not sure."

The ringing strengthened to clanging. Someone was

beating her heart on an anvil. "Thirteen years, and you are not sure?"

His smooth face tightened. "It was never— Your mother—"

"Thirteen years, and you never told me?"

Fear in his eyes, uncertainty. Things she had never, ever seen before. "I . . ."

That was all he could say. Her mentor, her teacher. Her *father*? He had always known what to say. What to do. And now, nothing. Providence had given Gwath back to Ruby, but he wasn't Gwath anymore. He stood there, bald in the moonlight, looking like some strange, broken automaton.

She pulled her hand from his. "Fine." The hurt roiled about in her belly, a terrifying storm threatening to eat its way out. She couldn't keep talking to him. But she couldn't go. Not now. He wouldn't let her leave him. Gwath would follow her and probably raise the whole camp for good measure. Besides. Two fathers. Was one real? Was one *not*? Her head whirled. She took a step back toward the cave, then looked over her shoulder. "You coming?"

He sighed a deep, deep sigh and stood.

"Yes, but—"

"You want me to keep this a secret?"

He nodded.

"Why? Why?"

He parsed the words out as if dropping them on the ground would break them. "I don't trust Alla Ferra. I want to protect you and the others. If I am revealed, we lose an advantage. If we tell . . . Captain Teach or your mother, their reaction might spoil the sharp."

More secrets. "Very well." More lies. She was beginning to loathe the things. Something scratched at the back of her brain: something shadowy and sharp. She turned to him as they walked back. He was Rafa again.

"Gwath?"

"Yes, Ruby?"

"Changers are liars, aren't they? They're liars."

It tore at her: seeing that look, so full of regret, not on Gwath's face, but on someone else's.

CHAPTER 5

Judge a man by his questions,
rather than his answers.
—Voltaire

Henry threw himself to the ground between two boulders, right next to Athena Boyle. The grass was still cool here under the trees, and he pressed his cheek into it. Their second day on the run had somehow been even more taxing than the first. Petra alla Ferra had set the whip to Los Jabalís's flanks, turning the rush through the forests into a headlong sprint. He turned this way and that on his back, trying to find a comfortable position for his leg; the day's march had it throbbing as if it were trying to send him coded messages.

The small and larger thumps just beyond his head had to be Ruby and her father, and the clattering on the other side of the boulder told him Cram and his bag had survived the punishing trek as well. Still on her back, Athena tossed a half-empty waterskin onto Henry's heaving chest. He patted her on the shoulder in thanks. The water trickled relief down his throat. It took an effort of will to give it back to Athena and another not to just fall asleep where he lay. Instead, he stifled a groan and maneuvered himself to an only mildly uncomfortable seat with his back to one of the rocks.

Los Jabalís had led them up a steep track into a boulder-filled grove atop a windswept bluff, perched above yet another burned-out village. The bluff commanded views in every direction, the better to spy pursuers, and yet the trees, boulders, tall grass, and the height of the plateau itself concealed the company handily from below. The mercenaries scattered about the grove at random, drinking water or just lying there, bits and pieces of them—a head poking above a rock here, some feet up a tree there—the only indicators that anyone was in the clearing at all. Their Catalonian companions had proved as adept at hiding as they were at flight. It had been a mad, looping getaway. As far as Henry could tell, they never maintained the same direction for more than a few hours, doubling, sometimes tripling back, crossing streams and rivers, tiptoeing full speed over scree fields. It seemed impossible that anyone could evade an angry flock of reeves, but they might just be doing it.

Cram's head popped over the boulder like a woodchuck. "What about a teakettle?"

"Cram, I told you." Ruby banged her head lightly against the ground.

"Now, Ferret, you told me you couldn't change yourself into a wagon, a bear, a church, a pudding, Lady Athena's sword, or me."

"So?"

"So you hain't told me you could not turn into a teakettle." The boy sighed. "I would truly love some tea right now, wouldn't you, Professor?"

"Cram—well, yes, I would adore a hot cup of anything not in a leather skin right now, but that is beside the point."

"Which is?"

It was all he had been thinking about all day. He lowered his voice, and the others leaned in. "We have rescued Ruby, yes, and Los Jabalís have sworn to take us to safety, but what kind of safety? Who is their mysterious employer?"

Athena seemed to come to a decision. "Well, I know the one paying the bills."

Henry blinked. "Who is it then?"

Her lips made a thin line. "Godfrey Boyle. Grand master of the Worshipful Order of Grocers. My father."

Henry didn't know whether to be encouraged or sick to his stomach. The Worshipful Order and Henry's old master, Fermat, did not get along. Not at all. What did this mean for him? "How long have you known? Why didn't you tell us?"

"Well, it didn't matter until now, did it? If we all were dead in the cellar of Reeve Mountain, no one would care who was behind this mad expedition."

Ruby frowned. "Well, can you just pull rank or something? Take control of this loony band?"

Athena hesitated. "I am not certain—"

Wayland Teach cleared his throat, drowning her out, and glanced about, checking for eavesdroppers. "The order doesn't work like that. Athena's being Boyle's daughter means nothing. Petra alla Ferra is doing her best to sneak us and her people to safety across an actual war-torn landscape. Besides, Los Jabalís don't answer to the order. They answer to the money they were promised. The only reason they helped us get Ruby was anticipation of a greater reward." His eyes flicked between them. "Anyone here secretly carrying a massive pile of loot?"

They all shook their heads, and a quiet came upon them.

The captain's joints creaked as he pushed himself up and grabbed an armful of waterskins. "I'm going for more water," he said, and wandered off.

Athena groaned and levered herself from her elbows onto her hands. Part of her braid had come loose, and a splay of straight black hair plastered itself to her cheek, wet with sweat. "I for one have a different question, a more important one."

Henry didn't like the look in her eye. "And what is that?"

Restraining a grin, Athena turned to Ruby. "Can you make yourself a bird?"

Ruby pulled up a handful of grass and threw it at the other girl. "No, I can't."

"But you made yourself a pumpkin?"

"Yes, but I didn't mean to at the time. I was scared, and it just—"

"What about other kinds of plants then?" She wiggled her fingers. "Sunflower, go!"

"Athena, it's not like that."

"Persimmon, go!"

"Stop it."

"Carrot, go!"

"Athena—"

"Rutabaga!"

"Athena, I swear to Providence if you name one more vegetable . . ."

But Ruby was smiling. She even laughed a little. It warmed Henry to see her thaw just a bit, but he could not relax. Couldn't they see? But when he looked about at them, the knowledge hit him hard. They *couldn't* see the challenge waiting for them, like a ball-tail cat hiding in a tree above the trail. "That's not the most important question," Henry whispered, talking himself through it.

"Well, what is it then, Henry?" said Ruby.

Someone needed to say it, terrifying as it was. "Ruby's power is important, but something has been eating at me since we've heard about the events at the fort." He chewed his lip. "Here it is. What does it mean that Ruby's secret—Marise's formula for pulling the energy out of folk— is loose in the world?"

Ruby went still. "And in the hands of a madman."

It had been hard the night before, hearing Ruby's tale. The man Swedenborg had turned her into an experimental specimen, a *thing*, not a person, and Henry had listened to one terrifying detail after the other with growing horror and rage. No, this adventure was not over. Henry shuddered to think of what a man like the Swede might do with such a powerful tool as this machine.

"Too many secrets," said Athena.

It broke Henry out of his thoughts. "I'm sorry, what?"

Athena plucked a handful of grass. "We need information. And Los Jabalís"—she glanced at Ruby—"and even the others like your father and mine . . . they are keeping us blind, perhaps for our own sakes. But we cannot allow that to happen. We need to know everything. That is why I told you of my father."

Henry chewed on his lip. She was right. Had *he* been entirely truthful? Had he told them enough of the spying he had done before he met them? Of Fermat's interests and Nasira's network of spies? He hadn't. *Should* he? "I'm not certain—"

Athena interrupted. "Ruby, there is something else you should know."

Ruby stared at her, and with her voice barely above a whisper she said, in time with Athena, "Gwath is here."

Cram's mouth hung open in shock.

Henry's head spun. "Who? The cook from your ship? Isn't he dead?"

Athena's eyes widened. "How did you find out? Did he tell you?"

Ruby scowled. "Well, *you* didn't tell me, that's for certain."

"It—it was not my secret to give." Athena looked about, but all the Jabalís, at least the ones Henry could see, seemed to be out of earshot. "Besides, when would I tell you? There are mercenaries in our boots, in our coats, up in the trees . . ."

"Doesn't matter." Ruby searched Henry's eyes and then looked at the other two. Her cheeks were flushed; she looked almost sick.

"Isn't this *good* news, Ruby?" asked Henry. Something was eating at her. Ruby was strong, but there was so much she was carrying.

She took a breath. "Gwath is not just my teacher. He's my father."

The wind whirred through the trees.

"Well, that makes sense," said Cram.

"Cram!" Henry said. "Have some— Don't just—"

"Well, it does, you know." His face scrunched up

like a raisin. "If you mull it about a bit, and the tension between the Captain and Ruby's Mam, and the way Ferret has Gwath's coloring, oh, and their hands. Hold up your hand, Ferret. It looks just like a little Gwath's—I never forget a hand—even the way the thumb has that crook—"

"Cram." Athena stopped him cold.

On seeing Ruby's face, the boy covered his mouth with his hand. "I'm so sorry." The voice came out muffled. "I didn't mean—"

Ruby sighed. "It's all right. He told me last night. I didn't know." The words came slowly, like the drops from melting ice. "I thought I was one thing, but I'm not. I'm . . . something else." Ruby shrugged.

She looked at Henry, and there was a sadness there so deep. He had no idea what to say.

Athena sat up, all business. "I have some experience in being one thing but having others think you are something else. There is a thing you must know." She moved over and put her arm around Ruby's shoulders. "You are you, Ruby. That is all that matters to us."

He and Cram nodded, but Henry kept worrying at it. He wanted to fix it. He wanted to say the thing that would make it all better, but the more he thought about it, the more a solution seemed inconceivable. It was just . . . hard. "How can we help?" he said finally.

Ruby eased back into Athena's shoulder and stared off into space for a while. "Keep this secret among us at least. Besides that? I don't know," she said, "but you can start by promising never again to ask me to turn into a carrot."

Henry woke to see Vera Medina looming over his bedroll, the first hint of dawn glowing behind her. "Alla Ferra would like to see you." She looked about at the little group. "All of you, except Captain Teach."

The captain grumbled but nodded his assent.

Henry, Ruby, Athena, and Cram found Petra alla Ferra sitting on the sunrise edge of the butte. Next to her, on a little flat rock, sat a tiny traveling chess set. The thick, heavy blade of her hunting knife moved as smoothly as silk as she sharpened it on an oiled whetstone, and the taut muscles of her forearm clenched and released in perfect rhythm. Coiled. Predatory.

Henry swallowed his uneasiness. "You summoned us?"

The heavy rasp of the blade on the whetstone did nothing to soothe his nerves. *Snick. Snick.* Only a hair's breadth away from cutting the tip from her thumb. "Yes," she said, eyes never leaving his.

"Why did we have to leave Captain Teach behind?" Ruby said. "If you wish to speak to all of us—"

"I agreed with Henry Collins that I would exchange the aid of Los Jabalís in rescuing you, Ruby Teach. For your cooperation as well as for his translation of the journal of Marise Fermat—" She glanced up at Ruby. "I believe you and Madame Fermat have met? As I said, I agreed to this exercise with *Henry* here"—she pointed the knife at Henry's left eye—"and my employer is the father of Lady Athena Boyle"—the knife shifted—"so she is here as his representative." She raised an eyebrow when none of them expressed any surprise. The knife shifted again to point at Cram. "And I find the servant amusing. Plus he did not disappear into thin air, like the woodswoman, so he must be trustworthy." She went back to sharpening the blade. "Captain Wayland Teach is not a factor in my decision making, and certainly Marise Fermat is not. It is to you four to whom I wish to speak. Would you like me to call your mommy and daddy so that they can hold your hands?"

When none of them answered, she pointed to the chess set. "Do any of you play?"

They each looked at one another. Henry ran his tongue along the back of his teeth. "I do."

She pointed the knife to the seat across from her. "Mr. Collins."

He sat. The pieces were scattered about the board, so he set them in order for the beginning of the game.

After a moment alla Ferra tapped the point of the knife on the board next to his hand. "Which side will you choose?"

From the look on her face, she was asking far more than whether he wanted to play the red pieces or the white pieces. He didn't know the rules to this game yet. He played for time. "Which do you prefer?"

"But I asked you, Henry Collins."

She was watching him so closely. Something else was definitely happening here. "I will play red then."

"Ah, you choose to go second, to respond, not to initiate."

Was he making the proper choice? But if he went back on his choice, he might appear weak. Nothing else but to be honest. "Yes. I wish to know the lay of the land before I act."

She nodded. "Good. Then perhaps you can tell me what you think of that lay of the land out there."

The red flicker of dawn crept over the valley below as if Petra alla Ferra had summoned it. At the far end lay two hills facing each other, both covered in trees. As the sun rolled up, Henry realized that they weren't trees. Their lines were too regular. "Soldiers," he breathed.

War. It was a battle below.

Alla Ferra nodded. "And not just here. You have seen the ruin of the countryside as we have traveled. Our long-range scouts agree. Fire and blood are the order of the day all over this land, in both the English and the

French colonies." Her lip curled. "So many skirmishes and battles to decide which faraway king gets to fly his flag over a burned-out landscape. My people sniffed this one out yesterday. This is a good vantage point, is it not?"

And then bugles rang out, just on the edge of hearing, and the lines began marching toward each other. It struck Henry, though, that each one of those little shapes was a person, a human, with family and friends and dreams. In the early light so far away it was difficult to tell the color of the uniforms or even the shapes on the flags. The tiny figures knelt. Then little puffs of smoke rose up from the lines, and a few moments later the popping sounds trickled in, like wood in a fire. Some of the kneeling figures fell down. This happened a few more times, and then one line charged the other, and Henry turned his eyes away because he couldn't watch anymore.

Cram cleared his throat. "Begging your pardon, Captain Alla Ferra, but which one is our side?"

Petra alla Ferra was staring at Henry. "That is the question, is it not?"

"You ask us whether we choose the French or the

English in this war?" Athena snorted in anger and disbelief. "I was born in London. I *am* English."

Alla Ferra chuckled, and she began moving the chess pieces, changing them out of their even rows into smaller clumps about the board. "Oh, but Lady Boyle, there are more than two sides in this game."

"I see two lines out there fighting."

"Yes, yes, but you all have been out in the woods for months, have you not? Almost a year?"

"So have you." Henry cut in. His blood was up. How could she be so casual, as if they were at a garden party? "You have been following us."

"Yes, but all my Jabalís have not been with us. I never travel unfamiliar territory without a few of my people keeping an eye on the neighborhood. A wise commander keeps her ear to the ground. I want to know the lay of the land. I am like you, Henry."

He looked at her, so at ease above a field of death, and suddenly realized that he hoped with all his heart that he would never be like her. But he could not let her know that. Los Jabalís were the only allies they had. And better them than the British, or the French, or the Reeve. Wasn't it better? Henry wrestled his attention back to the conversation.

Alla Ferra nodded at her lieutenant. "Vera, tell them what our people told you."

The tall girl shifted, pulling herself away from the trunk of the tree to stand straight. Her jaw was set. A shadow of alarm flickered behind her eyes.

"The gates to Philadelphi are closed and manned by armed guards. No one is to enter or leave the city, except by order of the crown."

Athena frowned. "Because of the war?"

Vera fingered her pistol. "Perhaps they anticipate an attack then?"

Alla Ferra's hands kept moving. There were three groups of pieces now, set out in a triangle on the chessboard. One was white. "The English," she said. Another was all red. "The French." A third was mixed red and white. "The Worshipful Order of Grocers." She looked up at Athena. "Your father's people. Their hand is on the scales heavily in this land. Rumors in strange places say that they may have *started* this war for their own ends?"

"What?" Athena looked genuinely puzzled.

"I prefer to know something about my clients before I work for them," said Alla Ferra. "Your father's people have been meddling with thrones and countries since before the Crusades."

Ruby chewed on her lip for a moment before she said, "Wisdom Rool told me something very similar before I . . . left."

"Ah," said alla Ferra. "Well, we are in this together. Am I missing anything else?"

Ruby leaned over to pull a white bishop out of the white clump and set it in a spot all its own. "Swedenborg," she said. "I do not think he cares a whit for king or country or anyone but himself."

In his mind, Henry set another figure on the board: Fermat, hidden in the center of the city like a powerful chemystral heart. He did not mention his old master, though. The crew needed to share their secrets with one another, no one else. He did not fully trust alla Ferra.

Instead, he asked, "But why would anyone start a war? Where did this come from?"

Petra sighed. "Who can say? Some governor wants more land. Some fur trader lord wants a better hunting ground. It's not them that suffer." She stared into the distance, where the tides of little figures still moved back and forth. "I don't imagine any of you have seen what happens to a country in war. In the capitals they talk of borders and troops, but in the fields, in the towns it is burning barns and blood in the mud." Something haunted twisted in her eyes. She shook herself and was suddenly back in front of them. "Perhaps it is chaos that these war makers want? Perhaps power? I suspect we will find out soon enough." She looked down at the board and its constellation of influences. "This is our situation. The gates to Philadelphi are closed. My contact is *in* Philadelphi. The person to whom you are to be delivered, who will grant you safety and give me my money. Can you help me?"

Henry was at an utter loss.

A coin purse thumped down in the center of the

board. "That is who I am loyal to," said alla Ferra. "I imagine you will need to decide who you are loyal to in the very near future. But we cannot answer any of those questions until we get into the city." She turned back to Henry Collins and set a white pawn down in front of him. "Well, Mr. Collins? Now is the opportunity to initiate. And we must be on our way quickly. Aside from the fact that it is not safe to gad about so near a battlefield, the Reeve may not be far behind."

Henry looked down at the cluttered chessboard, and his mind whirled. He and his friends, they were pieces on this game board, too. Many were searching for them, and not just the Reeve. If he were on his own, he would go straight to Fermat. If he could even get in the city. But what of the rest of them? Athena's duty was to her father. Cram's to Athena. And Ruby? Ruby was a weapon. The knowledge that lay in her blood still had power, even though the Swede had decoded it. And even if the Swede had solved her like some kind of equation, she still had the power to *change*. But she was also his friend. She had saved his life more than once, by Science, and she needed—they all needed—to get to some place of safety. But he could see no safety in front of them, no matter what path they chose.

Henry looked up at his three friends. They all looked as confused as he felt. Trapped. Frozen.

Then Athena's face crumpled into a kind of resigned disgust.

"What is it?" Henry asked.

"The Worshipful Order has a safe house in the city. And one of its entrances is outside the walls."

Ruby looked as if she had just eaten a toad. "You mean—"

Athena nodded. "Perhaps they can help us at the Warren."

Ruby rolled her eyes. "Barnacles."

CHAPTER 6

What does a king from across the sea know of my land? What does a fat merchant care for my brother's toil? What will a redcoat's bayonet find in the heart of a patriot?
—Thandie Paine, *Simplicity*

Ruby looked up just in time. A little breeze came up, and a piece of the roof just *fell*. She stepped to the side, and it plunked into the dry, dead dust. The Archer farm smokehouse had not aged well.

The rickety patchwork of spare wood, twine, leather, and in one case a surprised-looking ex-possum leaned together in a vaguely rooflike shape atop a shack that groaned in the wind like a grandpapa before a storm.

A sad weather vane hung broken from the roof, its iron rooster staring mournfully at the ground. More shards of pottery and wood lay scattered beneath it, planted in the loose midsummer soil like old headstones.

Ruby stood in front of the door, flanked by Cram and Athena, and a shiver ran down her spine. Had it been less than a year since she and these two had stood in this very spot, on the run from the Reeve, the navy, and Science knew what else? Was she even the same person? Were any of them?

With the city's main gates locked tight, Los Jabalís and the companions needed another path into the city. The Bluestockings—the Pennswood arm of Athena's secret society—just happened to have a tunnel that went under the wall and into the heart of UpTown. The chemysts and especially their leader, Madame Hearth, were prickly, unpredictable, and downright dangerous, but since the three friends had gotten inside once, and there were no other options, it had fallen to them to try to make nice.

Los Jabalís and the rest of the party, including Henry, had gone to ground in a small patch of trees a few hundred yards away. Not far, but certainly not close enough to help if there was trouble. Both Marise and Wayland (her mother and her, what, father? What about Gwath?) had insisted that with their more recent experience, Athena, Cram, and Ruby were the best choice to say hello. Ruby was not so sure, but the chance to get free of all three of her parents and the secrets roiling around them, even in the face of danger, was almost a relief.

They needed to fulfill Henry's debt, rid themselves of the Jabalís, and then go. . . where? The *Thrift*? Cathay? The moon? And what about the Swede? Would he simply shrug his shoulders and let her be gone? She shook herself. One deadly reeve at a time, Teach. She brought her mind back to the task in front of her: begging at the doorstep of the Bluestockings.

Athena coughed. "Well, I must admit a certain uncertainty regarding how the landlords will receive us. Last time you thumbed your nose at them and climbed out the chimney, and we disobeyed direct orders to capture you."

Cram didn't add anything, except to softly whistle a

little tune and sidle over a step—just to the right of the hole in the wall where a blunderbuss blast had almost blown him into sausage.

Ruby's stomach rolled, but she smiled grimly. "I may owe them something for my room. And I did break into Madame Hearth's office." She rocked back and forth on her heels. "Did I mention the money I stole from her pocketbook on my way out the secret passage?"

Both of the others turned to her, eyes wide.

Ruby straightened. "Well, then. Don't make too much of it. Perhaps they've forgotten." She knocked clearly, three times.

No sound but the wind.

Then something else. Not a sound, but a feeling. Eyes on them, from somewhere.

Athena glanced over at Ruby, and her sword slid from its scabbard, rasping against the leather. Cram eased his butter churn hammer from its strap across his back. Pulse pounding, hackles raised, Ruby put her weight forward on the balls of her feet as her reeve teachers had taught her.

"Mr. Abel Ward," Athena called the name of the

guard who had previously manned the shack. "We've come with a delivery of spices."

With a clack, the eyelid of the weather vane rooster opened. Inside lay a red jewel of an eye, whirling.

"Down!" Athena yelled, and Ruby threw herself to the side. The beak spit, and a pellet of something slammed into Cram's shoulder.

The boy had time only to cry out. A puff of red smoke bloomed up from his shoulder, but it grew, too quickly for him to move, until it surrounded him completely. With a crack the smoke hardened into crystal, and then the whole mass fell to the ground, Cram trapped and wriggling behind its crimson facets. Ruby gaped in horror.

The rooster kept spitting, once, again, again, and she and Athena launched into a crazed, rolling dance, barely keeping ahead of the pellets.

At the same moment they both yelled, "Inside!"

Athena kicked the door, and it shattered into bits. They both dived across the threshold, the pellets puffing harmlessly into the ground behind.

However.

The interior of the smoke shack was not as Ruby remembered it. On their last visit rows of game had hung on hooks in two rows to the back of the little house. Between the rows had sat an overstuffed chair and the sentry of the Warren, Abel Ward.

None of that remained.

As soon as Ruby landed on the driftwood floor, it cracked like the thinnest of piecrusts, and Ruby cursed her lack of care. She fell, speeding into the darkness, headed for poison spikes or some underground worm or worse.

Until something slammed into her, knocking the air out of her as if someone had hit her with a big, wide pillow. Cushioned, hanging in place. She struggled, fear and frustration fueling her, but she was stuck fast like a fly in a web. Indeed, she lay in a net of sticky gray fibers faintly lit from the doorway high above, strung across a pit that continued as far as she could see down into the dark. Athena slammed down next to her, her back striking the web with a wet smack.

Ruby bit her lip. "Top marks for strategy. We should be able to save Cram quite easily from here."

Athena tried to roll onto her shoulder, but she was stuck on her back just as fast as Ruby was on her stomach. Ruby had landed with her face to the side, so she had a perfect view of her friend's thrashing.

Suddenly Athena stopped struggling, and Ruby's blood ran cold at the horror blooming on her face. In all their time together Ruby had never seen her so fraught with terror.

"What? What is it? Athena!"

"Oh, no. Oh, Providence," was all the older girl said, over and over like a prayer.

With all her strength Ruby tore at the strands and freed her face. She craned her neck to look up over her shoulder, and there she saw it.

Framed in the light of the smoke shack doorway, staring down at them with a horrible rictus of a grin, perched a small figure in a butterfly-patterned gown.

"Greta Van Huffridge," Ruby breathed. Her heart sank.

The piping voice, like a little bird pecking at your eardrums, cut down the well and into Ruby's soul. "Well,

well, it seems we have some visitors to the Warren. What a delicious surprise." The girl stood. "I'll come back for you once I've finished my homework. Probably." She turned to go.

"Wait! Greta, please!" said Athena.

The tiny girl turned back, and the light struck a blue mask she wore over her eyes. She tapped it. "I'm sorry? To whom were you referring?"

Athena gargled. It sounded as if a gecko were caught in her throat. "Er, Journeywoman Van Huffridge?"

She turned immediately. "Yes?"

The words crept out of Athena with a kind of iron control Ruby associated with holding an anchor rope in a gale. "My serving man Cram is currently on your lawn, surrounded by some manner of red crystalline—"

"The coalescer? Brilliant, is it not? I designed it myself."

"Yes, it is brilliant, and full marks for the rooster-eye shooter—"

"Thank you."

Athena's voice rose in pitch ever so slightly. "However,

this coalescer has completely encased him, and I fear he may be cut off from air."

Greta Van Huffridge tapped her teeth in thought. "Does he come from a good family?"

"Science, woman, he is my serving man, and he may be dying out there!"

The girl clucked her tongue. "Lord Athen Boyle, you are slipping. You used to not be so easy to bait. What do you take me for, a monster?"

Athena's gargle transformed into a kind of soft, vicious muttering. Ruby identified the words *possibly* and *worse*.

"The boy will be fine. The crystal—my own design, did I mention that?"

"You did," said Ruby. This was not going well. The clock was ticking, and ratcheting up the fight would get them nowhere. Visions of Henry and her parents and the rest hounded across the wilderness danced in her head.

"You see, the crystal is penetrable to air, and so the capturee is in no danger of suffocation. In fact, the air takes on a scent mildly reminiscent of strawberries."

"Miss Van Huffridge." Ruby tried to weave a ship's hold of sweetness into her words.

"Oh, yes, and Ruby *Teach*." She flayed the skin right off Ruby's last name. "You have returned, as well. My old roommate. My chum. I had thought you would be my companion, my friend. Instead, you ambush me in the middle of the night, tie me up, and run loose to create havoc for Madame Hearth, the Bluestockings, and, most important, *me*. I am tempted to just leave the both of you there to rot, and no one the wiser."

Ruby's hopes fell further into the hole with each sentence. Yet the fates of too many hung on this conversation. "Miss Van Huffridge—"

"Your servant makes a lovely lawn ornament—"

"Miss Van Huffridge!"

"—but I am under strict instructions that if either of you surfaces, you are to be brought directly to Madame Hearth, and this I shall do."

"Thank you," Ruby and Athena said together.

"I will summon some sentinels, and they will get you out of those webs and into your shackles."

"But I am a member of the Worshipful Order," Athena said. "You cannot haul me into a refuge trussed up like some kind of—"

"Oh, but I can, Lord Athen, I can," said Greta. "The tenor of the moment is fluid, to say the least. As to your standing with the order, well"—her teeth glittered in the dim light—"we shall see."

Shame and anger flared in Ruby's chest. Athena had done what she had done for Ruby. Now she was being punished for her bravery. "You have no idea the lengths Lord Athen has gone to bring me back! All the while you lot sat here in your little hidey-hole and—"

"Quiet, Teach." Greta raised a shape in her fist, its silhouette almost familiar. "It feels so good to say that. Oh, I have been biding my time, waiting for this moment." The eye of the thing in her hand twinkled in the light of the doorway.

It was a small, terribly cute stuffed pony.

Ruby groaned, but it was muffled by the pony in her mouth. Greta Van Huffridge had been as good as her word. That infernal stuffed toy had been given to Ruby when the Bluestockings had decided to help her learn chemystry, and Ruby had given it to Greta when she escaped. Well, she had left it with Greta. In her mouth. While she was tied to a bed.

A few hard men and women in deep indigo cloth masks (Greta's bore a set of freshly painted scales) had emerged from a concealed ladder and lowered Athena and Ruby down the pit to the chemystrally smoothed and hardened earthen floor. They had relieved them of their weapons, then trussed up Ruby and Athena in more greasy gray rope. A boil-covered man carrying a vicious-looking ax that matched the image on his mask said, "Welcome back," and gave Ruby's knot an extra yank. Another Bluestocking was a squat, tough woman with a badger on her mask, who turned a filigreed quartz lens over and over in her fingers. A few moments later Cram was lowered down to the bottom of the pit like a loaf of red crystal bread. Two of the guards stayed behind to reassemble the whole intricate trap, leaving Greta, the Ax, and the Badger. The three Bluestockings loaded

Cram onto an iron cart and forged down the corridor, leading Ruby and Athena briskly down a narrow hallway.

Ahead of her, over Greta's shoulder, Ruby could see Cram's terrified face. He was not frozen in amber, like a fly, but some kind of goo inside kept him mostly immobile. He wiggled a finger at Ruby. She raised a hand back. Chem pots cast strange shadows across his face. Here she was again, neck deep in trouble and someone else suffering for her mistakes.

Ruby snuck a glance at Athena. No, Athen. She had to remember. Lord Athen Boyle. Since Ruby's friends and Los Jabalís had found her, there had been no sign that anyone in the party thought Athena was a boy. But when she and Ruby had met, Athena had taken great pains to conceal her identity, and it was days after they had met before Ruby discovered it, and then only because Athena was gravely wounded. Here in Philadelphi, though, and in London and the rest of the world, for all Ruby knew, it was still Athen. The person in question strode forward, lost in concentration.

The cart rolled to a stop in front of a door. It was big. It was brass. The symbol of the Worshipful Order of Grocers was carved upon it: a roaring camel. For some reason that completely escaped Ruby, the Grocers thought it fierce. A tinny voice, like someone talking high into a pewter mug, came out of the camel's mouth.

"Password, please."

Greta puffed up. "I pass with olefiant gas."

Athena snickered.

Greta threw her a look that could have skewered her to the wall. Heavy whirring and clanking sounded from deep inside the door, and it slowly opened, revealing at least a foot of thickness. Greta hustled them through and right past a boy with half his hair burned off. He held out a slate and chalk like a prayer.

"Journeywoman Scales, I need you to sign—"

"No time!" she called over her shoulder, hurrying down the hallway.

On this side of the door the halls were wider and well lit with soft blue tinker's lamps instead of the cheap chem pots. Much in the Warren, however, had changed. The orderly classrooms, once filled with students and teachers studying chemystral science, now sat dormant and dark. Tables once littered with beakers and alembics lay stark and barren, sealed boxes stowed underneath. They passed one room where the tables now held neat lines of bedrolls. In another classroom the furniture had been pushed back against the wall. A tall man with a heavy, oiled black beard, his mask sporting a wagon, had lined up a squad of students to toss stone flasks at painted targets.

"What are they doing?" Ruby asked. Actually it came out more like "Waffa buh hooing?" but Greta seemed to understand.

"Training," said Greta. "A chemyst can be the finest in the world, but it doesn't matter a whit if she can't actually hit something."

Through her gag Athena asked, "Hooba dey frooingah?"

Greta nodded, a glint in her eye. "That is indeed the question."

"No more chitchat, Van Huffridge," said the Badger. She had a gruff, no-nonsense voice and a West Indies accent.

"It's Journeywoman Scales, please, ma'am."

The woman simply glared.

"Yes, ma'am." Greta sighed, and she kept leading them down the hall.

Eyes and whispers followed them wherever they went, and Ruby's pulse quickened. These preparations had nothing to do with her or Athena. The Warren was preparing for a fight. But with whom? Her thoughts raced back to alla Ferra's chessboard. If they were fighting the French, why were they preparing in secret? Did that mean they were set to fight the crown? But why?

They were running before the storm, with no plan and no prospects. She had to seize control of the wheel before they were smashed upon the rocks.

They stopped at the end of a little side corridor at a depressingly familiar, featureless door. The only thing that stood out about it was the doorknob, an intricately carved stone imp, claws outstretched. The imp had been scrubbed clean, but it still held the faintest traces of red burned into the stone around its eyes. The last time she had seen that imp it had been clutching at her hands, dripping acid, and yelling, "*Thief! Thief Here! Thief!*"

Ruby mouthed a curse around the pony. Well, it wasn't as if she hadn't known that this was where they would end up.

Greta rapped sharply upon the door.

It opened immediately, and a big man poked his head out. It was hairless as an egg, and his mask bore no sigil.

"Pate, I have visitors for your mistress," announced Greta.

Pate looked them up and down, eyes widening slightly as he recognized them. He nodded and then opened the door wide.

The silver bookshelf samovar still bubbled in the corner. The armoire still loomed against the wall. *She* sat at the table. She smiled, and the cracked paint crinkled around the fireplace symbol on her mask, but the smile promised nothing pleasant.

"Ruby Teach," said Madame Hearth, "I have been waiting such a long time to see you again. Welcome back to the Warren."

CHAPTER 7

The enemy of my enemy's friend's enemy is my friend. Wait. The enemy of my friend's enemy is occasionally my— Oh, hang it. If it shoots at you, blow it to flinders with a cannon.
—Precious Nel, Scourge of the Seven Seas

Madame Hearth's tea was just as terrible as Athena remembered.

She took a sip. After a moment of misery she was able to summon the will to offer "Delightful. Is this"—*Arsenic? Rotted mushroom? Diseased cat?*—"an herbal mixture of some kind?"

"Please don't try to get on my good side, Journeyman Boyle. That ship has long since sailed. Tell me right now why the two of you are here."

Even though the room was quite cool, Madame Hearth fanned herself vigorously with a fan the Athena of months ago would have found desperately unfashionable (a pattern of peacocks and abacuses, so very ten years ago). She was pleasantly surprised to find that she cared very little about the fashion of Madame Hearth's fan or indeed about the opinion of Madame Hearth.

So Athena pointed at Cram in his jeweled prison, propped up against a far corner in what was most definitely a washtub. "I will say nothing until you release him."

Hearth's eyebrows arched, and icicles hung from her words. "This is not a Sunday market, Journeyman Boyle. We are not bargaining for potatoes. The three of you broke into *my house*, and I will hang that crystal, along with that boy, from a chandelier for a hundred years if you do not answer my question to my satisfaction this instant."

Athena cast a glance at Ruby, who glared an unreadable message at her. The last time they had been in this room, Athena had been torn between duty to her father and the order and caring for this ferocious friend.

And what had happened to Athena since? Well, for one, she was not so nearly attached to her pride.

She swallowed that pride and cast her eyes down at the floor. "Madame Hearth, forgive my outburst. I cannot speak for my companion, but one reason I am here is to apologize."

Hearth started in surprise. "Apologize?"

"For defying your orders and"—she couldn't resist—"eluding the pursuers you sent after us."

"Well, you didn't elude them as much as set up house in the tower of a seemingly immortal chemyst."

"Touché, madame. Additionally, we would like to request passage through your Warren."

The fan paused. "You wish to pass *in*to Philadelphi?"

The question threw Athena for a moment.

Ruby stepped into the gap as smoothly as if shot from a musket.

"Madame, I would *not* like to apologize for my behavior. We have at our disposal a mercenary company, full of hardened clobberknockers, stashed in secret just outside your door."

Hearth's eyes hardened. "Do you now?"

"Oh, indeed, madame. And they are ready to move at a moment's notice." Ruby's face went innocent. "They can be quite violent, you know. Very difficult to control."

Hearth went quite still. "Teach, are you threatening me?"

Athena's heart stopped, and her mind raced. Had they come all this way just to have Ruby get them thrown back into a Bluestocking cage? But then the images began to pop in her mind: the preparations they had witnessed on their trip to Hearth's office. Before Ruby could stick a knife in their only chance, Athena lunged to interrupt.

"Hahahahaha, of course not, Madame Hearth." She reached over to give Ruby what she hoped looked like a friendly squeeze on the arm, but was in truth a grip of death. "You know what a trickster Ruby here is. She just cannot give up the jest."

Ruby covered well enough. "Ahaha, yes. Ow." Well, not so well.

But the pictures in Athena's mind were already running rampant: the bedrolls, the target practice, Greta's tight-lipped nervousness, the air of tension and preparedness in the passageways. The Warren was going to war. Athena's words were just seconds ahead of her thoughts, and she hoped she could keep pace with them. "That is why we are here. As a gesture of goodwill we would like to offer you the opportunity to acquire the mercenaries' services."

It seemed as if Ruby's indrawn breath took a year. She licked her lips and stared straight ahead. "Yes."

Hearth sipped from her tea, face expressionless. "Are they well armed? Veterans? Know their business?"

Ruby and Athena exchanged a glance. *Could* Athena commit alla Ferra's people? But never mind *could*. She already had. "Well, yes, if you call crossbows, muskets, arm's-length knives, an intimate understanding of corners and shadows and bringing down prey . . . if you call that knowing their business, I would say that they do," said Athena. Would Petra alla Ferra even agree to any of this? That was a question for another time. For this first pass of the duel, get Hearth to commit. "I could not help noticing that you are preparing for some kind of—"

"How can I be certain of your word? What if these

soldiers are agents of the crown? What if this is all some sort of sly betrayal?"

Athena hesitated. How could she prove that Los Jabalís were trustworthy when she didn't even know that for herself?

Ruby took a deep breath. "Also with them are two people you know, Wayland Teach and Marise Fermat."

Hearth stood, mouth agape. "Marise is here?"

Ruby's eyes went wide and innocent. "Yes. Not a quarter mile from your door."

Without a moment's hesitation Madame Hearth said, "Very well. I accept."

"What?" said Athena.

"What?" said Ruby.

"Impossible," said Greta Van Huffridge.

Hearth turned to the bald steward, Pate. "Release them." She was already halfway out the door. "Do it as we walk."

Greta Van Huffridge bristled. "But madame—"

"We don't have time for these games, Van Huffridge. You, of all people, should know that."

"Yes, but madame, they humiliated you."

The woman raked a glance across the two friends, and Athena struggled to meet it. "That is a debt for another time." Pate cut Athena's bonds from her wrists with a single pass from a monster of a hatchet, then coiled up the remainder. Hearth continued, quickly and urgently. "Can you describe the location in which they are hidden?"

They nodded as one.

"Good. Pate, take Badger and go with all haste to this place. Tell them that their people are safe and that the mistress of the Warren would see them without delay. Time is of the essence. I will meet you at the first smokehouse door after I show these two what they must see."

"Wait," said Athena. She pointed to Cram, who in response nodded so vigorously inside his crystal prison that it wobbled in its washtub. "There is the question of—"

"Your man will be fine, and free soon. Van Huffridge, start the dissolving process."

The girl grimaced, but to her credit she did not protest. "Yes, madame," she said, and then stuck some sort of metal needle into the crystal. It immediately began to steam.

"Come now. Time is of the essence," repeated Hearth.

They followed her down the hall. What is the hurry? What is she showing us? thought Athena. The passages ran narrower and narrower until with two abreast their shoulders were brushing the walls.

"Where are we?" whispered Ruby.

Hearth answered without a glance backward, "Earliest tunnels. No one comes here now; this way I can keep things a bit more private."

It was impressive the way Hearth had put her grudge aside without a second thought. Wherever they were going, it felt as if something larger were happening. Something more important than personal ill will. Athena sped up to walk with Greta Van Huffridge. The girl gave her a grim shrug and motioned with her chin for her to keep going. It was an inappropriate time to bring it up, but really, why let the appropriate get in the way of the true? "Miss Van Huffridge, please let me apologize for our misunderstanding in London so long ago. We were both a good deal younger, and I may have misstated my family's—"

"Our parents wanted us to marry, and you said no."

Greta forged forward, keeping her eyes on the chemystrally hardened earthen floor. "You thought yourself too good for my family of hayseeds. What more is there to say? You have another round of insults prepared?"

It rankled at Athena. She had had very good reasons to refuse the match, mostly revolving around the fact that Miss Van Huffridge, daughter of Lothor Van Huffridge, secretary-general of the Rupert's Bay Company and one of the most powerful men in the colonies, was most likely neither inclined toward nor interested in marrying a young man who turned out to actually be a young woman. So Athena had done something shameful. She had publicly humiliated Greta, denied their engagement in front of hundreds of people. "There are innumerable reasons, Miss Van Huffridge—"

Greta snorted. "Innumerable, you say? The reasons for scorning me are infinite?"

Behind them Ruby stifled a chuckle. "I have to admit that—"

"Ruby, please." Athena blinked. "Greta, that is not at all what I—"

Hearth stopped. "We are here. Please quiet yourselves."

Ahead of them in the hallway lay a stout wooden door, the kind of door whose maker's philosophy was most likely "You can have your frills and carving. Give me something that will keep out a hungry werewolf." Scarred, thick, and functional. In front of it stood a warden Athena recognized from their previous visit. Reed thin and sharp as thorns, his bushy beard jutted out of his mask, which bore a single flame. Two over-the-shoulder belts crossed his breastbone, holding a crowd of clinking vials and flasks.

"Why the walking laboratory?" whispered Ruby.

"Whatever is beyond that door has someone scared spitless, that's why," whispered Athena.

Madame Hearth looked back at them. The front of confidence was gone. Even half hidden by the mask, her face was so nakedly afraid that it set Athena reeling. "Indeed. I have no understanding of what is beyond this door, and it frightens me immensely." She turned back to the guard. "Flame, we'd like to see our guest, please."

"Of course, madame." He pulled a brass key from a pouch and placed it against the lock. The key flowed effortlessly into the very incompatibly shaped keyhole. His jaw set, he held the door open. "I'll be right here."

Hearth nodded and stalked into the room, screening their view for a moment. She stepped to the side.

It sat on a cot in the corner.

A thing out of a nightmare.

Black veins crept up its neck from beneath its functional frock. It looked at Athena with vacant eyes, shot with tendrils of slate where the bloodshot should have been. Its hands peeked out from the heavily mended wrists of its blouse, lying there in its lap like cold fish. It looked exactly like a young woman, like a mother perhaps, but everything else about it screamed *wrong*.

A faint odor hung in the air. Sickness. Or rot.

Beside Athena, Ruby swallowed a curse, working hard to control her breathing, muttering, "Nonononono," over and over again.

The thing slowly raised its hand.

It waved.

"Hello, my name's Penny," said the thing. "What's yours?"

Athena's hand strayed to her hip for her missing sword. Her pulse pounded in her ears. The thing (Penny?) made no threatening moves, no hostile gestures. It just sat on the cot, smiling slightly.

"Madame Hearth, what is this?" Athena managed.

The leader of the Bluestockings braced her back against the corner of the cell farthest from Penny. Hearth had picked up a curve of hardened cloth from a small table, and it crackled as she twisted it back and forth. Her nostrils flared. "You tell me."

"I have no idea. Why would I? I've never seen anything like this," said Athena. "Why did you bring us here?"

Hearth looked down her nose at Ruby. "Call it a hunch." She held up the torn bandage. "We found this wrapped and hardened about her head. And this"—in her other hand lay a small chemystral device—"wedged into her ear. These mean nothing to you?"

"I tell you, no."

Ruby hadn't taken her eyes off the gray woman, the chorus of noes unceasing.

She did know, obviously. She had known the moment they walked in the door. Athena could see the knowledge mixed with terror and guilt plain as a child's first steps. "Ruby, what is it?"

No response. She was hypnotized.

"Ruby." Athena touched her shoulder.

"Hello, my name's Penny—"

With a start Ruby looked up to meet Athena's eyes. "What?"

At the look on Ruby's face Athena's shoulders crept down her back. "Do you know what this is?"

The words came haltingly, as if she were waking from some terrible dream. "I think so. I—I know someone else who was made like this."

Madame Hearth leaned in. "In Philadelphi?"

"No. In the mountains."

"The *mountains*? Where have you been, Ruby Teach?"

Ruby ignored the question. "Where did you find this woman?"

"She is the sister of one of our teachers. He brought her in. She's a fishwife. He went to visit her in UnderTown and found her like this."

She knelt and put her hand on the woman's knee. The gentleness of it surprised Athena. "Penny, can you tell these two friends what you told me? About the shop?"

Penny smiled at Hearth. "They pay you. Not much but a little. It feels good. You go to sleep, and you walk out a little bit richer." She kicked her feet back and forth like a child.

It didn't make sense. Athena turned to Ruby. "Like an opium den? But you pay them, not the other way around?"

"I don't think it's an opium den." Something deep and sad and scared lurked behind Ruby's eyes.

Hearth twisted and pulled at the bandage. "Can you help us solve it?"

"Possibly. As soon as they arrive, please bring a boy named Henry Collins." Ruby flexed her hands. "And my mother."

CHAPTER 8

*Chemystry is Nature's Gift to all, without reservation. To grant it
to some and deny it to others is as to Hoard Sunlight or to Parcel
out the Seas. I shall not allow it.*
—Francine of Torres, founder, *the Bluestockings*, 1692

Henry's nostrils quivered. He placed a hand on the cool
corridor wall next to Marise Fermat's shoulder, not to
reassure her but to brace himself.

"What is it?" Her voice rang hollow inside the metal
mask.

He blinked. His eyes were in truth watering. He
leaned down to whisper into the narrow air vent nearest
her ear. "Mix a tight underground corridor with a pack of

Jabalís who have not bathed in weeks, and your product is an acidic fog that could knock over an oliphant." He made sure to keep breathing through his mouth. A small chuckle emerged from the mask. Henry counted himself lucky. The trip east had not been easy for his new master. She had come willingly enough after Ruby when Henry, Athena, and Cram had arrived on her doorstep asking for aid. But since then it had been a plague of the worst kind of luck. Her brilliant cottage, a chemystral wonder complete with a vesicle that carried it across the sky? Ruined. Her own self? Imprisoned. Her daughter, for whom she had sacrificed so much? Estranged. He could not blame her if she was angry.

"Why have we stopped?" she asked.

Henry hunched down to speak into the mask's ear. "We have stopped at a large chemystral door, embossed with the seal of the Worshipful Order."

Marise's snort echoed. "That stupid camel." She shifted from one foot to the other. Henry smiled ruefully. Her body could stay no more stationary than her mind. Just like Ruby. In that way and so many others.

"The Warren. Here I am again," she said to herself.

Henry glanced about at the hard, chemystrally smoothed earthen walls and the intricate engraving on the great door. He had heard about the Warren. Pierre Fermat had dim opinions of the chemysts who worked inside it. It gnawed at Henry's calm, which was truly never very calm. "You know this place?"

"That door you're looking at? I helped build it. This was my home laboratory for years before—" The mask tilted slightly.

"Before your journeys with Captain Teach?"

"Yes."

Wayland Teach stood up near the door, talking quietly and intensely with Petra alla Ferra and her two lieutenants. With them stood a pair of Bluestockings, one in a badger mask, holding some kind of crystal artifice, and the other bigger, balder, and carrying a hatchet. Those two had appeared at Los Jabalís's hiding place in the trees, waving a white handkerchief of parley (actually some very busy lace, thrust like a pike above the head of the woman) just as Henry was about to gnaw straight through his lower lip for worry over Cram, Athena, and Ruby.

The pair had escorted the troupe under cover of darkness to a strange little house made up of random boards, then down a side stair next to a very deep pit into a highly sophisticated set of tunnels. But Henry's brief candle of hope had quickly dissolved into an oily slick of worry. Where were his friends? Were they being herded into a trap? The camel's mouth in the door looked as if all manner of fiery and deadly effects could be shot through it.

He picked at the stains on his fingers.

They had been waiting too long.

With a great groan of gears and mechanisms the door slowly opened. "Something's happening," he said to Marise. A woman appeared in the doorway. She was completely unremarkable: medium height, unkempt brown hair under a faded blue mask adorned with a drawing of a fireplace. She walked straight up to Petra alla Ferra, however, and stood nose to nose with her, talking a good long while. The hallway remained silent. The two women spit on their hands and shook. A deal had been made.

The mercenary captain parted the middle of her company like a heated stylus through salt metal. She stopped in front of Marise, the Bluestocking leader trailing behind her. In tones so low only Henry could overhear them the woman said, "Madame Fermat?"

"Devil Woman?"

Alla Ferra smiled grimly. "Today the sun smiles upon you, but do not think I will stand by and watch you harm even a fingernail of one of my people." She raised her voice to fill the hallway. "In exchange for safe harbor in this place, until the matter of our compensation is resolved, I have agreed to free you from this mask, if only for our time in hiding here." She turned her eyes to Henry. "Do not forget your pledge."

He swallowed. "I haven't."

She raised an eyebrow. "I would have you say it."

It was the price that he had been willing to pay. Why did it seem so difficult to say out loud? He cleared his throat and forced it out, filling the corridor as alla Ferra had. "I have sworn that we would accompany you to your employer and that I would aid in translation of Marise

Fermat's journal, in exchange for your aid in saving Ruby Teach. You have held up your bargain, and I will hold up mine." He glanced at the woman behind alla Ferra. "This is not your contact?"

"His representative is within the city walls. These are— They are—how do you say?—in cahoots with the one who has my money."

"With Godfrey Boyle." He chewed at his lip. Athena had told Henry much about her father, and none of it was reassuring. Boyle was loyal to the Worshipful Order, period, and Henry was not a member. Nor, for that matter, was Ruby or Marise.

Alla Ferra's eyes shackled his. He could not look away. "As you say." She took the green metal key from around her neck and dropped it into his hand. She turned and walked through the huge brass door into the Warren with her head high, trailed by Los Jabalís.

Vera Medina leaned in as she walked past, her mouth just at the level of his ear. "Never trust a chemyst, Henry Collins. Let alone a hive of them." She winked and moved on before he could reply.

He felt a sharp jab in his ribs. Alaia Calderon looked up at him with a scowl. "I have my eye on you, Collins."

"Thank you?" he ventured.

Without another word alla Ferra's other lieutenant hurried off after her companion.

Before he knew it, the hallway was empty save him, Marise, and the woman with fire on her mask. Wayland Teach hovered out of earshot in the shadows near the door.

The woman looked Henry up and down with interest, eyes lingering over the burns and scars on his chemystry-stained hands.

"Well?" she said.

"Pleased to make your acquaintance. My name is—"

"Open the mask, boy."

He blinked. "Yes, ma'am." Of course. He should have done it as soon as he had been given the key.

And so Henry put the key in the keyhole, right next to the temple. It turned easily, and a handle popped out.

The faceplate opened easily on its oiled hinges, and Marise Fermat stared back at him. An older, blonder Ruby Teach.

She sported the remains of a quite substantial black eye.

"Hello, Henry," she said.

"Hello, Master."

Her eyes flicked behind him. "Hello, Alice. Lovely mask. Still given to overblown theatrics, I see."

The woman smiled icily back. "Hello, Marise. Still biting the hand that protects you, I see."

They stared blades into each other. Henry tried to fold himself back into the wall.

"Well," said Marise, "that was a lovely reunion. Let's be off to whatever it is you desperately need me to help you with. Henry, be a love and remove this cursed bucket from my head."

"Of course."

The women waited for Henry to take the heavy contraption off. "What should I do with this?" he said.

Marise looked speculatively at the other woman. "Bring it along. I'm sure we'll find some use for it."

He held it awkwardly to his chest. The Bluestocking woman was staring at him again.

"I am Madame Hearth. You are welcome to the Warren," she said, in a way that made it quite clear that he should not get used to it. "Follow me, please." She turned and left at a brisk pace, not waiting to see if they followed.

"What was that about?" said Henry.

"I stole her boyfriend," said Marise.

"Who was he?"

"I believe you know my husband."

". . . oh."

They set off down the hall after her.

Captain Teach waited just inside the doorway. He fell in next to them.

"What are you doing?" said Marise.

"Hearth wants to show us something or other," said Teach.

"I don't recall inviting you to come with us. Henry?"

Oh, no. The relationship between the Teaches was one that Henry still could not understand, and he generally tried to blend into the background when they came near each other. "Yes ma'am? Er, Master?"

"Did I miss something? Did I ask Captain Pickpocket to walk along with us?" From up ahead, where Madame Hearth walked, came a chuckle.

"No, you didn't."

"You see?"

Henry chewed his lip. "But I'm not certain the captain requires your permission."

Teach smiled through his bushy mustaches. "Good lad."

Marise snorted. "Henry, you are now officially notified that I am initiating a search for a more obedient apprentice."

"Duly noted, Master."

And so they followed Madame Hearth through a bustling collection of passageways, full of classrooms and young people, surrounded by older folk in masks. He had heard rumors of these chemysts. The Bluestockings ran a school for students who wanted to learn chemystry but did not meet the Tinkers Guild specifications—to wit, male, of the gentry, and English by blood. They wore masks because the practice of educating these other students was outlawed, and the teachers here undertook their task at great risk to their families. Henry drank it all in hungrily as he passed.

He had been part of a School of One.

The old man—Fermat, Marise's uncle—had taken him on as a student, and Henry had never met or even seen any other chemysts close to his age. Well, with the exception of Athena Boyle, but she was really more of a dabbler; he felt guilty for thinking it, but it was true. In fifty feet of hallway they passed more chemysts than he had ever seen in his life. And the smells! Cram could go on and on about this wildflower or that, the scent of a particular strain of rabbit scat, and he was welcome to it. Henry breathed in deeply. The sharp bite of aqua fortis acid. The deep base mushroom scent of carbon. The slightly fruity tang of blue vitriol. The smells sang to him, wrapping him in a rich song of Science. They took him back in time to Fermat's laboratory, and with a sharp ache he realized he deeply missed his old teacher.

He caught Marise Fermat watching him out of the corner of her eye. "It's like home, isn't it?"

He blushed.

On her other side Wayland Teach wiped his red, watering eyes with a handkerchief. He blew his nose. "Providence, I hate this place."

They could not catch up with Madame Hearth, who arrowed down the halls like a runaway tinker's carriage. As quickly as they strode, she moved more rapidly. She led them by twist and turn deeper into the complex, into a maze of older, rougher, narrower passages. They turned a corner to come upon a hard-looking guard and, next to him, looking shaken, Ruby and Athena. The guard bore a single flame on his mask and wore a veritable arsenal of chemystral flasks. Without a word he unlocked a stout door, stood aside, and motioned the group past. The others went through, but the captain paused a moment next to the guard.

"Hallo, David," he said.

The man smiled and nodded. "Wayland."

From inside the doorway Madame Hearth's voice rang out. "I would ask that you respect our customs while you are in this place."

Teach rolled his eyes. "My apologies, Madame Hearth!" And in a quick, low voice he said to the guard, "Why her?"

The smile vanished. "She's pure iron, Teach. And we need someone like that in these times. Loyal, too. A rare quality nowadays."

Henry had never seen the captain blush.

"You were a Bluestocking, too?" Henry asked.

"A sentinel. A bodyguard of sorts, like Flame here." Teach nodded at the guard and then sighed. "It didn't really take."

The guard cleared his throat. "Go in now. This is something you all should see." He waved them through the doorway.

Madame Hearth, Marise, Ruby, and Athena stood inside, crammed around a cot with a straw mattress. Cram was nowhere to be seen.

The other person in the room? He would not be able to forget her face for a very long time.

CHAPTER 9

Beneath my cypress, a startling smile.
Wondrous sweet, it bears no guile.
—Taki, first poet to the Tulip Sultan, 1712

Even after a few hours it reassured Ruby to see Henry. And her father. Or should she say Captain Teach? Blast it.

Seeing her mother was quite another thing.

"Stop staring at me," said Ruby.

Teach frowned. "Ruby—"

"It's all right." Marise Fermat had somehow rid herself of the mask Los Jabalís had stuck her with, and now Henry was toting it around like an anchor. Ruby wasn't certain she approved of the change. Marise flicked her blue eyes away from Ruby to study Penny. Madame Hearth had left Ruby and Athena in the custody of the guard Flame, while she collected the others, and he had responded to their questions with only grunts. So they had watched Penny through the little grate in the door. The woman had sat quiet, smiling vacantly, ever since. "What is your name?" said Marise.

"Penny. What's yours?" Her eyelids flicked closed, then open again. The gray skin was almost translucent.

Being near Penny gave Ruby the shivers down to her marrow. The skin, the black tendrils, the hollowness. It was very like Evram Hale back at Fort Scoria, and what that might mean had her scared spitless.

"Is this somehow a fruit of your research, Marise?" asked Hearth.

"I suspect it is, but I'd like to observe while my apprentice asks a few questions. Then we can compare our observations to any you have made?" There was a strange formality between them, as if they were following a set of mysterious rules.

Madame Hearth nodded. "Very well. Proceed."

She passed Marise a kind of magnifying glass, and Ruby's mother knelt in front of the woman. "My name is Marise." She looked up at Ruby, and then her eyes slid past her. "Henry, could you help me, please?"

A quick spike of something stabbed Ruby in the gut. She wasn't sure what to make of it. Was she jealous? Of Henry? She couldn't give two shillings for her mother's regard, and now she was pining for it? She gave herself a mental shake and tried to pipe her mind down.

Henry, who had jumped ship from old Fermat to a new master before you could say "fickle," wove his lanky frame through the tightly packed cell and knelt down in front of Penny. He hesitated.

"Just ask her about what's happened to her, please," said Marise. "This is an opportunity for your education."

Henry chewed his lip for a moment, and then he turned back to Penny.

"Hello, I'm Henry. May I ask you a few questions?"

The smile widened, strange and just flat wrong on her terrifying face. "Of course."

His eyes searched hers. "How did this happen to you?"

"What?"

His gaze shifted to Marise, who nodded encouragement. "Your skin seems to have some . . . discoloring to it . . . and your eyes. Have they always been like that?"

Penny laughed, a completely innocent sound. "Oh, no. This is what happens from the juicing. It don't hurt, though." She rubbed her hands over her arms. "Feels right nice. Smoothlike."

Henry forced a smile to match Penny's. "I see. 'Juicing,' you say?"

"'S right. Some tinker fella set up a flash little shop. You go right in, and they sit you on a nice sofer, and then they give you a kind of contraption for your face—"

"Like this one?" Henry pointed to Marise's mask, lying on the floor.

Penny laughed. "No, silly, just for your mouth. And it has tubes and the like on it, and you lie down, and breathe easy"—she demonstrated—"and you have the most wonderful dreams, and then they come and wake you, and they gives you two whole shillings for your trouble!"

Ruby's stomach rolled. All she could think about was Evram Hale, skin mottled like Penny's, but even worse—not talking and just staring—the first victim of the Swede's machine. For all she knew he was still sitting there back at Fort Scoria. Where she had abandoned him. Her cheeks flushed. Evram had helped her at every turn, even putting himself in danger for her, and she had left him behind.

Henry leaned closer, looking closer at Penny's features. "They put a mask over your face?"

"Yeah, you breathes in, and it tastes like flowers or somethin'. Then feels like someone's sucking your air out your mouth, but soothing, like. So nice. You should try it."

Henry's chuckle was strained. "Maybe I will, Miss Penny."

Ruby could not keep herself or her thoughts still. How long had it been since she escaped Fort Scoria? A fortnight? Had fourteen days been enough for the

Swede to get the apparatus into the city? If he was using it already . . . She tried to keep her voice calm. "The machine, Penny. There's a ticking kind of hum? And a thump in the air, against your skin, like a heart is beating somewhere?"

"That's it. You know."

Ruby's heart fell into her boots. "That's it. It's the Swede's machine."

The woman yawned. "I'm sleepy."

Marise shook her head in exasperation. "Ruby, please. We do not know for certain. We need to discover exactly—"

How could she say that? It was *her* invention they were talking about! The plans for this, for what was sitting in front of them, had been put into Ruby's body by her mother and then ripped out by the Swede. "Of course you know what it is. Of course you do. Of course you do."

"Ruby—" Captain Teach said.

She turned on her father, her chest tight with fury and guilt. "Father, of course the great inventor knows her work.

Why not take credit where it's due for this wonderful—"

Madame Hearth interrupted. "We should let Penny have her rest. But before we go, I would like you to observe one more thing." She turned to the woman on the cot. "Penny, please stand up."

The woman smiled, then stood up.

Athena frowned. "What does this have to do with—"

Hearth ignored her. "Penny, hop on one leg."

She picked up her foot and began hopping, a distant smile still plastered on her face.

Ruby didn't know why, but it disturbed her. Something about the vacancy, the emptiness there. It wasn't the emptiness of the Reeve. It was something scarier.

"Penny hop up on the bed."

She did.

"Penny, flap your arms and squawk like a chicken."

She did.

"Penny, choke yourself."

Henry turned to Hearth, eyes wide. "What?"

Penny put her hands about her throat and began to squeeze.

"Stop her," Ruby said. Her voice shook.

Penny continued, and she started to make small gurgling sounds in her throat. Her eyes bulged.

"Penny, stop!" said Ruby.

Penny pulled her hands away, easy as you please.

The room was silent, save for the sounds of the woman heaving in great gouts of air.

Ruby wanted to scream. Or retch. She turned back to Hearth. "Why did you do that?"

Hearth's eyes were granite. "You needed to see it. Now I suggest we all retire to my study and let Miss Penny here get some rest."

Penny immediately yawned. "Thank you!" And she curled up on her bed, ready to sleep.

Hearth led the pack of them down the corridors back to her office. Silence preceded them. Students stared. Masked adults tried to pretend not to. Whispers spread behind their passage like the wake of a ship. Everyone was looking. But they were not looking at Ruby or Athena. Every eye followed Wayland Teach and Marise Fermat.

Athena leaned over to Ruby as they walked. "Well, this is different."

"What do you mean?"

"They're not gawking at us."

Ruby scanned the halls as they walked. These people did not know Marise Fermat and Wayland Teach as her father and mother. To them they were something else. Something apparently important. On Ruby's first visit Madame Hearth had said her mother was a brilliant alchemyst and had implied her father had stolen Marise away from greatness. Was that the truth? Did Ruby even know them? That big, bearded man up ahead had always been her rock in the storm, a pillar of strength. But he wasn't what she thought he was. Was he? A wave of dizziness struck her.

Athena was there to steady her, taking her elbow. "You all right?"

She nodded and squared her shoulders. "Just— I'm reeling, Athena. I don't know what to think. Wet is dry and dry is wet."

Athena smiled sadly. "We have to keep up. Can you

make it, or will I have to carry you? I can do it, you know."
Her eyebrows shot up, perfectly innocent. "Then perhaps
people will start looking at us again."

It brought Ruby back to the world. They walked on.

They arrived at Hearth's office and arranged
themselves on the battered furniture. Cram was there,
sitting on a wooden chair, wide eyed as a new colt. The
washtub next to him was full to the brim with strawberry-
smelling ooze. He sat wet and shivering in a robe, small
pieces of pink goo still hanging from his nose and ears.
Ruby hugged him in relief.

"Easy, Ferret." He smiled shakily. "Take care you
don't tarnish your hard reputation."

Athena and Henry greeted him as well, but the
whole group quickly subsided into silence and their own
thoughts.

Hearth busied herself with the samovar. "So."

Ruby saw no reason to be tactful. "So what kind of
cruel madness was that?"

"Ruby, I think Madame Hearth was correct. I think
we needed to see her—" Henry said.

"To see that woman choke the life out of herself? I suppose we have been a bit starved for entertainment out in the wilderness, Henry, but why not some old sea shanties? Don't you think those might go down a bit more smoothly?"

"If you cannot keep a civil tongue, I will have all the children removed, and the adults can continue this conversation," said Hearth.

"*Children*? Why, you gussied-up bag of—"

"Ruby." The shards of glass in her father's tone stopped her short. He was still her father to her, but in the days since Gwath's revelation it had not gotten any less confusing. And where was *Gwath*? No matter who knew what, he should have been here. With her other father. Ruby's pulse raced. The room was vibrating.

"Fine." She waved her hand airily in the direction of Henry and her mother. "The chemysts should speak. Tell us about the Swede's work, will you? Of excellent quality, is it not? He seems to have made some modifications since his first experiment. Evram Hale couldn't even speak when I saw him. Charming woman Penny is, don't you think?"

Marise stared at her for a moment, face unreadable. "Henry?"

He hesitated.

"It's all right," said Marise. "You can speak candidly. Obviously my work is no longer a secret. Report your findings."

The young chemyst cleared his throat and looked about nervously. He steadied himself on Hearth's table. "From her description I believe that woman to have been subjected to some variation of the process you discovered, the one encoded into Ruby's blood, the process that harvests the chemystral energy from living subjects."

"Juicing, she called it," said the captain. He kept on looking back and forth between Ruby and her mother, tentative and pained.

"But how did the process become known?" Hearth asked. She turned to Marise. "If you were hidden in the mountains, and Collins here had the journal—"

"It was Swedenborg," said Ruby, "the chemyst from Fort Scoria." She wanted to throw something. The words tasted bitter on her tongue. "He . . . harvested the plans from my blood. He must be in the city. Somehow he has reached Philadelphi before us."

Marise rolled her eyes. "Chemysts can move quickly if they choose. I'm certainly not the only one to ever have created a flying house."

Athena frowned. "How long has this been going on?"

"A few days perhaps," said Hearth.

"How many people?" said Teach.

"No way of knowing. There is at least the one shop in UnderTown."

"Why— I'm sorry." Athena cleared her throat, and Ruby could read the disgust on her face as clearly as if it were on her own. "Why were you telling her to do those things?"

"Penny is susceptible to suggestion. Highly susceptible. I wanted you to see."

"Swedenborg added that little hint of spice to your recipe, Mother," Ruby managed to get out. She wanted to scream. "Now the machine sucks your will right out along with your Source."

Henry said, "With just one of those machines the

amount of chemystral energy they could be harvesting would be, well, significant."

"Significant? Really? Is that all you care about?" Ruby ground her teeth. How could they all just be sitting there, drinking their tea, discussing it so calmly?

"No, but with reserves of energy like that, a skilled chemyst could do, well, almost anything."

"Skies open, fire from the heavens, cracks of doom, that sort of thing?" said Athena.

Henry blinked. "Well, yes. Exactly that sort of thing."

They stared at one another. Ruby held herself completely still. It was the only way she could stop herself from throwing things.

Madame Hearth turned back from the samovar and plonked a tray of steaming teacups down on the table. Henry picked up a cup. Everyone else, who had tasted this particular tea before, found somewhere else to look.

"And with a populace subject to that sort of suggestion, there would be no resistance to the exercise of such power." Madame Hearth sat in her chair and sipped her tea. "There is something else you should know."

Henry sampled his cup. Choked. Eyes watering, he managed to ask, "And what is that?"

"Well, a few things actually." Hearth produced a sheaf of papers. Wanted posters. Drawings stared up from them: Captain Teach, Marise, Ruby, Athena.

"No Cram or Henry?" said Ruby.

"Henry and Cram are apparently less of an official priority," Hearth said. "But the rest of you are wanted. In Philadelphi and abroad. Enemies to the crown."

Ruby's eyes narrowed. Hearth was no idiot. Why would she show them the posters now? To soften them up? For what? "Being wanted is nothing new to us. You said a few things?"

Hearth stared at her for a moment. "Your arrival is fortuitous." She spooned sugar into her cup. "You are a formidable set of folk. I know this from our history together and from my experiences with you and Lord Boyle there. Not to mention the company of mercenaries you have brought with you, currently squatting in my hallways. You are a walking collection of balance shifters."

"Thank you?" said Ruby. Shifting the balance. Hearth sounded eerily like Wisdom Rool. She dug her fingernails into her palm.

"I hope you also know that I am showing you a tremendous amount of trust by allowing you to enter the Warren at this time and by introducing you to our . . . guest."

"We thank you for it," said Ruby's father.

"Well, then. Here it is." Her cup clanked down on the table. "War is coming. This you know. Militias on both sides are setting fire to towns, salting fields, sowing terror. Boston itself is half burned to the ground. For some time now the people of Pennswood and several other colonies have chafed under the rule of the crown. The Worshipful Order has fed the fire of the current unrest. We see it as the perfect opportunity."

"For what?" said Henry.

"A rising. To name our own monarch. A king in America."

Ruby's jaw dropped. A king. She certainly had no love for the English crown. It had hunted, captured, and filleted her. But throwing off a king would not be easy. It would cost lives.

Her father had a distracted look, too, as if he were doing sums in his head. "Who?"

Hearth put down her cup. "Lothor Van Huffridge."

"Greta's *father*?" Athena shook her head in wonder. "It works. He is strong, admired by many, has relationships throughout the colonies, even in New France. . . ."

Henry cut in. "Does what happened to Penny have something to do with this? If I wanted to take the fire out of a revolt—"

Hearth nodded bleakly. "I might attempt to make the people amenable to do whatever I told them to. Even if they were harming themselves. Yes."

All at once everyone was talking. Questions filled the room. Madame Hearth looked about and waited until they all became quiet. "If you are with us, you may stay. If you are not, I will expect you to depart forthwith, with your mercenary accompaniment. You will be allowed to depart in peace." She stood. "I imagine you wish to discuss this among yourselves. You may use this room to plan your road forward. You have one hour."

She knocked at the door. Pate opened it, and she flowed out.

The door clacked shut.

They stared at one another.

"Well, I do know one thing," said Henry.

"What's that?" said Ruby.

"This tea is terrible."

CHAPTER 10

When Freedom wakes in the New World,
it will not be put back to sleep.
— Elizabeth de Toqueville, *Travels in the Colonies*

Ruby shook her head. A strange little whistle hung in her ears, just on the edge of hearing. "Did she say—"

"A king?" Henry said. "On this side of the ocean? Besides Greta's father, who is Lothor Van Huffridge?"

Lost in thought, Captain Teach stared at the wall. "Van Huffridge, yes." He shook himself, waking from a dream. "The head of the Rupert's Bay Company. They do all of the fur trading in the colonies. Powerful man.

Savvy. I met him once, outside a tavern in UnderTown."

Ruby squinted. He had on his it's-not-my-fault look. "In the street or the alley?"

Teach licked his lips. "Alley."

"So you robbed him?"

"Well, he had so much money—"

"You robbed the king of America?"

"He wasn't king at the time."

Cram shook himself like a dog after a bath. Pink goo flew. "Mayhap he will be, though, Captain."

"Hold on," said Marise. Her hand flew up, as if to ward off demons. "Are you lot actually considering *staying* here?"

"What do you mean?" said Ruby.

"I mean, this city is about to explode. People will die. Many people. Colonial revolts do not succeed. They get squashed." She pulled her hair out of the greasy band that held it back and started to regather it into a tight bun. "It's out of the question for any of you to stay here."

Ruby laughed, a long, low, bitter chuckle. "Out of the question? Marise, who are you to tell us what is or is not in our futures?" Besides, Ruby was completely flummoxed by the news. She loved Philadelphi, but a rising? A revolt? A strange excitement flared at the base of her spine. If the English crown was the Swede and Rool, perhaps this rising would rid the city of them. Or the countryside. What if the crew didn't have to stay on the run? What if they could make a place of, of refuge?

"I am your mother, Ruby. This is no time for petulance."

Fury pulled her out of her chair. "What do you know of petulance? You feared for your precious secret. You feared for it so deeply you hid yourself away for over a decade. You *left* us!"

"Ruby, this is not the time—" said Athena.

"No, no, Athena. She left me and him"—Ruby waved her hand at Captain Teach, who leaned against the edge of the sofa; he looked ill—"and the crew and, and"— she took a shuddering breath—"and Gwath, and she ran away." She whirled back to Marise. "Would you have us do the same?"

The scorn was gone from her mother's face. Now she

measured the rope of her words, knot by knot. "I would. Because despite what you think of me, Ruby, I did and do care for you. And Wayland. And yes, Gwath." There was something in her gaze, a machete of a look. Did she know that Gwath was here in this place?

"Stop it, the two of you," said Captain Teach.

"Father, she is manipulating us right now. She—"

"Wayland, this has nothing—"

"*Stop.*" The captain's sledgehammer of a fist slammed down on the back of the sofa. It snapped in half with a loud CRACK. A storm of anger loomed in his eyes. Ruby stopped talking. Her father was a pleasant man, a nice man. But she had seen him angry. A hurricane. No one could stand before him. Beside her, Cram whimpered deep down in his throat.

Captain Teach blew out his mustaches and shook himself like a bull. "Now. You heard Madame Hearth. We have one hour, and we must decide; it is dishonorable to abuse her hospitality. Ruby, your mother is right. If the city rises, no one will be safe, including us." His glance cut short Marise's interruption. "But I consider you companions, not children. I shall not tell you what to do. You must decide for yourselves. Who will stay and who will go?"

"Wayland—" Marise interrupted.

"Marise. Please. Look at them."

Ruby followed her mother's gaze.

Athena stood before them. Even in her frontier leathers she cut a figure of valor. Her chin jutted forward with grace and resolve, an image of her warrior goddess namesake, carved from living stone.

Cram. Restless fingers worried at his bag, constantly checking to see that its knots were secure. Somehow he had found a plate of biscuits and a never-ending stream of them rolled into his mouth. His eyes never rested, though, always searching for a side door to guide them through or a safe haven to hunker down in.

Henry. An awkward beanpole of a wizard with chemystry-scarred hands, the deepest secrets of the spheres hiding behind his onyx eyes.

Marise's gaze finally traveled back to Ruby, and she imagined what Marise saw there: a willful child, fists clenched at her side, reckless and wild. But even so, she knew that however she might appear, she would never let someone else decide her fate for her again.

"Very well," said Marise. Suddenly she was all smiles. She turned to Athena. "What is *your* assessment of our position, my lady?"

Henry cut in. "My apologies, but—"

"Henry?" said Athena.

"Shouldn't Captain Alla Ferra be a part of this?"

Athena raised an eyebrow. "Why should she?"

"I gave her my word, Athena. We have an arrangement."

"Created under duress."

"They had a literal knife to your throat, lad." The captain's face was *too* innocent. "Who could be held to such a bogus bargain?"

Henry glanced at Ruby. "They helped us save your daughter, sir."

Ruby would not, could not let them make this only about her. They needed to decide for themselves. "I didn't need saving," said Ruby.

Athena laughed. "Oh, that's right. You were doing perfectly well climbing down that cliff face. In the rain. And the dark."

Ruby flushed. "I was."

"I'm certain the Reeve wouldn't have caught you on that bridge."

"They would have never noticed! You tipped them off. That is the only reason they came after us. You and that great, galloping herd of Catalonians."

"They helped us save you, Ferret," Cram said with a wounded look.

"I didn't ask to be saved!" Ruby slammed her hand down on the table, sending teacups everywhere. Ruby blushed. Her father's daughter indeed.

Silence reigned for a moment. Cram went after the cups.

"It wasn't—" She *had* asked to be saved. She had dreamed about it and slowly her faith had dissolved into nothing, and then, against all hope, they had found her climbing down the wall in the rain and scooped her up like angels, but— "It wasn't you."

Athena snorted. "No, that's right. We just ran into you in the street, on our way to the coffeehouse."

"I don't mean that, Athena. You did. You did arrive and spirit me away"—a tornado of ideas was whirling around in her head just that moment, but one stood out, a candle in the dark—"but it was Rool who set me free."

"I'm sorry?" said Henry.

"It was Rool." The realization gathered steam, like Sleipnir at a full gallop. "Could he have released me, at least in part, because he knew I might come here to the Warren? Because he knew about the rising? Because he *wanted* me to be in Philadelphi at the time of the revolt?"

Athena's eyebrows were so knitted together they were touching. "But what benefit—"

"I don't know." She thought back to Alla Ferra's chess set; but Wisdom Rool was a grand master, and she was utterly lost. She barely understood the rules. "He said I was an agent of chaos, and that's what he needed me to do. *Be chaos*." She avoided her father's eyes. "Past that I haven't the faintest idea what he might want, and I'm not inclined to try to follow his lead. But what happened to Penny, to Evram . . . it cannot be allowed. I will help." She turned to Athena. "Athena, your father—"

"Wants us here as well. At least the person who hired Los Jabalís on his behalf is somewhere in the city."

Captain Teach took great care with his words. "The order—and therefore your father—are playing a part in engineering this revolt. He wants it to happen. But you are English. We all are." An unspoken question hung in the air.

Athena stared at him, then answered it. "In England, sir, I have pretended all my life to be a man, so that I might inherit my father's vast estate and continue his work." And then she was talking to Ruby, and Ruby could not tear her eyes away from Athena's. "But I find this landscape suits me. My friend Winnifred Pleasant Black, who was wise enough to leave us far behind, mind you, cares not a whit whether a person sees her as man, woman, or bear. I find that a position to admire and even emulate." She took a deep, sharp breath. "My concern is Ruby Teach, those of you in this room, and, only after that, the order. Currently I believe the goals of all of my priorities align. If sometime in the future they do not, well, I will reexamine them."

"I'm staying. I will help," Henry said. "Master Fermat is attached to the bones of Philadelphi. He is trapped here, and I am committed to him. Besides, whatever happened to Penny is a perversion of chemystral science and needs to be stopped."

They all looked to Cram. He cleared his throat, blinked, and then spit a piece of pink goo into his napkin. "I won't lie if I say I ain't been thinking about Mam. Boston is burnt to the ground. But even if I could get myself back there, no guarantee she and the other kids hain't already skarpered off. She never was one for the heat." His face set in a grim line, and he tipped his head gravely at Athena. "I set my lot with you, Lady Athena." He looked about. "And you folk. None can say that Cram ain't loyal. Besides, as far as I see it, a king an ocean away ain't much of a king nohow."

Marise Fermat had watched them with growing degrees of dismay. "Wayland—"

Captain Teach smiled. "I am not your ally in this, Marise. And any obedience I owed you has long disappeared. Until I can find a way back to Skillet and the *Thrift*, this"—he gestured to the four companions—"is my crew. I will not be separated from them."

Ruby could have floated through the roof with pride.

Marise Fermat shook her head slowly. "This is sheer stupidity. For you two, especially," she said to Henry and Ruby. "If the great powers get hold of you, it will be misery for the rest of your lives."

Ruby stared at her mother. They were declaring their allegiances. They were hauling their flags up the mast. But Marise would not see that. Or she refused to go along with them. In the end, it didn't really matter. Would it ever? "You helped my friends, and you helped me. Thank you. But if you wish to go your own way, please do. It seems that one of the things you are expert in is leaving." As soon as she said the last sentence, Ruby regretted it. But she would not take it back. It was a truth. And it ate at her.

The look on her mother's face was too raw.

Henry interrupted. "Master—" He hesitated. "Marise. You helped save us in the west. You helped save Ruby. You helped me. I am grateful to you, and I will never forget that. But I cannot leave these people and this place in danger."

Marise avoided Ruby's eyes and gave Henry a curt nod. After a moment she clapped him on the shoulder.

Because she didn't know what else to say, Ruby said, "It's settled then."

"War. Revolution. A mad chemyst. Arcane science gone awry." Athena looked about. "This is my kind of folly."

A wisp of a smile played across Ruby's lips. She put her hand to her mouth and called out, "All aboard the Good Ship Stupidity!"

Henry blinked. "How long did that take?"

Athena frowned. "I think all of ten minutes."

"Did she say she would return in an hour? Well, then." Cram sat down next to the tea biscuits. "I suppose we should all get comfortable."

As if by agreement they drifted apart to islands of

their own thoughts. Ruby didn't know what to do. She didn't want to talk to her mother. It was too hard to talk to her father. Gwath weighed on her mind. And Rool. And Evram. So instead, she just found a corner for herself and plopped down. With the furniture screening the rest of the room it reminded her a bit of her hidey-hole on the *Thrift*. At least there were two stout walls at her back. Nothing else was certain. Ruby reached into her rucksack and carefully pulled out the artifice otter that had been Evram Hale's parting gift to her.

Somehow Henry had not gotten the message about keeping to themselves. He hovered just out of reach, leaning against the wall in a bad attempt at casualness. He cleared his throat. "May I approach?"

Sometimes he was so formal. But just now the formality was nice: having at least one person treat her carefully. She gave him a Look for good measure but then nodded her permission.

He sat down next to her, his forearms on his knees.

"What is that?" he said.

She closed herself about the otter protectively. She

wanted to keep it to herself. The wounds with Evram and Sleipnir were too fresh. She had to say something, though. "It was a gift. From Evram Hale."

Henry looked about the room, and she followed his glance. The table and chairs screened the two of them from the rest. They all seemed lost in their own thoughts anyway.

"The young chemyst?" Henry leaned in, interested. "May I see it?"

She met his eyes, and they were so calm and friendly and wise that they unsealed a sadness so deep it shook her to the bone. The sad came pouring out of her eyes, and she let it.

He waited patiently.

She held the artifice out. He shifted to pull it into his lap.

It was a small automaton, just a bit longer than his forearm. It was delicately, beautifully crafted. The skin was brushed brass that looked and felt like living fur, if living fur was metal.

"It's an otter?" he asked.

She nodded, sniffling.

The dark chestnut of his fingers highlighted the deep blue of the otter's eyes. "Are these sapphires?"

She nodded again. "Chips. Cut down from the originals."

He was impressed. "Where did you get this?"

"I told you. A gift."

"Who was Evram?"

"He was someone who helped me. And didn't deserve what he got." She had left some things out back in the cave after the rescue, but she told him the whole story this time of the beautiful eight-legged horse automaton that had saved her life at the cost of its own and then the story of a boy who had helped her only because he thought she was a friend. It hurt her to tell it. But at every turn Henry didn't frown, or look askance, or pull back. He just nodded. And listened. "Swedenborg . . . because Evram helped me, the Swede did to him what was done to Penny. But much worse. I think Evram made this for me out of parts of Sleipnir before it happened."

The little otter lay across both of their legs as if it

were asleep. But it wasn't. No life stirred inside it.

"Would you like me to wake it up?"

"Her," she said.

"Her. I— It's impossible to know with these things how they'll animate. Gearbeasts—I think half of them go mad in the first moments. Knowing that . . ." He chewed his lip. "Would you like me to wake her up?"

Her heart caught in her throat. "More than anything."

He smiled. "Well, then."

Henry splayed his fingers out lightly across the artifice's backbone and closed his eyes.

Ruby stayed as still as she could. She felt like a deer or something caught in a thicket, hunters all about.

Henry muttered under his breath, "It's . . . complex." Something like awe tinged his voice. "And by Science, efficient. It will run for a long time on the smallest energy, but"—his voice roughened, and his jaw tensed—"starting it is a bit like pushing a boulder over a cliff." Cords stood out on Henry's neck, and sweat beaded up on his brow; but then his face changed.

He looked scared.

"Henry—"

"It needs a lot," he gasped. "A lot. I don't—" His muscles locked up, as if he had been struck by lightning.

The little otter quivered.

Ruby gasped.

The artifice blinked her blue eyes sleepily and then, curious, quirked her head up. Somewhere inside Ruby the sadness shifted, from raw to bittersweet. And there was something else, too, something she had not felt for a long while.

Hope.

She looked up at Henry, who was looking up at the others, their heads sticking over the table, watching what was happening. Marise Fermat gave him a proud nod.

Henry's eyelids fluttered. "I think it is time to sleep."

Ruby didn't know what to say, but she had to thank him somehow. So she said, just as sleep took him, "Her name is Evie."

CHAPTER 11

In the Chemystral Age, the idea of Family is a hopelessly antiquated concept, a primitive tribal behavior rendered useless now that we can build our communities with Science.
—Emmanuel Swedenborg, personal journal

Ruby watched as Henry smiled and turned his face into the wall. He was snoring before he even settled. She reveled for just a moment in the small fire of hope he had kindled.

Something tapped her wrist: the lightest of weights.

The otter artifice named Evie sat in her lap, gazing up at her, forepaw outstretched to rest on Ruby's arm. There could be no mistaking that look. *You are mine. You belong to me, and I to you. So pay attention.* The little fire of hope blazed brighter in Ruby's chest, and that gave her both an idea and the strength to follow it through.

"You two, follow me," Ruby said to Marise Fermat and Wayland Teach. She stood up and walked past them toward the far wall of the office. "Could someone please tell Hearth we are with her? I am taking these two people away to speak to them for a moment or two."

Athena frowned. "Ruby, Hearth said we can't leave. How—"

"I consider this"—Ruby rapped on the big armoire against the wall—"part of her office." She opened the door with a flourish, stepped into the big wardrobe, and then opened the secret door in the back wall, which let out into a steep passage that climbed upward through the rock. The effect was partially spoiled by Evie's darting about between Ruby's feet and chittering with excitement, but the others looked suitably impressed.

"So that's how you skarpered out the first time," said Cram.

She allowed herself a small spike of pride, and then she faked a bravado she did not feel. "Indeed. Now I would like a moment to speak to my parents alone, and the only way I seem to be able to do that with you folk is to resort to extreme measures. Athena, when Hearth returns, please ask Los Jabalís's cook to join us."

Athena's mouth dropped open.

So did Cram's. "You mean G—"

Athena's hand shot up to block his mouth. "I will do that," she said with a horrible attempt at innocence.

With that, Ruby pulled a small tinker's lamp from a hook on the back wall and began to climb briskly upward, ignoring the questions and exclamations behind her.

After a moment two sets of footsteps followed.

"Ruby—" Her mother called, but Ruby held up her hand without a backward look and kept walking. Her father said nothing.

She had to keep moving. The feeling was bursting at her rib cage, hammering to get out, and the things she needed to say she didn't want to say in front of the others. Not because she didn't trust them; this was simply a family matter. Well, and Evie. Never away from her ankles for long, the little artifice paced the trio in fits and starts, sniffing here, then rushing to catch up, then sniffing there. It was a good half hour of constant upward travel before they reached the other end of the tunnel, a small barred door cut into the rock. The bar was stout and well oiled and slid back easily. Ruby took a brief glance through a small viewing slit and then opened it and motioned the two adults through. Fresh night air greeted them with the smells of cooling flagstones and untended grass. She shuttered the lamp. The high summer moon cast plenty of light.

They were in a tiny courtyard with odd walls, one of those unused orphaned spaces between buildings that no one quite knew what to do with. Stars twinkled above in a cloudless sky. Windowless town house walls bordered the court on three sides, and a fourth wall stood before them, its only feature a locked wooden gate.

Her father quirked an eyebrow at her and murmured, "You know, your mother and I both knew about this tunnel. We used it plenty of times when I was a sentinel and she was a chemyst." He pointed over his shoulder. "Bluestone Square is right beyond that fence. Fancying a walk through the city? Making certain all our wanted posters are well distributed?"

"Ha. We had better stay quiet. Evie—"

The otter artifice skittered about, sniffing at corners with her brass-whiskered snout and turning over rocks with her paws.

How did this work? "Evie."

The otter looked up briefly and then went back to her business.

"Try this." Her mother held something out in her hand. It was a nugget of metal. "Pewter."

Ruby briefly considered ignoring her altogether but settled on taking it silently. She held out her hand. "Evie? Evie."

The whiskered snout popped up, and then suddenly the otter was at her side, forelegs on her knee, haunches on the ground, staring intently at her hand. Ruby tried to swallow a smile. "Good, er, automaton. Otter. Ottermaton." Then she held out the little nugget and Evie grabbed it in both forepaws and settled down right there to gnaw on it. A deep kind of pleasure—warm and satisfied—bloomed in Ruby's chest. She held on to it.

A voice in her mind named the grave, straight-on look Evie gave her. *Thank you.*

Both the captain and Marise were also looking at her.

"Ruby, what is this?" said her mother.

She didn't meet her mother's eyes but instead looked at her father. "Wait," she said.

"For once I have to agree with Marise. This is hardly the time to—"

"I had to get out of there, and I didn't sort the whole thing through. But now going back would be a waste of time, and I don't want to anyway. Thus, Wait."

So they waited. The truth was, Ruby had no cursed idea what she was going to say. A flock of pigeons were fighting it out in her belly, and she was sweating gallons. But all this running about in secret and suffering in silence, it couldn't go on. If Wisdom Rool himself had jumped out of the sky to try to skin them all alive, he would have had to wait. It all was just . . . unacceptable.

After about twenty minutes a form loomed in the doorway.

He was never loud. If they saw him, it meant he was choosing to be seen.

"Come out," Ruby said. "Show yourself."

Gwath stepped out into the moonlight.

"Providence," her father breathed. He launched himself forward to crush the other man in his arms. A tight knot spun loose in Ruby's chest: a knot she hadn't even known was there. Over her father's shoulder she could see Gwath's face. Never, ever had she seen him look pained or troubled, but that was what she saw as he hugged Teach right back just as hard and stared into the shining, stunned eyes of Marise Fermat. Ruby had wondered if Gwath had hinted anything to her mother. Unless she was a better actor than Ruby, he hadn't.

And then the captain pulled back and around to look at Marise. The two men stood there arm in arm, and her mother's face was so still and fragile, like a glass bird ready to take flight. All the confidence and pride and science were stripped away. She was scared, Ruby saw. Her mother was so scared.

Little claws scrabbled at her side, and without looking

away she reached her arm down and the ottermaton climbed up and buried her face into the crook of Ruby's elbow.

Wayland Teach stared at Marise, his arm around Gwath's, and then Ruby's heart burst with pride as he held out his hand to her mother. It was understanding, and forgiveness, and love. Had she been unfaithful? Had their marriage been for show? For Ruby, those were questions for another time. Right now Marise, sniffling, stumbled forward into their arms, and they stood there, the three of them, holding one another.

Then a wonder: they opened the circle and invited her in.

And wonder of wonders, she went. They folded their arms about her and Evie, and the knot in her chest unlooped and blossomed into something wonderfully new: contentment.

"Why now?" Marise asked a little bit later.

"When else?" The anger Ruby felt at her mother had taken only a few moments of rest before it bloomed back, stronger than ever. Was it possible to hate someone and still feel other things for her, too? She forged on. "It's like you said, Marise. 'People will die.' I didn't want to be one of those people who get shot or knifed or something and not have my family know one another. Especially since we all were wandering about in the Warren, bumping up against one another like cattle in a ship's hold."

Gwath, strangely, had brought a hunk of cheese, and they handed it around. The absurd thought struck Ruby: this was her first family dinner. The other three were quietly talking when she realized that Evie was no longer sitting next to her. The little artifice was standing at the gate of the courtyard, stock still and quivering, staring straight through the gap between the gate and the fence.

Ruby knelt down next to Evie. "What is it, girl?"

Evie chittered quietly without turning away.

Ruby tried to follow the otter's stare through the gap. A small block of buildings sat in the center of the square, a coffeehouse among them. It was busy even in the middle of the night, with outdoor tables full of patrons coming and going, most of them lively with conversation.

One table sat quiet. Two men and two women in

unassuming clothing silently sipped their drinks. The two facing the gate were good at masking it, but it took Ruby only a few moments to recognize that their eyes never strayed from the courtyard. This itself wouldn't have been of any note until those four people rose up to leave. At that moment, almost like a dance, four other patrons sat down at the table, and the two facing the gate took up the exact same behavior.

And the four new patrons at the coffeehouse table? Ruby knew them. They were dressed to blend in rather than in their standard uniforms, but there was no mistaking the matching white hair of Never and Levi Curtsie or, for that matter, even from behind, the ox-wide shoulders of Gideon Stump and the deadly grace of Avid Wake.

"Ruby?" Gwath and the rest had come up behind her.

"What is it?" said Wayland Teach.

Ruby took some small comfort in figuring that if any of the four could see her, they would have shown some sign. Still . . . "We'd best get back down the tunnel, and we'd best get to Hearth right away." She eased back on her heels and looked up at the rest of them. "The Warren is no longer a secret. We're being watched."

CHAPTER 12

A council is an excellent place for speaking.
I am one who is more for doing.
—Mother Greenfoot, Keepers of the Western Door, 1636

Athena could barely find a place to stand.

Madame Hearth's office was full. The Bluestockings called Badger, Ax, and Flame were there, and Greta Van Huffridge stood next to the leader of the Warren. Henry had fetched Petra alla Ferra, and she had brought her daughters. All three of them were giving Gwath the stinkeye.

And Providence help them all, there was tea.

"Do we have to take tea?" Cram and his ever-present

satchel had squeezed into the only remaining corner with his mistress.

Athena leaned over and murmured, "You see anyone else with cups? It's a keen group in here. If that stuff tastes any worse than it smells, this rising will be over before it begins."

Ruby looked as if she could barely contain herself, fidgeting between Gwath and Captain Teach, with Marise next to them. Athena felt a strange pang. For now Ruby had three parents, and Athena had not seen her one in almost a year. Did her father miss her or even know that his only daughter was at the center of a plot he had engineered to change the rulership of the colonies themselves? Godfrey Boyle had hired Petra alla Ferra and Los Jabalís to acquire Ruby, Marise Fermat's journal, and Henry, in that order.

Athena was not even on that list.

True, Athena's father *had* sent her expressly to the colonies to get Ruby, but then why hire Los Jabalís? Had he simply not trusted her with his entire scheme? Had he forgotten she even existed? Athena's gaze wandered back to Ruby. Perhaps that was for the best. After all, could Athena say her loyalties still lay with Godfrey Boyle and the order? If she were asked to choose between her friend and her duty, what would she do?

Madame Hearth loudly cleared her throat. "This was to be a private meeting."

Cram raised his hand. "I didn't tell no one."

"You were apparently the singular example." Hearth scanned the room and sighed. "It is good that you all are here. Ruby Teach has concerning news. Ruby?"

The whole room looked at Ruby. Something was slightly different about her, Athena thought. She stood taller. Or more rooted. A gleam had returned to her eye: a danger, a recklessness, that Athena realized she had missed. Whatever had happened to her, she seemed ready to fight, and Athena's spine straightened in response.

Ruby raised her chin. "The Reeve have a watch set on the door to Bluestone Square."

The office erupted into questions and exclamations. Athena's mind raced. The Reeve? If they were watching one of the (supposedly secret) doors, they were aware of the Bluestockings. And if they were aware of the Bluestockings . . .

The one called Badger raised her hand. "How do you know this?"

"You all know that I spent time as a prisoner of the Reeve over these past months. I trained with them. They even tried to recruit me. I know many of them by sight, and four of my former comrades are hunkered down at the Carpe Cacao coffeehouse like sailors in a crow's nest. And they're peeping just this way."

Ax leaned forward. "Wayland, is this true?"

Captain Teach put his hand on Ruby's shoulder. "I trust her eye with my life."

Madame Hearth nodded gravely. "And Pate has been up the tunnel and confirmed that there is an organized group of some kind keeping a watch on the Warren."

"What about the smokehouse door to the Dregs?" asked Athena.

"We don't know."

"Pate is checking on that now," said Hearth, "but time is our enemy here. If the Reeve have discovered us—"

Or if Rool did cut Ruby loose into the wild only to follow us here, Athena thought with rueful admiration.

The man was a thorn in their side, but she had to respect his strategic mind. He spun wheels within wheels and gears within gears.

Hearth pressed on. "If the Reeve have discovered us, then we have no way of knowing what else they have discovered. The rising could be at stake, and many lives along with it. We need to warn our allies."

Athena shook her head. "But if we warn our allies, won't the watchers simply follow us to them? They are watching our secret door. How can we avoid their notice?"

The samovar sputtered in the corner.

"What if they never see us leave?" asked Ruby.

A murmur passed through the room. Marise Fermat grabbed the bridge of her nose. "What do you mean, Ruby?"

Ruby forged ahead. "I'll go. I can sneak past the reeves, and I know the city. I evaded them for days not a year ago. We could cook up a quick sharp, a distraction, that could give us the time to get a few people through unseen."

Hearth shook her head. "The wanted posters. The patrols. The city is an armed camp, much worse than a year ago."

Ruby cast a quick glance at Gwath. "I can disguise myself," she said. "They will never recognize me."

Athena gritted her teeth. Ruby was talking about changing, she was sure of it.

Hearth searched her eyes for a moment, then looked over her shoulder at Wayland and Marise. They both hesitated, then nodded.

Ruby frowned. "This isn't their choice. It's mine."

"We're with you, girl," said Teach.

"I need my crew."

"Your crew?" said Hearth.

Ruby looked as if she were facing down a bear. "Henry, Cram, and Athena. I need them; otherwise, I won't—I can't—do it. The disguise is only a part of the sharp." She pointed to the three of them as she spoke. "We need skill, resilience, and courage to complete it." A thrill ran up Athena's spine. Rushing together headlong into the fire? Into the center of her own father's plans? Perhaps.

Badger chuffed like her namesake. "Children." She turned to Hearth. "This is a task upon which the fate of nations hangs, and you want to entrust it to—"

"The same children that made us all look like fools searching high and low for them? Yes, Badger. Besides, do you have another idea?"

The woman pressed her lips into a line.

Hearth nodded. "All right, then. There is a party being held tomorrow evening, at Lothor Van Huffridge's home. One of the guests is a woman named Thandie Paine. She is a Grocer, sent here to facilitate the rising and our connection to the Van Huffridge organization."

Alla Ferra stepped forward. "I see no reason to withhold the information that she is my contact as well, the go-between to my employer, Godfrey Boyle."

Several sets of eyes flicked toward Athena. She delivered her best unfazed smile. "Good old Dad."

"Boyle, you know this woman?" Hearth asked.

Athena blinked. "Yes. From Virginia, I believe? She has visited my fa—Godfrey Boyle numerous times. She is a . . . capable woman," said Athena. Then, because she might as well be as honest as possible, she added, "And by 'capable' I mean ferocious, uncompromising, and relentless. When last I saw Thandie Paine, she was sliding half of Quebec City into the St. Lawrence River. She thinks big. And brutal."

Hearth nodded. "Agreed. Very well." She turned to Greta. "Scales. You know the house. Is there an easy way to provide the four of them entry?"

Athena frowned. "It is her house. Can she not just get us invitations to the party?"

Silence fell.

Greta stared at her embroidered slipper.

Hearth cleared her throat. "Scales."

With a huff Greta said, "No, Lord Athen, I cannot just *get you* invitations. That would require going back to my house, and I would most likely never get there."

"Why not?"

"She is wanted by the crown as well," said Hearth.

"Ooooooooooo," said Cram.

"It was a judicious use of—" began Greta.

"You *know* the rules, Scales."

"That woman would have *drowned*, madame!"

"Nevertheless." Hearth used the word like a stop thrust. "Scales here's public use of chemystry in a crowded park in a very visible way has rendered her, if possible, *more* pursued than the rest of you. And so we have lost one of our primary ways of communicating with Van Huffridge House."

Greta stared straight ahead, her fists clenched so hard Athena thought they might just break off. Right or wrong, whatever the situation, the girl was convinced she had done the *only* thing to be done. Athena knew that look and what it felt like on the inside.

Greta rallied herself. "With the troubles in the city, soldiers check papers constantly. Up Town will be crawling with redcoats and guard posts. We need someone close by in Bluestone Square, who can travel freely past the soldiers, someone who they will never give a second look. Someone who also already *has* invitations." Greta tapped her teeth; then her eyes narrowed. She turned to Ruby. "You say you can disguise yourself?"

Ruby nodded.

"How well?"

"How well do you need?"

Greta looked her up and down. "Can you be taller,

beautiful, and look like a particular young man?"

Ruby turned to Gwath. He held her gaze for a moment, "Yes," he said. "I think so. We'll need the night."

Ruby swallowed. To Greta she said, "All right then."

Cram elbowed Athena and whispered, "Changing. But the Ferret—"

Athena gave him her best keep quiet, you look and tried to keep the worry from her own face. From the stories Ruby had told the crew, she couldn't summon a wart on her nose, let alone completely change her appearance. But Greta was no longer looking at Ruby. She was staring at Athena. With relish.

Van Huffridge chuckled deep in her throat and struck her tiny hands together. "I have it. If Ruby Teach can do what she says she can, I can get them in."

Cram murmured under his breath, "Am I the only one that don't find that encouraging?"

"Excellent." Hearth turned to Ruby. "You will make contact with Paine and, if you can, Lothor Van Huffridge and warn them of the possibility that our plans are known."

"And that I am ready to collect my money," said Petra

alla Ferra. "Please make certain to stay in one piece until you establish your delivery of yourselves to Madame Paine." She turned to Henry. "I must trust you, Henry Collins. I must trust that you will do us honor in this."

Henry chewed his lip. "I will."

"I hope this contract of yours will not be a problem?" said Hearth.

The mercenary revealed her teeth in a predator's grin. "I hope so, too."

Hearth sniffed. "And the rest of us will be here, waiting for your return and preparing for the rising." She scanned the room. "I hope you are not looking for a speech of some sort. Be off with you."

The others said their good-byes. Athena and Cram looked at each other.

"Disguises?" she said.

He shrugged. "Well, milady, at least we get to go to a party."

CHAPTER 13

Elizabeth Arbuckle pretended to be me when she was robbing that counting house. So I stopped pretending to think Elizabeth Arbuckle should continue to breathe, Your Honor.
—Testimony, Miss Aquila Rose,
Philadelphi Court for Capital Crimes, 1719

J ust a few hours later and just a few doors down from Madame Hearth's office, Ruby, prickling with anticipation, stood silent on the chem-packed earthen floor of the library. They would leave in the morning to try to sneak past the Reeve and to throw themselves into Greta's mad plan, but if it was going to work at all, there was something she had to learn to do.

Gwath sat smug and cross-legged on the Warren

library's big worktable, which had been pushed against the door. Its books packed away for the duration, the library was the only place they could find where they wouldn't be interrupted, even in the middle of the night. "Show me," he said. "Or are you too tired?"

Provoking her with anger had always been one of his favorite tactics. She closed her eyes and eased into the emptiness the Reeve had tried to shovel out of her at Fort Scoria. There was no library. There was no Gwath. There was not even a body. If you had a body that was a fixed shape, how could you turn it into a different one? No. There were only her friends and family, lined up in glowing formation. Edwina Corson had said, "You have to get empty only so you can know what to fill it with," and she was right. Once Ruby had lost everything, she saw that if she could keep her people in the forefront of her mind, the changing came easier.

The brass picks grew silently out of her fingertips.

She opened her eyes.

He was sleeping.

"Gwath!" said Ruby.

The big man blinked his eyes and yawned, stretching like a drunken parson. "My apologies. What did I miss?"

"You missed me almost poking your eyes out with these." She held up the picks.

He stared at them and cocked his head. "You woke me for that?"

She kept her words low and steady. She felt she might burst into flame. "I changed. Look at it."

Gwath chuckled. "That's not changing."

"You—" She clenched her fists. The picks sank into her palms. "Blast it!" The picks retreated back into her fingertips. "How is this not changing?"

"Well, you haven't, you know"—he flapped his hand about—"changed."

"Then show me!" Ruby dug her fingernails into her palm. "We're out of time. So stow this *mysterious gift* mumbo jumbo and tell me what I need to know."

Gwath flowed off the table and sat in front of her.

"And don't you dare try to *charm* me. Right now."

He held up his hands in surrender. "A story then."

Ruby flopped back down to the ground. "Fine."

He took her hands. "When we talked in the woods, you were right. I did not tell you the entire story. On the *Thrift*, after you escaped, I threw myself over the side. Rool was going to wear me down and either take me or kill me. As soon as the water closed over my head, I knew I was too weak to swim. I sank like a stone. So I changed. I gave myself gills."

The frustration evaporated like mist with the dawn. "Like a fish?"

"That's right. I landed on the bottom, and breathing with my new gills, I crawled, inch by inch, back to Philadelphi. But this is the danger. The shape you hold changes your mind as well. The beasts of the land are very different from us, and the ones from the water stranger still. When I changed into this half Gwath, half fish, I lost myself. I was gone. In my place"—he hesitated—"I don't know if I could call them memories or even thinking, at least as you and I know it. Through some instinct, for home maybe, or to keep after you, I ended up on the shore, flopping on the sand. I choked out the water and drew air into my re-forming lungs, but it took me much longer to come back"—he touched his temple—"up here. I was gone for a long while, staring at the sea, staring at the sand, the me just draining out. The Da Rochas found me on the beach and took me in. I don't know what would have happened if they hadn't."

He stared at her.

Ruby held on to his hands for dear life. How could she even want something like this? To change into some sea slug and die on the bottom of the ocean? But her crew needed her. "Go on."

"With people, the process is more delicate, like using a razor instead of a club. But it is the same at its base. If I were teaching you changing at my own pace, we would spend months strengthening you in here"—he tapped her chest—"and in here"—he tapped her head—"before we would ever try a full transformation. To take on someone's skin, you need to know them—how they think, how they feel, how they live."

"But how do you know what they think?"

He blinked, pretending exasperation. "Only by using all the skills I've taught you all your waking life.

You observe. You consider. You guess. You open yourself to the possibility of who they might be. How they are different from you. How they are the same as you."

"But that's so you can trick them."

Gwath pursed his lips. "But before you can trick them—"

Something shifted in Ruby's brain. "You have to know them. But if you know them too well—"

"If you believe too well that you are them—"

It fit. "That is where you lose yourself."

Gwath smiled.

He knows what he is about.

The voice wasn't Gwath's. And Gwath's expression hadn't changed. The voice had come from somewhere else.

Up here.

Evie perched on an abandoned shelf, chin on brass paws, staring at her.

Ohhhhh, no, thought Ruby. That can't be you. You can't sneak into my thoughts.

Evie cocked her head, then rolled over to scratch her back on the wood. *If you say so. Whether I'm talking to you or not, he knows what he's about. You should listen to him. He's trying to take you somewhere, to get you to see something.*

"Ruby."

Ruby blinked, then sighed. Whether Evie's voice was real or not, she was right. What choice did Ruby have? It was simple. And insufferably hard. "What do you want me to do?"

Gwath glanced up at the otter, who seemed blissfully unaware of him, and then back at Ruby. "The old way to teach changing is harder, and stranger, but quicker. My grandmother taught me like this." He moved the table away. He knocked three times on the door.

The door opened.

In walked her mother.

"No."

"Ruby—" said Gwath.

"No. Get her out of here."

Gwath and Marise exchanged a glance. Gwath put a hand on her arm. "Ruby—"

She shook his hand off. If she could have thrown him

through the wall, she would have. They were standing there together as if it were the most natural thing in the world. "We are not a happy family after one moment in a courtyard. Marise, you solved whatever equation you had to with—with my fathers, but you and I? We are not done. We are not solved." She gripped her fingers behind her back to keep her hands from shaking. She looked at her mother. "You need to go."

"I—"

"She stays," said Gwath. And he bulled on before Ruby could interrupt. "She has to. We need her for your training."

For my training? How could Marise be necessary for her changing training? Unless— "No."

You're being a child.

She glanced up at Evie. *What do you know about—*

I know what you know. If Gwath says this is the only option, then this is the only option, and you are wasting valuable time by acting like a spoiled little girl. Do you want to help your friends? Do you want to save people from the Swede's machine?

They were still staring at her.

Fury battled with need. Need won. "Fine," said Ruby. "Teach me."

Gwath sat mother and daughter down knee to knee in the hard-backed library chairs. Her mother stared at her, then looked away. Her blond hair half covered the fading yellow and purple bruise around her eye.

Ruby snorted. "You have to look at me, Marise."

Gwath sank to the balls of his feet between them. He glanced at Ruby. "You have a deep understanding of this process, do you?"

". . . no."

"Then you should keep quiet, too, and focus on the task at hand."

"Which is?"

Gwath turned his gaze to Marise. "Look at her."

"I *am*."

"No. I mean, truly look at her." Gwath slipped out of Ruby's peripheral vision until all she could see was Marise. "See her. Know her. The real Marise, not the person you've imagined. Not the story. More than simply your mother. Who is she? What does she want?"

Ruby's mother blinked, then glanced at Gwath. "What?"

"Quiet, please, Marise. Ruby, what does she want?"

"I have no idea. I'm not in her head. Besides, she—"

Gwath took her hand. "Unloose your anger. Let slip your fear," he said. "They are not useful now."

He sounded like Edwina Corson. But that, too, felt familiar. Ruby rolled her eyes and tried to make her way to the kind of clear seeing that the reeve lieutenant had. So she looked at her mother. Forehead lined with worry. Hands stained by years of tinkercraft. Tiny tracks about the eyes. Underneath that, though, it was a familiar face. Ruby's own. This was the curious part and the part that made her so angry. She kept anything tied to her mother behind a door in her heart, locked and barred with the stoutest steel.

So Ruby did what she had to. She unlocked it.

Marise Fermat had left Ruby when she was not even a year old and fled into the west, with never a note, never a contact, leaving behind only the strange schematic she had implanted in her daughter's blood. Ruby would never have done that. So how could they have the same *face*?

"Why did you do it?" she asked.

Marise's head jerked back as if she had been struck. She looked at Gwath. He shrugged. She closed her eyes and let out a low breath. "I—I had to protect the discovery."

"And not me." Ruby's shoulders tightened.

Marise opened her eyes. There were no tears. The blue was stone, her jaw clenched. The words twisted out. "It was all I could think of. If they found me, they would take me. The same thing almost happened to Fermat. The crown *took* Isaac Newton, you know. One day just gone. Ruby, they would have had me doing chemystry for them in a hole so deep that I would never have seen the sun again."

"So you left." Ruby tried to keep herself open. Tried to keep herself calm.

"So I left."

Something glassy and hard reared up in Ruby's belly. "Except before you went, you decided to make by

Providence certain your daughter would be hunted, too."

Icy resignation stilled Marise's voice. "Ruby. It *was* important. If something happened to me, the formula needed to be preserved."

Hearing it so naked hit Ruby like a falling mast. "So you turned your girl into a thing. An artifice. A recipe. A discovery. Were you more comfortable with me then? When I was—what?—Science? Did you love me more?"

Horror flashed across Marise's face. "Ruby—"

It was the horror that did it. For a moment, for the slightest moment, Ruby saw. Her mother wasn't evil. She didn't hate Ruby. Maybe she even loved Ruby in her own way. She had done a thing that she regretted, but she feared that if given the choice, she would do it again.

She did what she thought had to be done.

And Ruby *had* felt that.

The bottom opened up. Everything in Ruby that was Ruby rushed out through her toes, and the only thing remaining was Marise's fear, Marise's doubt, Marise's choice.

Her mother was staring at her, hand over her mouth.

Ruby looked down at her hands, now stained and scarred with chemystry. She pulled a lock of hair down from her neck. It lay there, corn yellow against the rough, pale skin of the hand worn by a lifetime of experiment.

She glanced over to Gwath, whose eyes were shining.

"I did it," she said. Her words were clipped, they came faster than usual, with a trace of ice. A kind of sureness washed through Ruby's veins. She could change.

She. She was Marise. The world spun. She had been talking to her daughter just a moment ago, but where was Ruby? The woman in the other chair was a perfect painting of herself.

Of Marise.

Gwath—her love? her sweetheart?—took her by her shoulders and put his face right in front of hers. "Ruby. You are Ruby Teach."

"But I'm not, Gwath. I'm Mar— Ow!" She looked down to see a brass otter, sapphire eyes whirling, teeth sunk into the meaty part of her hand. Ruby's otter. Ruby's hand.

"Ruby." She was Ruby, not Marise. The otter let go.

Her belly groaned. Her hands started shaking. The true Marise blurred in her vision, and she felt dizzy and tight all at the same time.

She blacked out.

When she came to, Ruby was on the floor, cradled in Gwath's arms, her mother beside them.

Gwath smiled. "You can do it. But you see how it is, yes? It will not be easy." He scratched between Evie's ears, and she chirruped. "Your friends must keep watch over you. Tell them to keep an eye out for closets. Bolt-holes. Places you all can retreat to if they need to remind you or, worse, wake you."

Invisible spikes poked through her eyes. "Can they help with this headache?"

Gwath smiled ruefully. "That is your own. Welcome to changing."

Marise leaned forward, concern written on her face. "Ruby— I . . . cannot take back what I have done."

"No. You cannot. But you could get me a cup of water."

"I would ask that you consider what I have to say

now, as—as one who has also been the target of forces beyond her control. Like you." She waited.

Like her. Echoes of Marise's guilt and helplessness and resolve still sat in Ruby like puddles after a storm. How could she not listen? She nodded.

Marise blinked, perhaps surprised. "All right. You have done much. You have seen much." She reached out her hand. "This changing. The way your friends speak of you. I know you are a formidable girl. A formidable young woman. I would ask that you consider walking away. We could take you."

"We?"

"Gwath and I." Her eyes flicked over Ruby's head to Gwath. "Wayland. Even Athena, and Henry and Cram. It is safe in the west. I have friends there. I could make you safe. You could be safe."

It pained Ruby to look at her. She could not think of Marise as a monster anymore. She *knew* her. And right now Marise's fire was banked; all that showed through was sorrow and regret.

Ruby did not shout. She tried to tell her the truth,

as clearly as she knew how. "Marise, Swedenborg pulled those schematics from *my* blood." She shook her head. "I have to try to help."

"People will die." Marise's desperate certainty chilled Ruby to the marrow. "A rising? A revolution? People will die, Ruby. And I could not live with myself if one of those people was you."

Ruby steadied a hand on the floor and pushed herself up. "Well, I had best not die then." She tried for a smile, but it withered somewhere on its way to her mouth. "We need to go. They'll be waiting."

Marise looked as if she were going to say something more. But she ground her teeth and nodded.

Ruby reached out and touched the woman on the forearm. "Mother."

Marise took Ruby's hand for a moment. Then Ruby let go, and her mother did, too.

CHAPTER 14

CATHERINE:	(Holding handkerchief to nose) Cornelius Thunderfatch?
THUNDERFATCH:	The same. Please take this fish.
CATHERINE:	It is heavy. And, oh, my, still alive. (Gathers self) Mr. Thunderfatch, I have come to beg of you a most remarkable undertaking.
THUNDERFATCH:	Woman, if you can keep a handle on two of those for one hour, I'll climb the very slopes of Mount Olympus to do your bidding.
CATHERINE:	Done. Please hold my gloves. Ew. Actually, feel free to keep them.

—Marion Coatesworth-Hay, *A Most Tenacious Flame*, Act II, Sc. iv

A hair-raising escape from Fort Scoria? Cram turned up his nose at such a thing. Convincing Ruby to leave behind her otter to distract the Bluestone Square reeves in their escape from the Warren? Piece of cherry pie. Slipping the notice of the same reeves at the café through a daring rooftop escape? Child's play.

But this?

Cram took a pin from his mouth, and his face screwed

up with worry as he eased it eternally carefully into the waist of the gorgeous ball gown.

"Ow, Cram!" said Lady Athena.

Not careful enough. "Sorry, milady."

Lady Athena took the pin. "Here, let me do it. This is humiliating."

Cram's mistress rejiggered the corset for the umpteenth time, and Cram sat back on his heels and tried to get his bearings. Their first stop after their do-si-doing the Reeve had been a fancy shop in the center of UpTown. Just after they had sneaked in the back door, Griddle Van Huffridge had unearthed for Lady Athena the most beautiful frilled and ruffled confection of a dress and insisted she put it on.

It was pale blue, and it fit her perfectly. Almost perfectly.

Henry and Ferret had found themselves seats in the viewing area of the shop and were pretending to try to be helpful, while Greta helped Cram with the fitting. Ferret had found a dish of cashews somewhere.

"Flounce more," said Ruby.

Athena glared. "A Boyle never flounces."

"Yes, I understand, but you just don't strike me as *womanly* standing that way." Ruby's face projected pure innocence, but Cram could see that underneath she was anything but. "That time you visited me down in the Smelted Grouse—"

"Saved you, you mean."

"Well, technically it was Henry who saved us."

"Quite right." Henry popped a cashew.

"At any rate." Ferret kept on. "You were quite flouncy then. You cooed and made faces and did all the lady things then. Now you look like a—"

"Don't say it," said Henry.

"—a depressed partridge."

Athena tugged at the corset again.

"I wish, milord, that you would stop doing that," said Cram.

"Milady," said Greta.

They all stopped what they were doing. Cram dropped a thimble; it clinked on the marble floor. He didn't know what to do. He thought about starting to sing. Or to stick Lady Athena with another pin. He cleared his throat. "Sorry, miss."

"You should call him milady," said Greta, around a smile that fair threatened to eat her face. "Start practicing now. Otherwise, you might make a mistake when you arrive at the party."

Lady Athena wore her counting-to-ten face.

Cram looked for a place to hide.

Finally Lady Athena said, "Good idea." Everyone started breathing again. Then she said, with infinite patience, "Greta, please help me understand, once again, why this little idea is an integral part of your strategy."

Greta spat one of the pins into her hand and went after Athena's hem. "Simple and brilliant is my plan. Reginald Shackleton, one of the most insufferable young dandies in Philadelphi, has an invitation to my father's party. His family's business is well known about town, and they are looked on favorably by the crown. Reginald will have no trouble navigating the curfew and the guard stations that are between us and Van Huffridge House. Ruby will, she has assured us, disguise herself perfectly as Reginald." She delivered this last with a dubious look. "But Reginald will require an escort."

Lady Athena looked queasy. "I could escort him as me, gallant fellow that I am and ever so comfortable with high society—"

Greta tsked. "I thought of that. It will never work. The party will be full of people who have spent much time in London, and you, however, as son of a noble— well, marginally noble—house in England and a onetime fiancé of the daughter of the host of the party would probably be recognized. We cannot have that."

"Then why can I not just go as a servant, like these two chubs?" Lady Athena waved her hand at Henry and Cram.

"Because, *milady*, you need to be on the floor with the guests. There are some parts of the house where servants will be out of place. Besides"—she sneered—"Reggie will need a companion not only for appearance but for expediency. If Ruby truly does look like the insufferable fop, he will draw far too much attention from the legion of mothers attempting to marry their daughters into his august household."

"—and you know that I hate this, and you wish to humiliate me."

Greta smiled. "This is only a scrumptiously delightful side effect of the plan."

Lady Athena took a few steps, the panniers swaying from side to side. The hoops were almost rectangular, and they stuck out of her waist like the walls of city hall. "I can't move in this," Athena said. "If we get into trouble—"

"You won't get into trouble," said Greta. "You are nobility. Nobility doesn't get into trouble. It gives trouble. Generally by ordering other people to deliver it."

"Don't tell me about nobility," said Lady Athena, but feeble-like. It was a surrender.

"It's a good plan, milady," said Cram. She looked down at him as if she were on a raft in the middle of the ocean, and he had just dropped a cannonball on her.

"Finished." Greta shook out the dress and got to her feet. She motioned to the floor-length mirror behind them.

Athena turned and looked at herself.

She was looking at the dress, but Cram could not look away from her face. Horror, then intrigue, then speculation, then distaste flashed like quicklime over her features. "I hate it," she said.

"I cannot believe it." Greta was staring in the mirror, too. "You were better looking than me as a boy, and now as a girl you are twice as pretty as I." She sighed. Her face relaxed for a moment, and something stirred there. Regret? Pain? She scooped it up again, too quick for Cram to be sure, and hid it all behind her mask of disdain. "Well, at least you hate it." Then Greta hurried toward the back door. "Come on. It's time to meet Reggie Shackleton."

Greta's lip curled up in a way Cram had seen her use only for Lady Athena.

Mam always said the best pies have unexpected depths, and Cram had been happy to discover that Griddle Van Huffridge had plenty. Once Ruby picked the lock to a back-alley gate, Griddle threaded them through an overgrown garden with the grace of a ball-tailed cat and squired them up a trellis, onto the balcony, and into the closet as if she were possessed by the spirit of Winnifred Pleasant Black. There was plenty of room. Reginald Shackleton had a closet the size of Cram's house. Plus Cram's uncle's house. Plus his grandmam's whiskey shack.

There was a problem, though.

Cram had to sneeze.

The tickle had started in his nose as soon as they climbed through the bedroom window, and it had kept on growing once the five of them had locked themselves into the capacious closet. It badgered him. It clawed at him, like a living, angry sneeze possum. He fought that possum with every scrap of his being.

He held his nose. And his breath.

Ferret looked over at him, her eyes flashing in the sliver of light creeping in through the closet door. She shook her head wildly and motioned to the three others in the closet.

Lady Athena turned him around. "Hold it," she whispered.

Out in the bedroom the door to the hall creaked open. A posh voice warbled, "I'll just change, and then I'm off, Grandmother! Don't wait up!" and then the door closed.

Cram stopped struggling.

The others relaxed.

Cram sneezed. It was a giant of a snort, one of those ones that shook you from your ankles to the top of your noggin. The closet shuddered. He thought he might have gone deaf.

Ferret wrenched open the closet door and launched herself across the room onto the shoulders of a strapping youth whose hand was just inches away from a bell pull. Before you could say "pemmican stew," Reginald Shackleton was bound and gagged on a fancy, cushiony chair in the corner of the room.

Lady Athena was breathing heavy and staring daggers at Cram. What had he done?

He sneezed again.

The window rattled.

They all froze.

Another swanky voice, this time an elderly lady's, rasped in from down the corridor. "Are you all right, Reggiepoo? Would you rather just turn in and send your regrets? I could have Withers bring you a warming pan."

Greta put her mouth right next to the boy's ear. "You owe me, Reginald. Don't think I won't tell your parents what I know about you if you cross me. Tell Grandmama not to worry. You are very well, thank you." On his other side Ferret set her knife against his neck. Ruby and Greta locked eyes, and Ruby nodded.

Greta pulled down the gag just long enough for the boy to call, "Er, no—no, Gramsie! No need to call Withers! I am fit as a French horn, thank you!" and then she pulled the gag taut again.

Cram thought he might sneeze again. He grabbed a pillow and put it over his face. It was very soft. Goose down. The Shackletons had excellent taste.

Ferret had walked around to the front of the boy, and she started to stare holes into his head, moving about from this side to that.

Reginald began to squeak.

"Pull the gag down. I need to hear him talk," said Ruby.

Athena had taken Ruby's place at his side, and she obliged. "Speak for the lady," she said low into his ear.

"Er." He coughed. "What should I say? Hallo, are you *robbers*? This is quite exciting, it is." He turned to Griddle. "Greta Van Huffridge? Aren't you away at school? Is this some sort of prank? Or"—a kind of dim cunning lit up his face—"induction into some sort of secret society?"

Griddle blinked. "Yes, Reggie. A secret society. Now, please answer this girl's questions."

"What do you treasure?" said Ruby.

The boy perked up immediately. The cords they had brought to tie him creaked slightly. Cram knew his type. He was a strapping kind of lordling, well fed, strong, emptily handsome, with the easy confidence that comes from never being denied nothing. Reggie clicked his perfect teeth in thought. "What do I treasure? Ooo, my glove collection."

"What is your secret desire?"

"I already told you, to be inducted into a secret society!"

"What do you fear, Reggie?"

The boy frowned. "Fear?" Then he smiled. "Hmm. Never really thought much about fear. Let me see . . .

I am desperately afraid sometimes that I might tear my favorite gloves when I'm riding. They are silk, you know, and—"

"That's plenty," said Ruby.

The professor had taken a listening post, guarding the bedroom door. "We need to do this quickly."

Ferret nodded and said, "All right." She took one final look at Reginald and then disappeared into his closet.

Lady Athena produced a little potion bottle out of her vest. "Drink this," she said.

"Are you poisoning me? But I don't want to be poisoned."

"No, you stupid boy," said Greta. "It's a sleeping draft. Don't struggle, and all will be as it was when you wake up tomorrow morning."

"Greta, I am so sorry I called you those things. I'll never do it again."

"I know you won't, Reggie." She smiled grimly. "I know you won't. And if you do, I'll come back with these fine people, and we'll do you so much worse."

Cram wondered if Reggie was feeling true fear for

the first time as he guzzled the sleeping potion, eyes never leaving Griddle's.

He was asleep before they could handle him into his bed.

"Ruby?" Athena whispered at the closet door.

"I'm not finished." A globbelly voice wobbled out from the closet. Sort of a cross between a frog and a pudding.

"I know. Are there any dressing gowns in there? We're putting him to bed. I don't want the servants to think anything is amiss if they come in during the night."

There were some shuffling sounds in the closet, and then a dressing gown popped out. At the end of a big pale arm the hand was still the Ferret's: little and olive.

They got Reginald ready for bed, and then there was nothing else to do but wait. They stared at one another.

"How do we get there?" said Lady Athena.

"I'm sorry?" said Griddle. She was sitting upright as a mast, fidgeting with a letter opener that could have bought Cram's family a new house.

"How do we *get* there, Miss Van Huffridge?"

"Oh. Of course. There will be a Shackleton carriage

down front, awaiting Lord Reggie here." The lordling took the opportunity to snore like a startled ball-tail. "You'll need to subdue the driver and attendant without anyone noticing and steal their livery."

The professor took a deep breath. "Of course. It just gets simpler and simpler."

"Of course." Griddle missed the sarcasm entirely. "Oh, and one other thing. I assume one of you can steer such a contraption?"

Cram's blood warmed. "Oh, I can, Miss Greta."

"Perfect."

And then, in a brilliant suit of party clothes, out of the closet, came Reginald.

"How do I look?" whispered Ferret in Reginald's body. Cram's jaw dropped. She even had his voice.

Athena looked New Reggie up and down, a smile creeping across her face. "Well, the nose is a shade fat, and one lip is a bit lazy. Besides that, I'd say you have it."

It still boggled Cram. A Changer. Here she stood in front of him the spitting image of that same Lord Reggie sleeping in that bed.

"How do you feel?" asked Henry.

New Reggie put a fist to his mouth and burped. "Strange. Sick. Not myself."

Cram stifled a nervous giggle.

"Can you hold it?" Athena asked. She waggled her hand. "The . . . shape?"

"I have no idea. We should get moving."

New Reggie flapped his hands around. "Remember, if I begin to act strangely—"

Henry blinked. "You mean, other than now?"

"*More* strangely, I may be losing myself."

Athena nodded. "Right. We keep a sharp lookout for broom closets, find a moment to slap you silly, and try to remind you that you're Ruby."

New Reggie nodded with a wild grin. "Tally-ho then!"

Griddle Van Huffridge stood at the balcony. "I am off as well. I won't be able to get back into the Warren with the watch on the door. The Birnbaums live nearby. Their maid used to work for my family and is a friend. That is where I will be." She smiled then normal like at New Reggie. Cram had never realized how tight she held her face until she didn't. The girl shook her head in wonder. "You are quite something, Ruby Teach."

New Reggie smiled a goofy smile and said, "Why, thank you, my dear. And it's Reginald."

Then fire bloomed in Griddle's eyes. "I am counting on you. My father is in great danger. Promise me you will do your utmost."

Lady Athena stepped forward bravely, but the effect was spoiled as she tripped over her hem. "We promise," she said. She hesitated. "Do you—do you have a weapon?"

Greta blinked. "Besides chemystry?"

Lady Athena held out her sword. Cram tried to pick his jaw up off the floor. "Take this. You might need it. Besides"—she shrugged and twirled the dress—"where would I put it?"

Greta Van Huffridge sighed. But she took the sword. And then she was gone.

"I'm not certain this is a good plan." The professor shifted his black and yellow Shackleton livery about on his shoulders, then fidgeted with the newly polished buckles on his shoes.

"Sit on your hands, sir."

"Kevin. Call me Kevin."

"Kevin. If you keep shifting about on that seat you will draw the wrong kind of looking, and that will be that." The professor stopped fidgeting, which was at least a bit of a blessing. Cram tugged at the cuff on his own livery and concentrated on steering.

It would not do to crash a tinker's carriage on a night like tonight. It had been the better part of a year since Cram had driven one of the horseless coaches, let alone a silver-plated one. He thought he should be enjoying it, but he was too nervous.

"Cram," said Henry, and Cram followed his nod to a street cart, a lady from UnderTown, hawking roasted nuts.

The chem-soaked bandages around her head bulged at the ears; little slate tendrils crept down from the fabric around her eyes. She looked up from a customer to meet his gaze, and her empty smile chilled him straight to his soul. "Is that—"

"Like Penny," muttered Henry. "If it's up here, it's spreading."

They saw three or four other Juiced, in pairs or alone, even as they rode farther into UpTown. As the houses got bigger, the streets got more quiet. But it felt like a quiet that might bite.

As the carriage trundled past an alley that proudly proclaimed PLATINUM WAY, five shapes detached themselves from the shadows and began following the coach. Their teeth shone in the dusk.

"Cram—"

"I see 'em." He had to keep his wits. If he started flabbering and jabbering, the professor would lose his head and then fricassee someone with a potion, and then they'd all be in the stew for sure.

"Why are they following us?" Henry eyed the flywheel amid the forest of levers and gauges in front of Cram.

"Nights like this, grudges get settled. Maybe some folk don't care for the Shackletons."

"Can we go faster?"

"Miss Van Huffridge said slow and steady. Nothing to see here."

"Yes I know, but—" Henry reached out for the flywheel.

Cram wanted to slap his hand out of the way. Instead, he said, in his best Madame Hearth voice, "Keep your wits, Collins."

Henry's hand froze. "Was that a Madame Hearth?"

"Yes," Cram said in the same fruity tones.

"Really spot on, Cram."

"Thankoo."

Henry reached out again.

Cram glanced back over his shoulder. The pack of folks was still there, just outside the light of the running lamps. Every tiny jot of him wanted to yell, "Whirl it, Prof!" and race away to safety. Instead, he said, "Quiet like, Professor. We ain't in a hurry to get nowhere. If folks is in a hurry, other folk wonder why."

Henry sighed.

They rolled around a corner, and there was nowhere else to go.

Across their path lay a sturdy split-rail barricade. And behind the barricade?

"The curfew." Henry whispered a curse. "Redcoats."

"Ice in your veins," Cram whispered, though he felt anything but. "This is the why of why we got Lord Reggie and his papers down below."

Their rear escort dissolved like watered wine. Before them a shadowy figure raised a tinker's lamp and opened its shutters, casting vivid blue light across the bearer's face.

"Hellooooo!" A ruddy moon-faced soldier trundled around the barricade and up to the carriage. Two others circled on the other side. "Lovely night tonight, innit?"

Cram started talking. Stopped. Then started again. "Yes. Yes, it is, sir. Lovely night."

The redcoat peered, smiling, at the curtained windows, which remained curtained. "Headed to the party up at the big hoose?'

Henry cut in. "Indeed. We cannot be detained. Very important passengers."

If they lived through this, he'd have to give the

professor a long lesson in bowing and scraping. Cram let out a laugh strangled within an inch of its life. "*Hahaaargle*. What Kevin means to say is that while we are on a bit of a tight shedjool, of course we have all the time in the world for His Majesty's scarlet heroes."

The little soldier grimaced and nodded, "Thank you kindly! Haven't heard a lot of such talk since we arrived here. We won't take long at all. Just need a little peek inside the coach, to observe the inhabitants and papers and all."

Cram hopped down to the cobblestones, all the while trying to quash the picture his head was giving him. The picture: Ruby a pile of Reggie-shaped goo, spread across the embroidered Shackleton cushions like yesterday's stew. He sniffed it away and stood up straight as he could. Time to cast the dice.

He rapped on the door.

"Yooooos, Kevin?"

"It's Karl, sir."

"What eees it, Karl?"

"Begging your pardon, sir, but we have come across a

wee roadblock, and one of His Majesty's soldiers would like a word."

"One moment, pleeeease."

Sweat crept down his back. He could smell it. He wondered if the redcoat had a good nose.

The curtain opened.

CHAPTER 15

Treat others as you would have yourself treated: with grace,
charm, and respect.
—Bethilda Fwallop, *A Young Tinker's Guide to Polite Society*

"One moment, pleeeease." Ruby's chin wobbled. It actually *moved* about on her chin, like a mouse under a handkerchief. She wrapped her fingers around it. It *shifted*. And then her elbow puffed up to half again its size. She grabbed it with the other hand. Perhaps no one would notice. "How bad?" she whispered.

Across the compartment, perched on a velvet cushion and awash in a storm of lace, Athena mouthed, "Bad."

Remember what Gwath said. Think Reggie thoughts. But between the strangeness of the new body and the panic she could barely keep her own self straight. Her sails were in tatters, and the hungry rocks awaited.

This was the time when Athena would draw her sword.

This was the time when Athena would kick open the door, knocking the soldier down into the street, and they would thunder off straight through the barricade with the redcoats on their tails.

Instead, Athena flounced up to the window, pannier hoops flaring out to fill the center of the compartment.

Oh, Providence. She was preparing to flirt.

Athena unveiled her teeth in something resembling a smile—the way a baboon would bare its fangs at an enemy—and pulled the curtain open. She unlocked the little window with a snick, and the sounds of night and street flooded in.

"Well, hello there," she purred. But her purring was more like she had a nut stuck in her throat and her eyes were too wide and she fluttered her eyelashes with military precision and—

The redcoat took a step back. "Gah," he said.

"Miss . . . Evallina Puddledump, at your service, my good sir." She flipped her fan at the soldier. Where had she found a fan?

"Ahem," said the redcoat. "Ah. Miss . . . Puddledump—"

"Of the Virginia Puddledumps." Somehow, impossibly, her smile had grown larger. Like a sinkhole.

"Yes. Well. Terribly sorry to disturb you, but your papers, please?"

Athena reached out without a glance at Ruby, trying to keep the focus on herself. Was Reggie's eyebrow still attached? Ruby handed over the papers and invitations, one for him and one for a guest. They were miracles of clockwork, more the thickness of a school slate than a piece of parchment, and embossed with all manner of gears that actually moved inside little crystal windows.

"Reginald Shackleton?" His mouth made an O of respect. "Of Shackleton's Shackle Town?"

Ruby risked it. "The same." Reggie's voice was close to his warble.

The man's eyes flicked over for a moment. "Well, milord, we do love your chains and manacles. Best quality in the colonies for keeping prisoners trussed up."

"Thank yoo. So much."

"And thank you for your patience. You are cleared to pass!" As he leaned forward to pass back the documents, he said, "Best to make your stay a short one? Dangerous night. There are rumors abounding. Good citizens like yourself most likely should stay in with doors locked and barred. I'm not certain it will be safe for anyone in the streets tonight."

The concern in Athena's "Oh, dear," was the first remotely authentic emotion Ruby had heard since the conversation began. "We will, sir, and good luck to you tonight."

Something fluttered behind his eyes. "Thank you, miss. And good luck to us all." He bowed, and Athena closed the window and shut the curtains.

Quiet descended. They were alone.

Athena collapsed back into her seat. "I feel as if I've sparred for hours." She made a face. "How do women do that?"

The low *thwock thwock thwockthwockthwock* of the carriage gears spun up, and they began moving again, cobblestones rumbling under the thick iron wheels.

Athena looked at Ruby as if she were china. "Are you all right?"

Ruby took her hands away from her parts, and they didn't waggle. "Progress," she said.

"No. I don't mean that. Can you go through with this? is what I'm asking. If you falter and your foot falls off in the middle of a Virginia reel, my fading flower routine will not be able to save us."

Athena's laugh was strained, but it helped. Her friend's courage helped Ruby focus. Bit by bit Reginald Shackleton solidified. She tried to wrap him about her like a cloak. Not just being a boy but being a boy who, when he sucked his thumb, was congratulated for it. Warmth bloomed in her chest, and she puffed it out. It felt good. It felt wonderful. There was nothing to fear here. Reggie was with his people, and Reggie's people were not suspicious of him. They loved him. Reggie grinned. Everyone loved him. "I'm ready," Ruby said.

"And with what the soldier just said—danger on the streets tonight—"

"Agreed," said Athena. "As quickly as we can, find Paine and Van Huffridge, warn them, get alla Ferra's money, and get out."

In her very best Reggie voice, Ruby said, "And snacks. We cannot forget snacks. I want a stuffed goose."

Athena gave her a sidelong glance and then leaned back from the other window. "I'm glad you've found your footing, Reggie, because we're here."

Cram's knock rang low on the thick wood of the door, and then it opened.

Sound flooded in: music from a quartet and people laughing and the clatter of dishes and the rumbling of tinker's carriages.

Cram and Henry stood at attention, and Reginald Shackleton stalked down the steps of the carriage, extending a hand to help Evallina Puddledump down as well. Before them lay the front porch of Van Huffridge House.

It would have been impossible to miss.

The clouds had cleared a bit, and the house, still wet from the rain, sparkled in the reflected light of a hundred tinker's lamps.

"Is that—" Ruby murmured.

"Yes," said Athena. "The outside walls are all alloyed glass."

The shining walls of Van Huffridge House rose up into the night sky: glittering panels supported by a crosshatch of silvery metal support beams. It perched on a corner of the Lid, jutting out over its edge like a crystal figurehead. A double line of footmen ran from the edge of the street, up the stairs, across the wide porch to the door. Milling about on the porch to either side churned a crowd of partygoers, panniers bustling, buttons gleaming, and witty chatter spinning. All along the glass railing, groups of men and women clustered to watch the new arrivals. They spoke with one another in hushed whispers from behind shining brass gloves and magnesium fans, all the while taking in the new prey. Which, currently, was Ruby and Athena.

Ruby smiled a wide smile that she hoped said, "I

am completely at ease here" and said, under her breath, "What now?"

Just then a little man hurried up, his eyes wide behind rose lenses. His purple and gray Van Huffridge livery was gussied up with so many ribbons it was hard to see the fabric underneath. "Welcome back to Van Huffridge House, Lord Shackleton!"

No room for hesitation now. Straight into the whirlpool. "Thank you, my good man! So good to be back. Er"—Ruby fluttered Reggie's handkerchief—"I am so terrible with names."

Sweat beaded his upper lip. "Clivens, milord. Third factotum of the western entrance."

"Well, I'm sure second is not far off now. Keep up the good work."

"Thank you, sir." He turned to Athena. "Miss?"

"Puddledump. Evallina Puddledump."

"Of course."

Ruby smiled. "Of course!"

Athena smiled all the way to the roots of her teeth and then stuck her arm out.

Oh. Ruby took her elbow, and the two of them flowed forward, past Factotum Clivens and along the row of servants. Ruby wanted to look back. She wanted to check to make sure that Cram was all right, and Henry. But she didn't.

Reginald didn't care about servants.

At her side Athena wheezed.

"Is everything all right?" Ruby muttered.

"Corset, that's all." Athena gritted her teeth. Her eyes bulged slightly.

"Evallina, everyone is looking at us. Like they know us."

"Just act as if you know them. Everyone is an old friend."

"But—"

"You were spot on with Clivens. No one will be so rude as to ask if you recognize them. Be vague as you like, but not overly familiar. You don't want anyone to feel invited to keep speaking to you. Above all, and this is most important, be pleasant."

"Pleasant?" Ruby nodded and smiled to a silver-nosed tinker who was waving madly at them.

"As if you had just spent the afternoon becoming fast friends while watching your falcons mate in your parents' two-hundred-year-old cypress grove."

"What?"

"Personal experience, sorry. Just assume you know everyone. More than half of them are doing the same with you, I guarantee it."

The silver-chased doors of Van Huffridge House were fifteen feet high if they were an inch. Two guards stood to either side; hard sorts whose swords and clocklocks gleamed dull and menacing against their party finery. Perched atop each guard's head was a freshly brushed coonskin cap. They looked as fit for the wilderness as a raccoon would in Clivens's tights. They flung the doors open, and waves of music and chatter washed over Ruby.

Flowers wound above on the inside struts, crawled in every direction, drooped drowsily from winding vines and jutted up from cleverly affixed pots. Gardenias and magnolias, iris and bee balm—everywhere Ruby looked there was a new one. The house was packed with them.

It felt like some kind of living thing. A wave of heat and moisture rolled over them, accompanied by a heady, thick mix of sweetness. Athena wobbled, grabbing Ruby's elbow for a moment. The foyer rose three floors of open air straight up to where rain had started up again fitfully tapping on the roof, spattering on panels that looked as if they could be slid back to let in the outside air. Bright, vigorous music filtered in from balconies wrapped in vine and creeper.

Transparent stairways of alloyed glass swept up in both directions out of the foyer, and Ruby and Athena had no choice but to join the tide of partygoers rolling upward. At the top of the stairs, next to a palm tree in a platinum planter, waited a serving woman adorned with somehow even more ribbons than Clivens. She held a cobalt staff of office and gave Ruby a graceful bow. "Lord Shackleton. Welcome back to Van Huffridge House." She turned to Athena. "And mademoiselle, welcome. How may I announce you?"

Athena fired off a stunning curtsy. "Evallina Puddledump, of the Virginia Puddledumps."

"Of course, mademoiselle." The woman flowed in through the doorway, plonked her staff three times, and proclaimed, "Lord Reginald Shackleton and Mademoiselle Evallina Puddledump."

Every corner was overflowing with the very finest people, a treacherous sea of rocks and monsters. Ruby looked down at Athena. "Ready?"

Athena's eyes tightened in a smile. "Always." Athena gave Ruby's wrist a squeeze. It would have been reassuring, but it left a pulsing divot in her skin.

Ruby swallowed. "Brilliant."

CHAPTER 16

Take my gold. Take my soul. Hell, take my children, if you like.
But if you look sideways at my steward? I'll keelhaul you and
leave you for the sharks.
—Precious Nel, Scourge of the Seven Seas

If the drive at the front of Van Huffridge House was a bubbling cauldron, the rear was a forest fire.

And Henry knew something of forest fires. He knew nothing, however, of the land of servants. The drive spiraled down and around a massive retaining wall, and as soon as they passed that border separating the front from the back, chaos attacked. Crowds of attendants hurried madly to and fro as if their lives depended on it, calls echoing from the vaulted brick ceilings. The carriage house was a castle in its own right. No fewer than three different grooms screamed garbled instructions at Cram, directing him and the carriage to various slots among a dizzying array of other coaches, spaces that seemed so narrow to Henry as to be completely impossible.

Through it all, Cram sat next to him silent and impenetrable as Bacon's tomb, his hands and feet like hummingbirds on the wheels and levers. He sailed the coach *through* the carriage house entirely and out into the court directly behind the main house. The carriage barreled past a fleet of wheelbarrows, casting a purple flood of fresh-cut violets to the ground and setting off a chorus of curses. They braked so hard that Henry was almost thrown from their perch, and then, nimble as a dancer, the coach sidled through the tiniest of gaps between two parked carriages. Henry could have reached out and tugged the quivering red mustaches of the driver on his side. For a moment he feared the man would tear him from his seat. Finally, as if by a fit of prophecy, Cram landed them in a space so recently vacated by a tart wagon that a bystanding groom swallowed a small scream of fear.

Henry opened the latches on his safety straps. "By Providence, Cram," he muttered, "that was well done!"

The serving boy nodded and coughed, covering a smile. He jumped down from the carriage and tied it up, hiding his words in the fierce motion of the ropes. "Follow me, *Kevin*. And don't say nothing to nobody, you savvy?"

"Why do they tie the ropes? There are no horses anymore—"

Cram rounded on him and hissed low, "It's just the way it's still done, see? Don't say nothing to nobody."

Henry cleared his throat. He was in Cram's hands now, Cram's world. He nodded. "Don't say anyth— nothing to nobody."

He followed Cram's lead and grabbed up a platter of tarts recently deposited by the tart wagon. When he turned about, a woman had appeared in front of him.

She was dressed in sensible wool, in the Van Huffridge purple and gray. Her eyes were bloodshot, and she bore a faint wisp of a mustache on her lip. She wore her hair in a forgettable bun and carried a battered, worn chain of keys and tools about her waist.

She bore down on them like a team of angered oxen.

"Who are you?" said the woman.

Cram instantly abandoned his air of authority, transforming before Henry's eye into a meek, polite nobody. "Begging your pardon, Miss Chatelaine. Lord Shackleton tasked us to help in any way we could, and the head groom said to help with the unloadings of provisions for the feast and the like."

A terrible skepticism hung about her like a cloud. "Head groom, eh?"

Cram's eyes and Adam's apple bobbed up and down in tandem.

"I will string up that oaf. I told him we could make do without the guests' folk pitching in. It don't look right."

"Yes, mum," said Cram.

Henry thought it would be good to nod.

As soon as he did, he knew he had made a mistake. The chatelaine's gimlet eye skewered him. "You think it don't look right?"

The details of hundreds of false people, some from books he had read, others from visions of his past life, coursed through his head like a raging river. He went on with the nodding.

Cram sighed, a sad sound. "Kevin, miss, he's mute these four years. Cain't speak a word."

Should he nod? Make a face? Start to cry? Science, he was terrible at this. He settled on a shrug.

The chatelaine sniffed like a coursing hound, eyes darting back and forth between the two of them. It felt like years passed. Finally she sniffed one last time. "Well, however it looks, we do need help. Those tarts will not move themselves, and they'll be ruined in this damp. Take them down to the kitchens."

The kitchens? Henry's eyes bulged. He tried to keep them in his sockets. Where in the name of all Science were the kitchens?

Cram seemed to take in all of this in a split second and tugged at Henry's shirt with his free hand. "COME ON THEN, KEVIN," he yelled. Directly into Henry's face.

They hurried past the chatelaine, already fixing her glower on some new victim. Cram walked ahead as if he owned the place through a massive set of ironbound oak doors. On the other side lay the maw of hell, also known as the kitchens of Van Huffridge House. Great ovens belched fire. Cooks and pastry chefs vied for counter space. Everywhere there was motion and chaos.

Cram scanned the church-size room, then froze like a hunting dog catching a scent. Henry couldn't hear what the other boy said over the din, but he followed nonetheless as Cram deftly maneuvered the tarts through the press to the far side.

A slight breeze trailed down two twin staircases, one with a stream of platter-laden servants traveling up and one for harassed folks coming down, bearing trays that looked as if they had been picked over by ravenous hyenas.

Cram marched up to a harried steward with eyebrows like bristle brushes and presented the tarts. "For Miss Paine?" he asked.

The steward barely gave him a glance. "Music room."

Cram nodded as if that were the most precise direction in the history of directions. "Of course, mum. We're with Lord Shackleton's people. Can you direct me to a particular music room?"

She gave a great gout of a sigh. "Four flights, long hallway. Second door, across from the tapestry of the lions eating the farmers."

A tall serving girl, her chestnut curls tucked up under a purple and gray cap, detached herself from a group of other servants and sidled up to them. "Those for Miss Paine?"

Henry nodded.

The girl made room on the platter for a pitcher and a single tankard. "Take those, too, will you please? Compliments of the house. In honor of the evening." She winked.

"Of course. Thank you, miss." Cram dived into the crowd of streaming servants. After the first turn he craned his head back over his shoulder. "Did you see that?" he whispered.

"Yes," said Henry. His mouth was dry as a bone, and

his pulse pounded in his ears. He risked a glance back around the turn at the clump of servants the girl had come from. A big one and the two white-haired twins. As if she could somehow sense him, the girl turned around and gave him a brilliant smile. All he could think to do was smile back and wave, as if he fancied her. He ducked back around the corner and tried, with all his might, to speak casually. "Those are reeves. That was the girl from the canyon."

Cram dumped the pitcher and tankard in a nearby plant. "We'd best move. We ain't the only ones masking as servants tonight."

CHAPTER 17

*What, you ask, is the Great Blight upon our new Age? It is
neither the terror of the Second Inquisition, nor is it the Hungry
Ghost of Poverty. It is that most horrible of scourges:
The Well-Attended Party.*
—Silence Dogood, *Boston Mercury*

Athena couldn't breathe. She rested her gloved fingers
on the table to hold herself up as another wave of
dizziness passed. She swallowed a grim smile, taking a
moment to imagine the faces of some of the women in
the room if they saw what lay underneath the tiny pearls
that marched all the way up to her elbows. Tan skin.
Chipped fingernails. Calluses at the join of the thumb
and forefinger, raised slowly and agonizingly after years

of study into her own style of needlepoint, the art of the blade.

Her vision cleared, and she found herself staring into the transparent maw of a roaring bear. Colonials took pride in their ferocious animals, and the ice sculpture centerpiece did not disappoint. Fully four feet high from the table, the beast was somehow chemystrally chilled by an artifice in the flat silver base. Silver, of course, because iron or even steel would not do for a party of this importance. The great finger-size fangs were so cold they did not even drip. She let the cool air wash over her as she got her bearings. The little balcony she and Ruby had found offered a better view of the packed main floor below, and a trellis full of morning glory offered cover from observation as well.

Anger at Greta boiled up through her cinched-in waist, forced itself through her manacled lungs, and trickled out in a swallowed curse. Athena flicked at the unwieldy panniers jutting out from her hips. Her artfully arranged hair tickled the back of her neck like the finest of water tortures. Her entire life she had worked to keep her distance from exactly this: being held captive in a bedamned prison of silk and lace.

Next to her, tall and handsome in a peaked way, Ruby Teach, in her guise as Reginald Shackleton, leaned over and warbled, "Barnacles."

Athena let her fingers play across a platter of radishes, bitter oranges, and anchovies. Country fare, but made up fancy. A wicked-looking knife had been artfully left in a loaf of hearty brown bread. She palmed it and secreted it among her ruffles. The familiar feel of steel against her skin helped her breathe a bit more easily. She smiled at a couple passing below, their hair tortured into a pair of overengineered matching ships. "I'm sorry?" she murmured.

"There are so many people. How are we supposed to find our woman in this logjam?" Reginald's voice quavered up and down on the last word.

The enormity of their task had Athena sweating. "I have no idea. Needle, haystack, that sort of thing I suppose."

There was a chuckle.

Athena turned to Reggie. "It wasn't that funny."

Reggie frowned "Then why did you laugh?"

Her blood ran cold. "I thought it was you."

The laugh came again from behind them, a low, gravel-filled chuckle filtering through the trellis of purple flowers, and a terrible scene reared its head in Athena's mind's eye: the *Thrift*'s windswept deck under a carpet of stars, blood on the boards, a merciless shadow looming over Ruby.

A scarred finger parted the purple buds, revealing the empty, feral smile of Wisdom Rool. "Why, *Athen* Boyle, you do clean up nicely. "

Athena flicked her wrist and dropped the knife into her hand. Next to her Reginald had gone very still, like a rabbit under a hawk-filled sky. How had Rool found them? Why was he here at all? Were they going to be taken here and now? "Sir, I am not certain to whom you refer. My name is Evallina Puddledump."

He raised an eyebrow. "Of course, of course. My mistake. Of the Virginia Puddledumps, if I'm not mistaken? Now, there's no need for conflict, Miss

Evallina. Perhaps you and your companion might come around to my side of things, and we could have a little chat."

Athena glanced out the corner of her eye at Reginald, who nodded. What else could they do?

Behind the trellis Wisdom Rool filled a glass-framed chair, one gnarled foot tucked up under his leg, shoes left adrift on the floor. A narrow side stair set into the wall yawned into the darkness behind him. He was not, however, dressed in his typical reeve blacks. Instead, he was stuffed into a set of Van Huffridge livery that threatened to pop open with his every move. At Athena's look he said, "I don't have to tell you what a challenging party this was to get into. Apparently something eventful is going to happen. Absolutely everyone who is anyone wants to be here this evening." His empty eyes glittered. "I had to convince some poor fellow to part with his livery and then sneak—sneak, I tell you—up the back stairs." His eyes flicked back and forth between Athena and Reggie. "But here the two of you are. Providence has certainly rewarded my lack of social graces."

Athena licked her lips. "What do you want from us? I warn you—"

"No need for warnings, Miss Evallina." He grinned. "Will you do me the honor of an introduction to your companion?"

Reginald cleared his throat. Or he tried to. It sounded like a frog gargling. "Reginald Shackleton, sir. My friends call me Reggie."

Rool stood, his eyes drinking in Reginald's features. He bowed. "A pleasure, Lord Reggie. And I am Wisdom Rool, lord captain of the king's Reeve. We are devoted admirers of your family's fetters."

Reginald bowed in return, a vapid smile on his face. "Well, Evallina, you do keep some high company! I am honored. And safe! I feel safe as a babe in arms! Why did he call you Athen?"

Well done, Ruby.

Rool stepped in smoothly. "She is a student of the classics, is Evallina. Athen is, if I'm not mistaken a shortening of the name Athena. Hellenic goddess of wisdom and strategy in battle, don't you know?"

"I—I see."

Athena's thoughts whirled. Why hadn't he sounded an alarm or called the guards? But he was in disguise as well. Did he recognize Ruby? Was this all some sort of game? She moved the knife into a more defensive position. "What are you about, Lord Captain? I don't imagine you're the type of man that can't bear to miss a society affair."

"Careful, Evallina. That looks to be quite a sharp little knife. I'd hate to see you cut by it." He smiled, a cat playing with two little mice.

Anger gave Athena strength. "But you don't want to be seen, do you, Rool? You think you can cut me with my own knife before I cry out? And before Reggie does?"

Rool raised his eyebrow in appreciation. "You reasoned that out, did you?" His eyes narrowed. "Well, here's a question for you. Why are you not sounding the alarm right now?"

Athena tried to keep her face smooth.

"I believe I can answer that. You are wanted by the crown, are you not? You and your friend Ruby Teach?

Perhaps you have as much reason for avoiding attention as I?"

Out of nowhere Reginald Shackleton's glove whipped out and smacked Wisdom Rool in the face.

Athena froze. Rool, ever so slowly, turned to face Reginald.

Reginald did not seem fazed in the least. "Sir, you have picked the wrong man's escort to bait. You are a cad and a bounder, and I challenge you to defend your honor. My seconds will call upon you to arrange a time for us to meet and settle this."

Rool was nose to nose with Reginald before Athena could blink. No time for thinking.

She stabbed upward, toward the heart.

It was a good blow, if a hand of iron was not already twisting her wrist, wrenching the blade out of her grasp. She took a breath to call out, but his two fingers struck her like a spear to a spot on her chest. She couldn't make a sound. She could not breathe. She stumbled into the chair, barely able to stand.

In that instant Rool's other hand had closed around

Reginald's throat. His eyes bulged.

"My honor, sir?" Wisdom Rool whispered. "You mistake your place, *boy*. Before this night was over, you would have known exactly what your place is, but now I fear you will discover it is six feet underground in a very fancy coffin."

"W-w—wa-i-i-it." Athena finally forced a whisper from her throat.

"Athena Boyle, it is quite impressive that you can make any sound at all. I will deal with you in a moment. Your friend here—"

"Not . . . friend." Her chest ached. Red flashed at the edge of her vision. "R-R-uby."

Rool looked at her. Then he looked at Reggie. "Truly?"

Athena could only nod.

The hand snaked out. Athena thought it was the end. Surprisingly she could breathe again. She pulled in great gouts of air.

"Don't try to call out." Rool's scarred hand still circled Reginald's throat. He peered into the boy's eyes. "Knock, knock."

Reginald blinked. "Who's there?" he whispered.

"Ruby Teach?"

Reginald frowned. Then his eyes widened, and he looked about as if he had just woken from a deep sleep. "Yes. Ruby."

"Why did you slap me, Ruby?"

"C-confused."

Rool smiled. "And what did I give you the night you escaped?"

"R-r-rope."

Suddenly Rool released Reginald, and he crumpled to the ground. Athena realized that his feet had been off the ground that whole time.

Rool checked the other side of the trellis to see if they were observed, then knelt to take them both in. "Well, now."

"Lord Captain—" Reggie began to speak.

"Ruby. Athena. It truly is a pleasure to see you. The crown is after you, but I have no interest in that hunt." He cracked his knuckles and turned to Athena. "Take this advice from someone who considers himself a kind of ally. Very soon it will be quite uncomfortable in this house, and the folk who will be filling it are not so kindly disposed to you. Whatever business you have in this place, you should do it quickly and be gone. If it is, as I overheard you say, to contact Thandie Paine, I suggest you make other plans entirely. If you are absolutely bent on self-destruction, I believe she is preparing to make an appearance shortly in the ballroom."

Athena's head spun, and it wasn't just from lack of air.

Rool was moving already, back toward the staircase. He turned in the doorway.

"Well done, though, Reginald," he said, and Ruby stared daggers at him from her stolen body. "I mean it. At least this time you didn't turn into a pumpkin."

And then he was gone.

CHAPTER 18

Strike first, and with all your ferocity.
—Manual of the Reeve of England

As Rool disappeared behind the flowers, a cold wave of fear washed over Ruby. Hearth had been right. The Reeve was on to all of them. Something was going to happen, something big, right here and right now. But what had just happened to *her*? She could remember slapping Rool, challenging him, but as if she had watched it in a theater. The memory was through this kind of terrifying veil. Ruby tried to stand, but Reginald's ankles rolled underneath her.

Athena grabbed her by the shoulders and forced her down into the chair. "Wait. Catch your breath."

She did. She looked down at her hands. Boy's hands still. She hadn't changed back. Not yet. But something was wrong. Like seasickness, but it was her mind that was at sea. Reginald's stomach churned. He couldn't think straight. "Ath—Evallina, I feel . . . not myself."

Athena snorted, eyes darting. "Not surprised. You're wearing someone else's shape like a shabby coat."

"Not . . . what I mean. I mean—" She tried to calm her racing pulse, tried to put what she was feeling into words. "I'm drifting. Like a boat or something. I can see me, but me doesn't hear exactly me, if that makes any sense."

Athena's brows knitted in concern. "No, it doesn't. Ruby. Ruby, you're scaring me."

Ruby. She was Ruby. Not Reginald. Reginald skin, Ruby heart. In her mind's eye Ruby was indeed in a little boat, rowing out to sea. On the shore, though, there was Athena, waving her arms, and the truth started flooding back. She was at the party with her friends. To warn someone. To help. Ruby started rowing back.

"Keep it fixed in your heart," Gwath had said.

I am Ruby. A body is just a body. It's not *me*. If it acts like Reginald, who cares? I'm him. But I'm me, too. And I have to stop something from happening. How did you stop something from happening if you didn't know what it was?

Ruby blew out through Reggie's lips. "All right."

Athena searched Ruby's eyes for a moment, and her smile brought Ruby all the way back. "All right." Athena helped her up, and they stood at the balcony searching the crowds below.

"Help me understand something," Athena murmured.

"What is it?"

"Why would Wisdom Rool just leave us?"

Why indeed? "Perhaps he knows that what we're doing is hopeless. Perhaps he wants us to know it." A thought struck Ruby. "Perhaps we are part of the trap."

"He said we should go to the ballroom."

"If we wanted to destroy ourselves."

"He said something was going to happen. He said Paine would be there."

"Yes, come on. It's the lead we have, no matter how small or perilous." Athena's jaw was as tight as a ship's rigging in a hurricane as she grabbed Ruby's wrist and hurried into the hallway. No more talk was possible as the press of party guests bore them down the stairs and into the great hall on a wave of perfume, sweat, and flowers.

The great hall of Van Huffridge House was a marvel. A cage of alloyed glass, it soared a full five stories high into the darkness. Rain from the billowing, clouded night sky spattered on its transparent panels. High above the floor of the hall hung a great chandelier, each of its hundred globes a tinker's lamp in its own right. The guests stood shoulder to shoulder on the parquet floor, arranged in front of a stage swathed in the gray and purple of Van Huffridge House.

On the stage sat a large *something* hidden under a silk curtain.

But Ruby's eyes didn't rest for long on the curtain because they were occupied with something far more interesting and far more dangerous, a vision from her worst memories. For directly in front of her, in the place of honor on the stage, stood a man. His white greatcoat, waistcoat, and shoes fashioned an island of snow amid the color of the hall. He chatted gaily with a steward, the silvery mesh that ran down the left side of his face, from his ear to his collarbone, glittering in the chandelier's light. In her mind she could hear the awful, cheerful gurgling tinkling of his breathing.

Dr. Emmanuel Swedenborg.

But why would the Swede be here? What kind of game was Van Huffridge playing to bring such a man into his home on the brink of revolt?

A chime rang three times, and the crowd fell silent.

A middle-aged male version of Greta Van Huffridge, knife sharp and focused as a hunting hawk, bounded onto the stage. His simple clothing stood in stark contrast with the opulence all around him, but the silence all about her told Ruby everything she needed to know. Lothor Van Huffridge was the biggest man in the room.

He stood motionless for a moment, eyes flickering across the crowd.

"Good evening," he said. "Friends and family. Brothers and sisters of our land. Thank you for joining us this evening. It is a tender time for our people, with wolves snapping at each other out in the fields. The French and English, forever at war, it seems, have carried their conflict further into our homes."

Uneasy whispers flitted through the crowd. Ruby desperately scanned among them, searching for a sign of something, anything out of place.

Lothor Van Huffridge smiled. "But tonight is not about conflict, dear companions. Tonight is a night of discovery! Dr. Emmanuel Swedenborg has agreed to show us something, well"—a brief smile flashed across his face—"you may have heard inklings of it coming from UnderTown. We seem to be on the edge of a massive change for our world. It sounds absolutely *magical*." The crowd laughed, at ease again. Ruby had seen many great sharpers in her time, including her father and Gwath, and this man was right up among them. The people were putty in his hands. A king indeed. Van Huffridge held out a hand in invitation. "Dr. Swedenborg?"

"Thank you, sir," Swedenborg lilted. "I hope we will not disappoint."

"I hope not, too," cut in Van Huffridge, and the crowd laughed again.

The doctor blinked, taken aback.

Beside Ruby, Athena's eyes never stopped moving, searching every corner for Paine. "I don't see her," she whispered.

Van Huffridge smiled to Swedenborg. "Proceed."

"Thank you." The Swede turned to the audience. He reached up, grabbed a fistful of fabric draping the shape beside him, and pulled.

The cloth tumbled to the stage, exposing a dense basket of pipes, gears, and levers, crammed into a space about the size of a dinner table. A cloth hose emerged from one end, hanging on a hook from a kind of hat stand. Next to the whole thing sat a comfy chair, like one you might find in a rich merchant's study.

"Behold the future." He looked for all the world as if he were showing the assembled crowd his baby.

Ruby's stomach churned. She knew what was coming,

and she could not bear the thought of it. Her shoulders hunched.

"Is that?" Athena whispered.

Ruby nodded Reggie's head. She couldn't speak.

"I shall require a volunteer." He looked out at the crowd. "Luckily many have been bravely eager to further the cause of Science." Then he held out his hands and helped a young woman onto the stage. She was nervous, plain, and fair, in her best mended frock, certainly not a guest of the party. A seamstress perhaps or a young washerwoman.

The Swede smiled and bowed over her hand. "And what is your name, miss?"

She looked at him scared and, Ruby thought, a little mesmerized. She said something inaudible.

The Swede's mesh jingled. "Could you speak up, please?"

Her eyes darted out to the crowd. She blushed. Her voice carried, surprisingly loud now. "Laura Bowers." The crowd laughed, startled.

"And Laura Bowers, have we ever met before?"

"No, sir. I answered an advertisement. I—"

"Thank you. Now, Laura, if you would sit down in this comfortable chair? Good." He presented her with the trailing end of the cloth hose, upon which lay a palm-size cup, chased with filigree. "Now, then, Miss Bowers, I would like you to place this cup over your mouth."

She took it in her hand. "What will happen?"

"Nothing untoward. You will breathe and feel a slight pulling sensation, but then a wonderful warmth." The Swede smiled. He gestured toward Van Huffridge, who was off to the side, leaning against an alloyed glass pillar. "The master of this house has guaranteed your safety," he said. Van Huffridge nodded.

Laura licked her lips, then said, "Very well." She pulled the mask over her mouth.

The Swede stalked over to the other side and flicked a series of levers. "Now, you all know that one of the great engines of our society for the last hundred years has been tinkercraft. Wonders of energy and Science have been created using the power that tinkers have harnessed for themselves." He twirled a wheel on the machine, and it adopted a deeper hum. Laura Bowers twisted a bit in the chair and gave a small "ooh!" He gestured up at the chandelier. "Do you know, however, that the chemystral power required to keep this chandelier running is provided by the constant work of three Tinkers Guild apprentices, whose only job, night and day, is to fill the sparkstones that keep it lit? But only one in two hundred of us is a tinker, and so we are limited in the wonders we can create by our strength of will." He moved a lever with the tip of his extended index finger. The hum deepened, and the machine began to shake. Laura Bowers's eyebrows lifted. It was only because Ruby was watching closely that she was able to see the tiniest of veins beginning to creep down the woman's neck from the spot right below her ears. Gorge rose in Ruby's throat.

She hadn't noticed the globe of the tinker's lamp behind the chair.

She hadn't noticed it because it hadn't been lit, its bulb inert in the smoked glass.

But now it began to glow.

The crowd murmured.

Then it lit up bright, and the crowd gasped.

The Swede flicked a lever, and the machine came to a halt. He looked at them all. The room lay quiet, shocked.

That's when Ruby heard it: somewhere, up above and behind, a creak of leather, as if someone were leaning forward, and the faintest click.

A clocklock being primed.

Beside her, Athena stiffened, too. "Oh, Science," she whispered.

The two girls whirled, searching the glittering rafters.

"Now. I daresay, Laura has no tinker training. Is that right, Laura? You can remove the mask."

She did, and she shook her head with a tiny grin, as if she couldn't believe her luck.

"I don't see anything," muttered Athena. She was desperately running her gaze along the upper reaches of the hall, same as Ruby.

"And how do you feel?" asked the Swede.

"Wonderful," said Laura, and the sides of her mouth widened into a blissful smile.

The Swede turned back to the audience. "The energy

we just harvested from Laura will keep this lamp alight for a full day and night."

There. The black, round hole in the middle of all the glittering lights, the end of a musket barrel leveled by a shadow perched in one of the high crystal windows, leveled straight at the man leaning against the pillar.

"Just think of the wonders we could—"

"Oh, no." Ruby turned back and raised Reginald's hand high in the air toward Van Huffridge. "Sir! Get Down!"

His eyes were wide and intelligent and compassionate, and in that moment Ruby mourned never seeing what kind of king he would be.

Because right then someone shot Lothor Van Huffridge.

CHAPTER 19

"Take care when you fish in chemystral waters. You never know what might come up on your hook."
—Dores Da Rocha, 1718

Cram led Henry up the servants' stairs as fast as his legs could carry him. His heart kept pace with his feet.

"The Reeve, Professor," he muttered.

"I know, Cram."

"All gussied up like a Van Huffridge servant."

"I *know.*"

"That one got a mite close to us on the rope bridge. You think she recognized me?"

The only sound for most of a floor was their boots on the hardwood steps.

"I don't know, Cram. I don't think she did. Wouldn't she have sounded the alarm? Come after us?"

"No telling with them reeves. We'd best keep our eyes open and keep fires under our feet. Four stories up, this is us." They tumbled out of the door into a long carpeted hallway with wood-paneled walls holding smaller panels of cloudy tinker's glass, almost like windows.

Cram had a thought, and it stopped him dead in his tracks. "Professor?" he whispered.

Henry came up next to him, favoring his bum leg from the climb. His heavy breathing echoed in the hallway. "Yes, Cram?"

Cram tried to keep the panic out of his voice. "This house is packed to the gills full of party guests and servants, and yet this hallway is empty as a bucket with a hole in its bottom." It was an eerie kind of silence, like the quiet before a giant rock falls on your head.

Eyes wide, Henry looked at him. "Now that you

mention it . . ." As one they started up again, hurrying down the hallway.

The tapestry of the lions eating the farmers was there, as promised, and it was even more scary than Cram had imagined it would be. The door next to it was heavily carved with notes and images of horns and mandolins and things. Cram eased the door open with the faintest of clicks, and then both of them sneaked through into the anteroom.

As he slid the door back into place, something feather light landed on his neck.

Someone said in his ear, "Don't move." It was a low voice. A woman's.

Cram froze.

"Turn around."

He did.

The cutest little razor lay up against his neck, and holding it was a tall woman sporting a thick, curly shock of salt-and-pepper hair who had a chin that could cut glass. In her left hand she held another razor—both were inlaid with mother-of-pearl, very fine—and that one rested across the professor's Adam's apple. A single drop of red had pooled up along the blade.

"Who are you boys?" said the woman.

Cram licked his lips and held out the platter. "Tarts for Miss Paine?"

"Who are you?" The tickle at his throat deepened a hair. It stung.

"Cram. Cram Cramson, milady, and this here's Henry Collins."

"Henry Collins? The boy with the journal?" she said.

Henry chewed his lip. "That is I," he said.

"And the journal?"

"Safe," Henry said.

"And Athen Boyle?"

"Here, in this building."

"And Ruby Teach?"

"With Athen."

The woman's eyes flicked back and forth between them, and then her face lit in a wide grin. "Well done! That is hero's work and a magic trick all in one." She tucked the razors back into the folds of her party dress right quick.

Her dress was the finest silk, white as milk. It contrasted well against her brown skin, and when she smiled, the cords on her neck flexed, witness to a life of hard work.

"Thandie Paine, at your service. The whole of the colonies and much of the rest of the world are looking for you, all the while trying to let no one else know that they're doing it." She fingered a small vial around her neck. "Is alla Ferra here? She and her boars were certainly worth their king's ransom."

The room behind her was large and filled with a gravichord, a cello, and a party-dressed crowd of two dozen or so of the hardest, meanest folk Cram had ever seen. They gathered around a far door brandishing an array of clocklocks and hand weapons, ready to spring into action.

"Er, hello," said Cram.

"Where are my manners? Cram Cramson, Henry Collins, meet the Committee for Local Coronation."

"Coronation?" Henry sputtered. "Miss Paine, do you mean to tell me—"

"We are crowning Lothor tonight."

Cram's heart stopped for a moment. Then it swelled.

Before he could say anything else, something behind Thandie Paine wobbled precariously on the edge of a little table, as if she had quickly set it down before almost slicing them into bacon. Cram grabbed it, saving it from falling before he recognized what it was.

A crown.

Cram had never met a crown face-to-face before. But he knew what crowns were like, golden, shiny things with long, thin points and crusted with jewels and such. A piece of gleaming candy to top the robes and furs and to remind everyone that your people was richer and powerfuler than the rest. A sign that Providence had chosen you to make grand edicts and gad about castles, sauntering from feast to boar hunt and back again.

This crown was nothing like that.

It was iron and hickory, all of a piece and of a weight such that you could knock a fella out with it or hammer a nail into a board if you wanted. The tinker that made it—this was no jeweler's work—had raised pictures into the iron, but not of seashells or lions or castles. Here was a man plowing a field with oxen. There was a woman pouring metal in a foundry, and scenes all about it of hunting, and making, and mending, and, well, living. Out from the front of it, right at the center of the forehead, preened a ferocious, wild—

"I'm sorry, is that a turkey?" said Henry Collins.

"It is." Thandie Paine was looking at Cram. "You know what that is, lad?"

It could be nothing else. Cram felt ten feet tall. "Well, it's the crown of the king of America, ain't it?"

She nodded, face as serious as an avalanche.

"But a turkey?" Henry's brows knitted in thought. "Not, you know, a bear? Or an eagle? Something more . . . noble?"

Cram could barely keep his heart inside his chest. "Professor, maybe let that go, considering what we got to say?"

Henry turned to him aghast. "Oh, yes. Right. How to begin?"

There was no time for politeness. "Lady Paine, you're in trouble," said Cram.

"Call me Thandie." She took the crown back from Cram. "What do you mean?"

He just dropped the whole of the story on her head. "We been sent by the Warren. The Reeve and the crown got a watch on the secret door to Bluestone Square. And if they know the where of the Warren—"

"They may know the rest of our plans." Paine finished his thought. She shared a worried glance with the rest of the folks in the room.

Henry sputtered. "But wasn't the plan for the rising to happen tomorrow, with the Warren and the rest of the city? Why now? What if they're just waiting for you to—"

She cut him off. "Henry, well done for getting here and the heroic journey and all, but I have a revolution to start in just a moment and a very important machine to steal as well. The rest of the rising will happen of its own accord. We have that machine within our grasp! This kind of opportunity will never happen again. If we steal the device as colonials, we're criminals. If we take it for our new country, we're patriots. If the coronation happened in secret, the crown could control the information. Now is the time for a bold public gesture, and we'll pick up our plan along the way." She pointed at the far door. "The ballroom is right out there, and Lothor will give the signal any second. We are committed, no matter what they have planned for us. When we leave, lock this door, and don't let anyone in or out unless it is me. You understand?"

Suddenly it all clicked into place. "Thandie, wait." Cram grabbed her arm, and she whirled back to face him, lightning quick. "There are reeves here, right now. In this building. In the kitchens we saw four gussied up like servants."

Paine's eyes widened. "The hell you say."

"This ain't your trap you're springing. It's theirs."

Somewhere beyond the door, a shot rang out.

The door to the ballroom crashed open.

Cram's world turned in on itself.

In the doorway stood the reeve with the red hair, the one who had almost caught them at the bridge. Corson, that was her name, and behind her was a wall of rough folk, some in Van Huffridge livery, some in the blacks of the Reeve. Corson tossed a little copper flask over the Committee for Local Coronation's heads, and it landed in the center of the room with a clink. It was smoking.

Paine, eyes wide, tore open the door to the hallway and yelled, "Go!" Cram and Henry dived through, and she was only a split second behind.

There was a huge sound, a BLORK, and in an instant the doorway to the music room filled in with solid amber. Thandie Paine hung in the air, stuck in it up to her waist. "Help me!"

Cram and Henry grabbed her arms and heaved with all their might, but she was stuck fast.

Cram turned to Henry. "Can you melt this, Professor?"

The other boy shook his head. "Not quickly. It would take—"

Just then Avid Wake and the other disguised reeves emerged from the stairs down the hall.

"Stop!" yelled Avid.

Quick as a wolf trap, Henry popped the cap on a little clay pot from his belt and hurled it down the hallway. There was a flash, and then a curtain of crystal shot out of the pot, slamming into the ceiling and walls, sealing the passage.

"That's right!" Cram yelled. "We got ourselves a tinker, too!"

As if in response, the lattice shuddered with impact and cracked. Shadows on the other side were throwing themselves into it.

"Cram." Thandie Paine forced two things into his hands. One was the small flask, torn from a chain around her neck. "This is alla Ferra's payment."

The other was the crown.

"And this must be protected." She smiled, grim and proud. Not a surrender but a challenge. "Now go."

Cram's heart was in his boots. He couldn't think of nothing to say, but he nodded; then he and Henry lit out down the crystal hallways, now filling with crowds of other people racing who knew where.

"Where are we going?" yelled Cram.

"I have no idea!" Henry yelled back.

"Excellent!"

They rounded a corner into the main ballroom.

It was a pulsing, heaving madhouse.

A British soldier and a woman in an evening dress

wrestled over a musket. An old man stood alone on the parquet floor, tears streaming down his face. Fights everywhere. Chaos reigned. They ducked behind a tapestry just in time to dodge a jogging squad of redcoats.

"I have no idea where to begin," whispered Henry.

Cram flogged his brains. Lady Athena. "Look for the floofy dress!"

Henry craned his neck about and then pointed. A torn tuft of lace hung from a balcony on the floor above. They wrangled their way up some stairs and checked doorways until they found Lady Athena and Ferret— still in Reggie's body—tucked into a corner behind a wall of purple flowers. Next to Lady Athena a pair of boots attached to an unconscious soldier stuck out from behind a potted plant.

"Thank Providence," Athena breathed. "I thought we might have lost you."

Reggie looked up from a lace handkerchief, eyes red.

Cram grabbed her shoulder. "What is it, Ferret?"

Reggie yanked his shoulder away. "Unhand me, churl! Do you not know? Someone shot Lothor Van Huffridge."

Cram saw red. "Listen, Ferret, this ain't the time for—"

Lady Athena held up her hands in despair. "I think she's trapped in there."

"In where?"

"Reggie."

"Who is this she you keep referring to, Evallina?" Reggie warbled angrily.

"Just— Here, I found a toy soldier. Play with it."

"Excellent!"

"Did they really shoot Van Huffridge?" asked Henry.

"Someone did. From the rafters. Then everyone went mad. The exits are sealed off. We beat a track back up here to try to avoid the redcoats. Rool is here."

"And more reeves." Henry poked his head up over the sofa.

Athena pointed down to Cram's hands. "What's that?"

Cram held it close. Its weight was the only thing reliable right now. "The crown of the King of America."

"Well, he won't be needing it. We have got to get out

of here right now." She pulled herself over to Reggie. "Ruby, it's time. You're going to get Cram and Henry captured if you don't come back."

Reggie looked about, clearly uncomfortable. "Who?"

Lady Athena held him by the face so he couldn't look away. "Ruby, it's Athena. And Henry. And Cram. Your crew. We need you."

Reggie looked up at Athena with limpid, soulful eyes.

And threw up.

And then his body wriggled and wraggled and bubbled and did some things Cram didn't have no words for.

Within moments it was Ferret who sat there in a pile of clothes three sizes too big for her. She squinted and winced. "Well, that was awful."

Athena produced a knife, and they cut the legs off the breeches and belted down the rest.

With a wheeze Ruby pushed herself to a crouch. Cram clapped her on the shoulder in glee. "Welcome back, Ferret!" She fell over. He helped her up. "Er, can you do this?" he said.

She gave his arm a squeeze, eyes bleak. "Well, I have to, don't I?"

They lit out down the empty hallway outside the balcony. "Down!" Athena whispered, and they all got down on their bellies and peered out of a floor-to-ceiling window. Below lay the great drive they had pulled into only a few hours before. Carriages lined it again.

But these were not the tinker's carriages of Philadelphi's finest folk. Each had two hulking dray horses at its front. And they had bars and stout locks and were fair covered in redcoats. As Cram watched, a crowd of party guests was herded inside, and then a grizzled sergeant with one eye slammed the door home and locked it tight with a massive padlock. He pounded twice on the side, and the carriage clattered forward. The next pulled up, ready for its load of prisoners.

"They're taking them prisoner. All of them."

Ruby whistled. "That's a neat sharp. Just gather together the whole mess and then sort out the rebels later."

"So Paine wasn't the only person who thought a

public event would be useful," said Henry.

Ruby turned to them. The color had come back into her face. "Well, we can't go that way."

Cram racked his brains. Garderobe tunnels. A place this posh, with running water, would have to have sewers. "Follow me," he said.

They stood to go, and from across the hall a call stopped them in their tracks.

"Sweetling!"

She was perched on a balcony a floor up and on the other side of the great hall. It was Avid Wake.

She and Ferret locked eyes.

Something passed between them. The reeve girl looked angry and . . . scared. She looked scared.

With a shake of her head, Avid waved them on, walking back into the shadows.

The friends looked at one another for just a moment.

"Let's go then," said Ruby.

Cram led them on a tense path, starting and stopping and twirling back down through Van Huffridge House, dodging several patrols, which were thinning now that most of the guests had been rounded up. It was a shock how quickly the house had gone so empty. Food left half eaten on crystal plates. Untouched wine in cobalt goblets. As they sneaked behind the now-abandoned stage, Cram climbed over a fallen chair. Tree branches wound up its sides in an intricate dance with scenes of labor and virtue. It had to have been carved by the same artist who had done the crown in his hands.

It was a throne.

They left it behind as he led them down into the basement and the tunnels below.

It wasn't hard to find the sewers. There was a big metal plate over a hole in the floor, and when they got that up, a ladder descended down into the darkness. There were no reeves or soldiers down this far. Perhaps they had missed it, or perhaps they just thought whoever would duck down a sewer wasn't worth their notice. Cram wondered what was happening out in the streets. The crown had not been caught unprepared. It had sprung its own trap. Something withered inside him.

The professor and the Ferret had gone on ahead.

Lady Athena waited for him in the doorway. She laid a comforting hand on his shoulder. "Strategy, Cram. Moves within moves. One must think ahead of one's opponent at all times."

The words came out of his mouth before he could stop them. "It's people, milady. Not pieces on a board."

Athena blinked, eyes wide. She grimaced, then nodded. "I am sorry, my friend."

Cram sighed. "Let's get on with it then." He followed her into the tunnel and shut the door closed behind him.

He took the crown, though.

CHAPTER 20

It is that Reflected Idol, Ambition,
that is the greatest danger to a chemyst's soul.
—Sir Francis Bacon, Invisible College, London, 1628

They bolted through the sewers like scared rabbits, and it took no time at all for them to be lost. The tunnels twisted and turned, and Ruby tried to keep her fears at bay by imagining the cellars and storerooms they passed as they followed their course through the Lid, the great ceiling that separated the UnderTown of Philadelphi from its UpTown. It turned out that the tinkers who had pulled the stone into place over the city like a blanket had left all manner of pockets and holes inside it, as if it were a great piece of crusty bread.

They finally found a staircase that wound back upward into a coal cellar that opened onto a deserted UpTown side street. To get back to the Warren's door, they had to go through at least part of the upper city. Bluestone Square was a terrible option, but it was their only one. With the trap sprung at Van Huffridge House, the Bluestockings had to be in danger as well, and that included Ruby's family. With any luck the reeves were still occupied rounding up the rebels, and the crew could beat them back to the square. Fear gnawed at Ruby as they ducked and dodged through the well-gardened lanes and boarded-up shops of UpTown, avoiding patrol after patrol of soldiers and reeves that appeared as if from nowhere. Once the four of them barely ghosted past a coffeehouse, its door hanging on one hinge, a broken, flickering tinker's lamp peeking out of broken shutters and illuminating the cobblestones. Grenadiers in their red coats wrestled bound and hooded figures out of the doorway and into yet another lockwagon.

The rain had started again, and its cool fingers trailing down her neck only heightened the urgency. She pushed ever faster, fighting down the upset stomach and the dizziness from her change. The party had been a disaster. When Van Huffridge had been shot, she had blacked out, lost in Reggie. Gwath had warned her against it, but she'd had no idea it would be like that.

Up ahead, finally, Lancaster Avenue opened into Bluestone Square. At its other end the little courtyard and the door to the secret tunnel down to the rest of her family.

They were too late.

Bluestone Square was a battlefield.

British soldiers and reeves had hunkered down behind improvised barricades in a circle twenty yards or so from the courtyard that held the tunnel entrance. Three big tinker's lanterns, each the size of a man, blazed with the harsh white light of the Swede's tinkercraft, picking the little gated wall out of the dark. It was peppered with gunshot holes. Just then two groups of redcoats, bayonets leveled, vaulted over the barricades and rushed toward the wall, their cries high in the distance. Ruby's heart jumped into her throat.

Two figures—Hearth in her blue mask and Marise with an unmistakable flash of blond hair—appeared above the little barrier; vials and missiles sailed through the air. They struck one of the groups full on, and the soldiers disappeared in a blanket of smoke and goo. When the vapor cleared, nothing moved on the cobblestones.

The flasks sailed wide of the other group, and the soldiers rushed on, blades gleaming.

Captain Teach and Gwath tore through the gate into the charging mass of soldiers, shrugging off clocklock fire and blades equally as if they were so much spun sugar. In moments it was over. But as soon as the last redcoat fell, volleys thundered from the surrounding barricades. A ball took Gwath in the shoulder. The captain grabbed him and hustled him back behind the wall. It was a standoff.

Silence.

The four friends looked at one another.

"What do we do?" Cram whispered.

"What can we do?" Athena shot back. "They are surrounded. There is nowhere to hide out on that square. If we try to take them from behind, the four of us against seventy, they will mow us down. Or worse, they could take us and then use us as hostages."

"We can't just leave them there." Ruby started forward, but Athena caught her arm. Ruby dug her feet into the cobblestones and wrenched with all her might against Athena, but the bigger girl had her in a grip of iron. "My parents are in there!"

Henry added his hands to Athena's. "She's right, Ruby."

Athena shook her. "You'll be shot down before you get twenty feet past this corner."

"Let go of me. Let *go*." A storm of urgency thundered into her. She had lost Gwath once. Her father had been taken from her before. Her mother had never been part of her life. She had to get to them.

From his post at the corner Cram said, "Hsst."

Something in his voice—fear or wonder or sorrow—cut through the storm. Ruby went still.

There came a far-off tinkling, like bells. The wind whirled across the cobblestones.

A shape appeared in the lantern-cast shadows at the far end of the square.

Slowly, as if it had all the time in the world, it solidified out of the mist and into the lamplight. It was a wagon of sorts, pulled by a string of piebald tin and copper chemystral goats. In the bed of the wagon, unmistakable, lay a larger version of that same engine that Ruby had seen in Van Huffridge House, a heap of tubes and pistons, gears and wires. Behind the machine gathered a score of figures, some standing huddled near the engine, some with legs dangling like children sneaking a ride on the back of a coach; but their heads were wrapped in chemystral bandages, and each of their mouths was covered by a mask, and each mask connected to a tube running back to the engine like a huge spider's legs.

At the wagon's front sat a little driver wearing huge quartz lenses over his eyes, swathed in a cloak far too large for him.

Gods, it was Evram.

Horror bloomed. She had thought he was done. She had *left* him with the Swede.

Next to him, Emmanuel Swedenborg lounged, white-clad legs crossed casually over the side. He wore a large coat with bulges rising up from the shoulders. The cart came to a stop between two of the barricades. Fear and loathing tore at Ruby. She was a fawn in the woods, and the Swede was a nightmare of a hunter, swooping in for the kill. Swedenborg stood up on the seat of the carriage. He waved a white handkerchief above his head and held up something to his mouth.

His voice boomed across the square.

"HELLO THERE. EXCUSE ME, BUT I SEEM TO BE A TOUCH LOST. COULD ANYONE DIRECT ME TO THE BURROW OF SOME TRAITORS WHO DABBLE IN CHEMYSTRY?" It echoed back and forth among the town houses. Curtains twitched as some townsfolk peeked out their windows. Storm shutters slammed closed from others. A terrible dread crawled up Ruby's legs and into her chest.

A head popped up from behind the wall. Marise Fermat's voice was clear but seemed infinitely small compared with the Swede's amplified rumbling. "I'm sorry, we're not taking callers this evening! Please come back tomorrow. We'll set you out a nice tea!"

The Swede's tittering laughter shook the cobblestones,

the approach of a flock of giant parakeets. "AN EXCELLENT JEST, AND FROM MARISE FERMAT NO LESS. WHERE HAVE YOU BEEN HIDING, MY LADY?"

"In a place where monsters like you cannot pervert the practice of chemystry." She pointed at the machine. "That . . . monstrosity should be wiped from the face of the earth!"

"ALAS, YOU DON'T UNDERSTAND THE IMPORTANCE OF THE WORK THAT WE—YOU AND I AND YOUR DEAR DAUGHTER—HAVE DONE TOGETHER. AFTER ALL, THIS IS YOUR INVENTION, MARISE. I MERELY MIDWIFED ITS BIRTH." He patted the seat delicately, then took out a pocket watch. "I AM SORRY. THIS IS A DIVERTING CHAT, BUT I CANNOT SPEND TOO MUCH TIME CONVERSING WITH YOU. I HAVE BEEN TASKED WITH YOUR SURRENDER TO THE CROWN." He gestured at the carnage about the square. "YOUR UPRISING HAS BEEN SQUASHED. VAN HUFFRIDGE IS SLAIN BY AN ASSASSIN, RECENTLY IDENTIFIED AS ONE ARUBA TEACH. SURRENDER YOURSELVES TO THESE SOLDIERS OR FACE THE CONSEQUENCES."

Marise jumped atop the wall and raised her arm. "She is no assassin, and you are the traitor—to Science!"

A star flashed in her fist. "I have your answer here!" Her voice disappeared in flaming thunder. A two-story-high wheel of blue chemystral fire blasted outward from the wall. It burst through a barricade like high tide through a sand castle. Soldiers dived out of the way, and the ones who were too slow turned to ash in a moment. The wheel rushed on, straight toward the Swede's cart, a trail of blackened, smoking stone in its wake. It blasted into the wagon and exploded in a wave of fire and steam so bright it blinded Ruby. When she could see again, any relief turned to ashes in her mouth. A perfect globe of water surrounded the cart, steam rising into the night. Inside, its passengers were completely undamaged. The Swede was not burned. He had taken Marise's blow on the chin and was smiling about it.

Spent from the chemystry, Ruby's mother crouched on her knee atop of the wall. Ruby's fathers and Hearth appeared, crouching above her.

Swedenborg raised his hand to his mouth again. "VERY WELL. THANK YOU FOR YOUR ANSWER. I MUST ADMIT I WAS VERY EXCITED TO TRY MY NEW SET OF TOYS." He shrugged off his coat, revealing a braid of tubes running from his back into the machine in the wagon.

"He's stealing the Source from those people and taking it directly into himself." Henry sounded as if he were going to retch. "Vampire," he said.

Evram scuttled down to the ground and flipped a switch.

The machine hummed, and strange lights flicked across its face. At the rear of the wagon, the crowd of passengers moaned and swayed in unison.

The hair on Ruby's forearms rose up with dread.

A small, low shape raced out from the wall. It was Evie, somehow, speeding through the rubble, twin blue stars shining above her snout, hurtling toward the edge of the square.

The Swede lifted his hand like a conductor.

The entire square erupted in an explosion of earth and stone, half a hundred feet high. It hung suspended, swimming. Ruby could barely see the tunnel entrance through the hanging debris.

The Swede flicked his fingers.

The curtain of earth raced forward with a roar.

Figures squirmed and struggled back toward the tunnel entrance like ants hurrying for their hill, but they would never make it in time. They were done. All of them.

The curtain stopped.

The tons of stone, impossibly, bounced back *up* into the sky, held at bay by a tiny bubble of air and chemystry surrounding the little courtyard.

A single shape knelt atop the wall as the others ran for the tunnel. Marise Fermat, her hand upraised in refusal. In her other hand lay a locket. It was the compass, the chemystral device her mother had used to track her across the continent. Something tore open in Ruby's chest. At that moment, when all was lost, she was looking for Ruby. Marise turned toward her daughter. They locked eyes, and Ruby saw something there that she had never allowed herself to see. It was love. Not the kind from the stories, and not what Ruby got from her fathers, but it was there. Marise smiled and raised the hand with the locket to Ruby, as if to say good-bye.

The Swede cried out in anger, clenched his fist, and slammed it toward the earth.

The rock wave smote down, smashing through the

bubble and into the tunnel entrance with a titanic roar.

Ruby cried out again, but her voice could not compete with the shredding of bedrock.

When the dust cleared, in place of the little courtyard stood a tower of rubble and debris. Nothing else.

"WELL, THAT WAS EXCITING."

The wagon turned about and drove off the way it came, leaving behind a field of death.

Ruby struggled in Athena's rigid arms, but it was all for naught. The others might have escaped far enough into the tunnels, but not her mother. A mountain of earth and stone lay piled atop of what had been the entrance to the Warren. Ruby sank to the ground.

Evie came into her arms, chittering softly.

Ruby did not move.

Her friends lifted her up by her arms. They dragged her away.

Through the haze of rage and loss and disbelief she heard Henry say, "We must get to Fermat."

CHAPTER 21

WANTED
For crimes against the crown, including
ASSASSINATION and TREASON
The SCOURGE OF PHILADELPHI has Returned
The most Clever, Strange, and Dangerous Aruba Teach
also known as Ruby Teach has Struck Again!
Of dark complexion, small stature and
with features fox like (as drawn below)
READY MONEY REWARD FOR HARD NEWS
Inquire at Benzene Yards, Building 221

Henry tore the poster from the alley wall. "How do they get these up so quickly?"

"They must have some sort of midnight print shop somewhere," said Athena.

She crumpled it up, dropped it in the muck, and stamped on it. She looked as frazzled and lost as Henry felt. Marise—how could anyone have survived that?

Athena cursed. "Here we are again then. On the run,

with no friends, in Philadelphi." She tugged at the stolen overcoat, which did very little to obscure her dress, and looked back down the alley.

Henry followed her gaze to where Ruby sat on a box, staring into nothing, Cram trying to get her to eat a piece of cheese out of his bag. The ottermaton, Evie, hanging out of a pocket of Ruby's coat, was batting at the cheese with singular intensity. Ruby had been nearly spent *before* Swedenborg dropped a square on her mother; now she hovered in a strange half emptiness between there and nowhere that Henry liked not at all.

He snuck a peek over his shoulder across the alley to a narrow door tucked between two huge bakeries, to a little window with a scale brimming with spices. "Well, I hope not *no* friends."

Athena glided up next to him. "Are you certain of this? I know that you'll be welcome, but the last time we were here, I—"

The rest of her sentence was cut off by a massive pair of chem whistles, blasting into the once silent night. Before you could count five heartbeats, the cobblestones were awash with people. The doors of both bakeries thudded open, vomiting a tide of workers into the narrow street. Flour-covered men and women trudged, feet dragging and hunched, toward the end of the street and the stairs to UnderTown, a procession of ghosts filing past another, cleaner crowd surging up the street toward the bakeries for the coming shift. Apparently it took more than a botched uprising to stop the gears of Philadelphi industry.

"Cram!" Henry called as softly as he could. "It's time!"

Cram already had Ruby up, and the two of them moved forward, his arm protectively over her shoulders and his eyes everywhere.

"With the stream, not faster or slower, and follow me when I switch." Henry tapped Cram on the top of his head. "And keep this down."

With that he grabbed Athena by the hand and shouldered into the stream of workers. It was an old dance, one he hadn't done in months. The old man, Fermat, had gone on unceasingly about secrecy. Henry had been allowed to come and go to this, his place of apprenticeship, only during the shift changes at the bakeries. "Clothe yourself in the masses," Fermat had said, and Henry had taken those lessons to heart. It had not passed without notice for him that even through all the spying on the navy and the tinkers that he had done for the old chemyst, it was only when Henry took up with his three friends that he had encountered a series of mishaps that would apparently never end. He fell into line behind a middle-aged woman, the rough-spun cloth on her shoulder barely showing through the thick layer of flour caked atop it. The flour cloud from the bakeries hung thick in the air, like morning mist, covering everyone in a snow of off white.

He glided toward the center of the street until all the people to his left were passing in the other direction, back toward the bakeries and the spice shop. He could sense Athena moving behind him, and he had to assume Cram and Ruby were following. He could not risk a glance back. The true nature of Fermat's little spice shop had been divulged to the Warren almost a year ago, and with the unmasking of the Bluestockings fresh in his mind, who knew what eyes were still watching?

The four friends weaved and nudged their way through the crowd until they grouped up behind Henry at the spice shop door. Once they had landed, the stream of workers slid grimly around them. Cram's black eyes stuck out against the cake of flour, and Ruby still stared at the ground.

Henry knocked at the door.

Once.

Twice quick.

Then three times regular.

It had been the pass knock during his apprenticeship, and he dearly hoped it had not changed.

A shadow passed across the little window.

Locks twisted and rattled.

The thick door opened slowly, and they tumbled in, desperately trying to appear nonchalant.

Behind them the door closed with a hiss and a pop, and then Nasira was there, lifting him in the air like a child.

He was home.

Hands like hickory wrapped around his shoulders and moved him out to arm's length. The bald woman peered at him out of a sun-leathered field of wrinkles, and she flashed a smile. "Welcome, boy. You have been sorely missed."

He grinned so hard that he thought his face might break. He could not help himself. Even through all the sorrow that he had so recently seen, through all the trouble and hardship, it was so good to see her.

"Nasira, I believe you know my *friends*?" He took special care to emphasize the word. Nasira was a fierce guardian. It would not do to have anyone falling down pits today.

Relief washed over him when Nasira smiled at the lot of them. "Of course, of course! Any friend of Henry's is a friend of ours, even if we have had our quarrels in the past."

"Thank you." Athena's jaw was taut, and her eyes were wary. "I do apologize for my . . . impoliteness when last we met."

Nasira waved it away with a wolfish look. "Bygones. You were only doing what you thought right. Besides, it was nothing a fall through a trap couldn't cure." Her gaze slid over the other two, lingering on Ruby, but to her she said nothing. She took another gander at Athena and ambled over to a wall of tiny drawers that rose up into the darkness. Every wall of the little room was covered with the same.

She clambered up a wheeled ladder to its top, opened a drawer with a faint pop, and deftly scooped something into a fold of paper. She directed the ladder to the corner of the room with a push of her toes and rescued something else from a different drawer into another envelope. She was back down the ladder before they could blink.

"Hospitality is important where I come from. Ruby is family, but you two, please. Eat of our salt and rest in our shelter. With a wink she added, "But salt is so boring." She presented the papers to Athena and Cram. "These are for you. I am never wrong."

Henry couldn't see what was in Cram's. It was in his mouth already. The boy's eyes first went wide with surprise and then all dreamy.

"Vanilla bean, from the far south," said Nasira.

Athena stared at a little pile of light green powder in her palm. She looked about before extending a tongue. Her face remained unreadable, but she snorted in surprise. She took another taste, then bowed to the old woman from the waist.

Nasira smiled and bowed in return. "Cardamom. From the Moghul Empire. I hope you will accept my apology. Your last visit I—"

A door behind the counter burst open, and a lanky windmill of ancient man exploded into the room. "*Bien-aimée*, I am trapped in a torturously delicate experimental quagmire! Can you come down and—" He stopped, staring at the group before him.

He clacked his teeth. His quicksilver eyes whirled. "You are sorely late, apprentice. What have you to say for yourself?"

Henry masked his face, creating an image of smooth professionalism.

But the grin came back, larger than ever.

"That smirk is highly inappropriate, young sir."

"Yes, I know," said Henry, and for a moment he set aside the sorrow and the guilt because he was once again in a place where no matter what madness was happening outside, he *knew*, beyond a shadow of a doubt, that he was safe. And then he threw himself into Fermat's waiting arms.

They all stared at Ruby, who stared at nothing.

Fermat had led them all back through the door at the rear of the shop down the great stone spiral staircase that circled the outside of his tower. Henry had never been quite sure how deep the tower went. Certainly through the Lid. Most likely far into the earth below UnderTown. The tinker's lamps, each one more strangely fashioned than the last, cast a low blue glow over the intricately carved walls, packed with elusive equations and pulsing strata of arcane symbols. Henry had seen many strange and fascinating things in his travels, but Fermat's tower still filled him with wonder.

Nasira had led them into the sitting room, which Henry had ever been in only to clean. He helped remove the sheets from the old elaborate furniture, while Fermat hurried off to brew some of his famous nettle tea. It was honestly Nasira's nettle tea, but she allowed him to pretend it was his when they had visitors. Finally they all sat down, and Henry told the story of where they had been and what was happening on the outside. It was hard. He stopped and started several times.

The two old people listened intently. An onyx raven perched above them on a stone outcropping, listening or not, Henry could not tell. It depended on the day.

After Henry had related their arrival at the door of the spice shop, the two looked at each other.

"Marise returned," Fermat said.

"And also . . ." said Nasira.

"The rising destroyed," said Fermat.

"The Bluestockings eliminated, or at least declawed," said Nasira.

"And this Swede running amok with his machine." As Fermat looked at Henry, the skin around his quicksilver eyes tensed. "You see? You see how this works, Henri? A discovery comes into the light, and then people crush one another to ruin themselves over it."

Henry said nothing. What could he say? He had been thrilled to translate Marise's journal, to offer his aid. The possibilities were so great. Machines to harvest crops, putting an end to slavery. Engines to build and make and grow. Happier people living better lives.

How could he have been so stupid?

Fermat stood. Then he began stalking back and forth, muttering to himself in French. It was too growly and too fast, but Henry was able to translate "too much to bear" and "stuck in this great, Science-forsaken rolling pin" before ignoring them, Fermat stalked out of the room.

Nasira flowed to her feet with an apologetic look. "You all are of course welcome," she said. "Henry, your room is still as it was, and Ruby can have her old room as well. Could you please help situate our guests? Linens are in the usual places, and I think some of my sparring gear will fit Lady Athena," she said with a bow.

"Of course," said Henry.

"Thank you," said Athena.

Nasira paused at the doorway. "I will be upstairs awhile, casting my net to take the measure of the town."

She looked at Henry. "He is upset. He will rally."

Henry nodded. "He will come back to us when he is ready. I will make sure our guests are well taken care of." *Our* guests. Well, this was his locus, he realized. Marise's cottage had been a resting place of sorts, but this truly was home.

Nasira hesitated, then stalked over to kneel in front of Ruby, her hands on the girl's knees. "Ruby Teach," she said, "I am sorry for you. Patience, my girl. Only with patience will your path be revealed."

Ruby looked up at her, her eyes focusing for the first time. She took great care to enunciate when she said, "Bugger that."

Nasira blinked.

Ruby stood up. "I thank you for your hospitality, Nasira, but you're wrong. Patience gets you caught. Patience gets you killed. I will wait, but only because we have nowhere left to go." And with that, she stalked out of the room.

CHAPTER 22

Let go your grief. It is the weakest of blades.
—Halvard d'Anjou, *Bastionado*

Despite Ruby's declaration, the hours turned into days. Four days, in fact, since Nasira had sent her minions—an army of orphans, workers, chambermaids, and chimney sweeps—out to get the lay of the land, and in those four days Ruby's grief had been replaced by a growing, deliberate rage.

Her room was comfortable enough. The sheets were soft, Evie had found a perch on the intricately carved headboard, and the fancy chemystral bath was just as wonderful as she remembered; but trying to lie still even for a few moments was torture. As soon as she was in the bath, she sloshed back out again. The *Thrift* had been hired once to transport a panther from the West Indies up to the animalium of some muckety-muck in Montreal; she had spent hours on deck watching it pace back and forth in its cage. It never rested once. It was in the wrong place, and it knew it.

She was that panther. Except her type of panther was apparently caged up by her friends. She flicked at a carving on the door, an eagle whose feathers were all equations. She buckled her belt—Nasira had somehow turned Reginald Shackleton's ruined, stained party clothes into a serviceable set of breeches and vest—and she wrenched the door open.

"Evie, let's go." The ottermaton was fascinated by all things chem, and she currently had her paws wrapped about a clever teacup that somehow kept its insides warm. She gave a little metallic chirp and dropped the cup back onto the tray with a clang. Evie took offense at the noise and began chattering at the tray, giving it what for.

"Evie, come *on*," said Ruby.

The otter squeaked and then was pure motion, flowing over the closely set marble tiles and clambering up Ruby's back to her preferred spot on the shoulders, wrapped about her neck like a high lady's stole.

"Good girl." Ruby flourished one of the pig iron nails she had found in a storeroom, and the ottermaton grabbed it eagerly and settled in, gnawing away. Evie didn't eat as such. She got her energy from the sparkstone Henry said he would eventually need to recharge. But she did love to exercise her teeth on metals of all sorts, and the nails kept her focused for at least a moment or two. Training the little creature had been at turns frustrating and exhilarating. At times it seemed that Evie could read her every thought and nod of the head, seeking out tokens Ruby had hidden about the room or even retrieving a book from the tower library. Other times she was unable (or unwilling) to accomplish the simplest of commands. Perhaps it was simply the little mechanical's personality, and Evie followed Ruby's will only when it suited Evie.

She couldn't blame the ottermaton. Sleipnir and

Evram had followed Ruby's lead. If only the boy and the gearhorse had not encountered her. . .

Best not think about that, Evie clucked in her ear. Or her head.

"Fine," Ruby breathed, and set off down the stairs.

She wasn't certain whether Evie was really speaking to her or those were simply her own thoughts, but in a world of changing, and chem, and upside-down towers and dead parents, she didn't much care.

The circular shelves of Fermat's laboratory rose into the darkness, packed with scrolls and papers and tomes from a hundred different countries and eras. The room itself was dominated by a scarred black slate worktable, covered by a salvage yard of scales, alembics, and vials. Ruby herself had sat, lain, stood, and—in one highly uncomfortable instance—hung over the thing as Fermat feverishly experimented on her to attempt to discover the secret in her blood.

The secret that was now sowing terror all over Philadelphi and—who knew?—perhaps even the entire continent.

The ancient alchemyst had not had time to ferret out the secret, as Athena and Cram had barged in, and then they all had run off in a dither to save her father. Which led to many other things, none of which was very pleasant. And what good had it done?

Perhaps it would have just been better to stay here.

No. Evie sounded off on her shoulder. *You had to try. It would have been worse if you had stayed.*

Ruby snorted at that. Evie coiled down her legs and skittered over to a clutter of Fermat's alchemycal devices. She couldn't get enough of them, as if they were a kind of strange kin to her.

At the foot of the table stood Fermat and Nasira, talking intently with a third person. Nasira saw Ruby and stood aside, revealing—

Greta Van Huffridge.

Before Ruby could think of what to say or what to do, Cram, Henry, and Athena tumbled down the steps and into the laboratory. "She's not in her room, she—" said Athena, and then she stopped when she saw Ruby and Greta. "Oh."

"Oh, indeed." Fermat's quicksilver eyes glittered.

Athena started over to Greta, hand outstretched. "Greta, I'm so sorry—"

"Don't touch me."

Athena jerked to a stop. At some point since their arrival she had cut her hair short. The fine black strands whispered across her jaw.

They all looked about at one another.

Fermat clacked his teeth, but the sound was different somehow. Impatient. Angry. "All right, my little chicks, settle in and listen, for Nasira and this young lady have news of the outside world."

"You want me to—" Nasira said.

"You must," he said.

The old woman sighed and turned to them, brows furrowed. "The city is an armed camp. English forces patrol the streets. Curfews are even more strict than they were. During the day no one can be out in the open without papers, period. If you are caught, you are arrested and detained. Those who are detained do not return."

The crown tightening the screws. Or the Swede. Who was running the city? "What of the Warren?" asked Ruby, her heart in her throat.

Nasira's eyes were a dark sea. "My people could not

get outside to reach the other entrance, at the smokehouse. There is still a watch on the former tunnel entrance in Bluestone Square. No one is clearing the rubble, and"—she cleared her throat—"my people talked to numerous folk who live in the neighborhood. No one has come out of it."

Her mother. Her fathers. Los Jabalís. At least fifty other people possibly trapped down in those tunnels or worse. Ruby shook her head. *Should* they have run? Her mother had said it. *People will die.* A cold, stinging regret washed over Ruby. She had never truly thought that some of those people might be the ones closest to her.

"Ain't no one lifted a finger to help?" Cram asked.

Nasira sighed. "They have their own problems. Many of the guests at Lothor Van Huffridge's party are still missing, taken into custody in the Benzene Yards. The governor has disappeared. Several speeches have been made by a captain with red muttonchops."

"Torvald," said Henry. "He commands the *Grail*. In my time as a midshipman I never heard an ill word said of him. He is well respected, even loved by his command. Is his tinker battleship still in port?"

"Indeed, and armed to the teeth. Anyone approaching within firing range gets a musket ball for their trouble."

"Are there troops outside the walls?" asked Athena. "What of the French and the other English?"

"No one knows. Philadelphi is an island now. A walled prison." It was Greta who spoke.

"What of the people?" Cram asked. "The crown just killed one of their own, plus a mess of other folk, and they thrown hundreds in the lockup. Are the rest just *sitting on their hands?*"

Nasira took a deep breath. "The juicing has spread like wildfire. Much of the city now, and each of those folk do nothing but wear their smiles and do the Swede's bidding." She looked down. "The people will not help."

Greta wiped her nose on her sleeve. The fire had gone out of her, Ruby thought. No, not gone out but changed somehow. Before, she had burned bright with ruthless certainty. The fire was still there, but it was strained, guttering, as if consuming the last of the fuel in a vain attempt to keep burning, right before it flared out. Ruby admired Greta's gumption, but the look of it and the feel of her desperation felt woefully familiar.

The heir to the Van Huffridge kingdom cleared her throat.

"After I left you all at Reggie's I made my way back to a house I know off Bluestone Square—the Birnbaums. They are—were allies of my father. They keep a small room in the cellar for Bluestockings who might occasionally need a hiding place."

Greta blinked as if she were coming up from some kind of dream. "In the middle of the night there was a great commotion in the street. Voices yelling outside, people running, bedlam from all corners. I opened the basement window to see what was the matter. A—A man ran past. He was yelling, 'They shot Van Huffridge! They shot him!' and then"—she adjusted her filthy skirts—"everything went dark for a while. Sometime later I heard Swedenborg in his cart—the Birnbaums are on Sauce Street, just north of the square—and then the—" She waved her hand. "Well, the aftermath." She glanced up at Ruby.

Athena put a hand on Ruby's shoulder, and she squeezed it. It didn't stop the ache in her belly, but it helped a little. Ruby nodded for Greta to continue.

The other girl sighed. "Melissa and Ezekiel Birnbaum were huge supporters of my father. They didn't come back. The house was in chaos. No one knew what to do." Her lips tightened. "One of the butlers went out to get the lay of the land and came back with money, a smile under his bandaged ears, and black tendrils trailing up his forearm. He started whispering to the others and wouldn't meet my eyes. Soldiers came the second day and ransacked Ezekiel Birnbaum's study, looking for papers. They were also looking for me." She frowned. "The cook didn't give me away, but after the soldiers left, I had to go." Her face went flat, her eyes far away. "I went to the square, I didn't know what else to do, and I saw the—" She covered her mouth with her hand. "I wandered away, through the alleys." To Athena, she said, "I lost your sword. I don't know what happened to it. I'm very sorry."

Athena shook her head. "It is nothing. I can find another."

Greta nodded. "At some point I just sat down in a doorway. That's when Ben found me." She sent a grateful nod over to a young boy Ruby hadn't noticed, standing quietly in the corner. "He sussed straightaway who I was, and he brought me here." She blinked and then drew herself up, all four and a half feet of her. "Where are my manners?" She dropped a graceful curtsy to the ground, somehow including both Nasira and Fermat. "I am grateful for this sanctuary. You have my thanks and the thanks of my family for taking me into your home. The Van Huffridges will not forget."

Cram huffed, like a steer clearing its head after smashing into something. "Any news of Thandie Paine?"

The boy Ben perked up. "Miss Paine, the Reeve took her with the rest of the committee. I watched them carried out, like flies stuck in amber, and loaded into a wagon."

Cram had taken something out of the bag and turned over and over in his hands: the crown.

There was a clatter from the corner.

Evie looked up, eyes guilty, caught in a tangle of tubes and silver she had pulled down from a shelf.

"Evie!" said Ruby. "Now is not the time for—"

The little ottermaton stared at her for a moment and

then turned back to struggling with the artifice, a kind of circular silver mirror.

"Evie, put that down."

"Oh, Science." Suddenly Henry was across the room and kneeling next to Evie. The ottermaton looked up at him and pulled uselessly at the heavy thing, chittering in what was obviously a request for help.

"This is—I think that—" Henry looked up at Fermat "Master Fermat—"

Ruby had seen the old man's face light up like that only once before, when he had so diligently and ferociously experimented on her in this very room. "Excellent, *Henri*!" He swept his long arm across the black stone worktable, scattering ancient and delicate devices everywhere. "Here. Set it up here."

"Henry, what is it?" said Athena.

Henry ignored the question and gathered Evie, the mirror, the tubes, and everything else in his arms and plopped them all on the table, whereupon he and Fermat descended into a complicated dance of arranging machinery, talking over each other in an unknowable mishmash of chemystry and French, and avoiding the insistent ottermaton, who nipped and chittered at them in imperious direction.

"HENRY!" Ruby yelled.

Everything froze.

She wanted to wring the collective throats of everyone in the room, and she desperately wanted to be in on whatever was obviously of huge importance. "What . . . is . . . happening?"

Fermat ignored her and went back to work. Henry opted for an addled combination of continuing their work and explaining. "This artifice"—scrabble, scrabble, twist—"can access the memories of some automatons"—scritch, tighten, indignant chitter—"It's how we discovered what was happening to you when your father was taken"—squeak, cursing in French, taptaptap.

Final tap.

"And if I'm not mistaken, Evie pulled down this particular artifice because she wishes us to do the same with her." Henry stepped back, and Evie—a tiny silver caliper at each temple, her tail and hindquarters attached to a twist of tubes, all running into the now-upright mirror—chirped smugly in the affirmative.

At least one of you in the room has a brain.

The room was silent for a moment.

Cram grabbed a chem-stained wooden chair from the corner and dragged it screeching across the floor, clunked it down in front of the worktable, and then sat down in front of the mirror. From somewhere he had produced a bag of nuts.

He popped one in his mouth. "Well, let's see it."

The rest of them gathered around the table.

Henry scratched Evie on the ridge above her eyes. "I don't think this will hurt, but it might feel . . . odd. Ready?"

Evie chittered, clearly unimpressed.

Henry flipped a switch.

Evie twitched, then froze, suddenly a statue. The surface of the mirror flickered mistily, as if someone had breathed on it, then resolved into a face.

And then Ruby was crying, and she didn't care who saw it. Because it was a face she hadn't thought she would see again. Her mother.

Marise Fermat looked out of the mirror, her features awash in smoke and grime and alight with fear and desperation. "I've used a variant of my compass and worked it into Evie here"—there was a chirp from offscreen—"so I hope this will get to Ruby Teach. If not and this is someone else watching"—she laughed sharply—"well, hello."

She paused, and musket fire, curses, and screams filtered into the workshop. The sounds of battle.

Behind her, several shapes hurried past. Petra alla Ferra scrambled up, Alaia Calderon leaning on her shoulder, grimacing in pain, an ugly wound in her thigh. The mercenary captain gripped her hunting knife in her other hand, its blade slick with red. "We go, Fermat. The way will be clear. On my honor."

Marise took a shuddering breath. "And we will hold here. As long as we can."

Alla Ferra barked a laugh. "Against mere soldiers and no reeves? I think you will be here until the next century." Then she turned and looked directly into the workshop. "Henry Collins. Athena Boyle. Cram Cramson. Listen to me. I want my money." And then she winked, and she was gone.

A closer voice—Captain Teach—called out, "Marise! They're readying another surge. Quickly, please."

"One moment!" Marise knelt back down. "They are coming. Here it is then. We are holding this courtyard, while Los Jabalís and the rest of the Bluestockings try to punch through whatever watch is on the smokehouse door. The Thrift is in some place called—Wayland?"

"StiltTown!"

"Yes, and we will meet you there. If we can. From there, we hope, maybe back to Catalonia." She pressed her lips together. "Leave this, Ruby. All of you. It is over."

"Marise!"

Ruby's mother leaned in so close to the mirror her face was practically touching it. "I'm sorry," she said. "I love you."

She swiveled out of view, and there was Madame Hearth crouched at the top of a set of makeshift stairs, an arsenal of chem on the steps around her. And there were her fathers, the captain and Gwath, backs against the little stone wall, dirty and bloody, heaving gouts of air.

They were staring into the workshop, and both opened their mouths to speak; but then there were battle cries beyond the wall, and the two men leaped up and out of the picture.

The empty wall was all that was left for a moment, and then the picture shuddered and went dark.

As soon as the picture stopped, Evie burst back into life, insistently chittering at Henry. He gingerly disconnected her from the artifice, and the ottermaton raced down the table and up into Ruby's arms. She stared at Ruby steadily and reached out one paw to rest it lightly on Ruby's forearm.

I am here for you.

Ruby hugged her close and tried to breathe.

Fermat inclined his head: a thoughtful giraffe.

He was looking at Ruby.

It was an odd thing when Pierre de Fermat looked at you. With most (well, all) other people, you could see if the iris focused. With the old chemyst, though, his eyes were balls of liquid quicksilver. But you didn't need to see the iris. When Pierre de Fermat looked at you, you *felt* it.

"What will you do, Ruby Teach?"

Ruby could barely keep her knees from buckling, so she turned it back on him. "What will you do?"

"I will stay in my tower because if I leave, I will die." He gave a sad smile. "I ask again, What will you do?" He ticked off his fingers. "Will you stay with us? You are welcome, of course. We can keep you safe for a long time." Nasira smiled. "Will you leave the city, possibly with no way to return, to search for your parents or your ship?" He ticked off another finger. "Or will you walk into the lion's den and stop this man Swedenborg?"

They all were looking at her. Looking *to* her. Even Greta. Ruby was their leader after all.

She hadn't known that. Not until now.

They knew her better than she knew herself.

Her parents had wanted her to go. And her parents knew her, *loved* her: Gwath and the captain, and even Marise.

But someone knew her even better than her friends. The man who knew her best was the one who had hounded her through Philadelphi but then given her his trust over and over: Wisdom Rool.

A wild wind. A fire in the field.

Rool had named her such in the belly of Fort Scoria. Ruby was a spark, a Changer, an ax in a forest. This city had a disease at its heart. Ruby was a knife. How could she look in a mirror again if she left that knife in its sheath? The way to protect her crew from danger was not to run from it. It was to remove it.

Her father had once said to her, "Who you are is what you do." Well, she would run no more. It was time to start cutting.

They were still looking at her.

Fermat asked her a third time, "What will you do, Ruby Teach?"

"I'm going for the Swede."

CHAPTER 23

Air of Saffron. For infection. EXTREMELY potent. One pinch if you must, two pinches if you dare, three if you want your arm to blow off. This is not a jest.
—Inscription, spice box

Athena watched Cram as Cram did the things that Crams do.

More specifically she watched him try to open the vanilla spice drawer with the power of his mind.

Or will. Or something. He stood, leaning forward on the balls of his feet, tip of his nose brushing against the brushed brass of the pull knob. His eyes squinched down tight, his fists balled up, and the boy shook from head to toe.

He opened his eyes, took note that the drawer had not opened, and then chose a different tactic: whispering. Athena had seen lovers onstage in theatrical productions, but this whispering took the prize for woozy slobberiness. Cram was obviously in deepest love with Mistress Vanilla, and she was having none of him.

Athena adjusted a strap on a traveling pack Nasira had summoned from somewhere. "Cram."

The boy kept his eyes fixed on the drawer. "Yes, milady?"

"Those spices are quite expensive. What will you do if that drawer does pop open?"

Cram inhaled a great gout through his nose, as if he could with the power of his lungs breach the tight seals on the drawer. He paused for a moment, then deflated. "Well, milady, if you must know, Mam always said that if it falls out of the wagon of its own free will, who are you to force it back where it ran away from?"

"Are you saying that your stomach is a safe haven for runaway vanilla?"

He sighed pitifully. "The safest." He wriggled his

fingers at the drawer, as if to cast a spell. "Now, if only—"

Henry emerged out of the stairwell behind the counter, in a slightly too short greatcoat that clinked and rattled when he walked. "They're coming."

Athena gave the strap one final pull, then stood up. The storerooms of Fermat's tower were deeply stocked for guests, and Nasira had found her serviceable (if slightly out-of-fashion) breeches, tunic, and vest. Excellent boots, too. If she never saw her old dress again, it would be too soon. Alas, her trusty dueling sword and its scabbard lay somewhere unknown on the other side of Philadelphi. After what Greta had been through, she could not blame the girl. Not at all. Still, she could not help feeling the absence on her hip.

"Cram."

The boy jerked his nose back from the drawer. He cleared his throat. "Ready, miss." He shouldered his new rucksack, also provided by Nasira, a massive thing that would have no trouble toting an oliphant, a brass band, or a smallish cottage.

Ruby stalked out of the stairwell, a dark traveling

cloak covering up breeches and shirt, her hair bound tightly back, followed closely by Nasira and Fermat. After a moment Greta, pale and still, appeared in the doorway. The boy, Ben, was a shadow behind her.

The quiet lay upon them, filled with things unsaid.

Cram shifted his foot.

Athena caught Fermat masking a smile. "We must say our good-byes then, must we not?" said the old chemyst. He closed his eyes, hiding the quicksilver. He looked, for a moment, simply like a very old man, and not a legend walking alive out of the history books. He opened his eyes, though, and that all went away. "Good-bye to you, my friends. I hope we may see each other again, but—" He waved his hand out at the street and did not finish. "We wish you safe journey and the blessings of Providence and Science upon you."

"Before we become all moony eyed"—Nasira lifted a long finger—"we have gifts to send you on your journey." She shrugged. "Small things, to help you in some small way."

She sidled over to Athena and produced, from behind her back a plain leather scabbard.

The blade fairly leapt from the sheath. It was a strange sword, slightly curved in the middle, single edged with a hooklike hilt, growing wider toward the point. Athena moved it about. There was something dense about it. The glow of the chem pots leaned into it. If she had been superstitious, she would have said it ate the light. The balance was exquisite. Athena was struck dumb. She had never held, never seen its equal.

Nasira had been watching her. The old woman showed her teeth. "Damascus steel, yes? She is a *yatagan*, a sword of my people. Her name in my tongue is Aksam. It means 'night.' It was crafted to be counter to the alchemysts of the time. It is said that it can cut through chemystra."

Fermat snorted. "Wives' tales."

"I am an old wife, and I am telling it," said Nasira.

"I cannot accept this," said Athena, though it pained her. "This is a queenly gift."

Nasira's eyebrows went up. "It is a warrior's gift. You are a warrior." She said it as simply as "My name is Nasira." "I am giving it to you, and I will be very insulted if you do not take it. Besides"—her strong, gnarled hands pulsed into fists—"I have little need for it these days."

A kind of stillness descended on Athena. She was made for this. "I cannot properly thank you."

"Do not fail its spirit. Use it to protect those in need. That will be my thanks."

Athena strapped it to her hip. It was slightly shorter than some swords, and it fitted as if it were custom made.

To Cram, Nasira offered a beautifully crafted wooden box, about two hand's widths apart. When he opened it, a strange and heady mix of smells wafted free. Ten small vials and containers lay nestled in cushioned holes.

"Some are for food, some are for healing, some are for . . . other things. All will be useful to you. Notes underneath them to tell you how they are used."

Cram flushed. "Ah—letters ain't my strong suit, Lady Nasira—"

"Self-confidence, Heavy cream, Yarrow," read Henry, pointing and peering over his shoulder. Cram looked up at him. "I can help," said Henry.

Cram's nervous smile disappeared. He nodded once

in thanks to Henry and then gave Nasira a deep bow.

Fermat stepped forward and took Henry's shoulders in both hands. "I did not think I would see you again, boy." He clacked his teeth. "You have grown, and not just upward." They were almost of a height, Athena realized, two towering reeds. Fermat wriggled a ring off one hand and held it out to Henry.

Fermat's hand was skeletal and wrinkled, more claw than anything else. Henry's was strong, filled with blood, slender. But both hands were covered with scars and burns, witness to their shared love of chemystry.

Fermat dropped the ring in Henry's palm. Henry's eyes widened as he recognized it.

Fermat sniffed. "My ring from the Académie Française."

"What does it do?" Henry asked, awestruck.

"Do?" Fermat thunked Henry on the forehead with his finger. "It doesn't *do* anything, boy. What else do you need besides that clattering array of reagents I hear under your coat?" Henry blushed. "I was given it to mark my achievement of rank in France long ago. The organization is long gone, but I wanted you to know." He clapped his hand on Henry's shoulder. "You are worthy."

He leaned forward again to whisper something in Henry's ears. The boy's eyes widened; then he met Fermat's gaze for a moment. Henry nodded fiercely, blinking away tears.

The old man turned to Ruby. He knelt in front of her, his eyes level with hers. The ottermaton's glowing blue eye peeked out from under the collar of her coat.

"I do not have a gift for you," he said.

A sad smile played across her lips. "No?"

"No. But I should return this." He reached into his dressing gown, mended in a thousand places. With a flourish he produced a worn book, tattered at the edges.

"Is that the journal?" Athena asked.

Ruby cocked her head and then shook it in wonder. "No. It's mine. *Bastionado.*" She took it carefully as if it were carved from diamond. "Where did you find it?"

"You left it here when last we spent time," said Fermat. "Even if everything did not turn out all right, it is a hero's story." He patted the worn thin volume. "It belongs with a hero."

Ruby leaped forward and hugged the old wizard, almost knocking him to the ground.

He chuckled, then squawked, and then gently untangled himself. "Go, stand with them," he said.

And then they were standing together in the doorway, opposite Fermat and Nasira. Greta Van Huffridge and the boy looked on, floating in the dim shadows of the stairway door. A kind of power hummed inside Athena. It was a time for leave-taking. It was a time for truth telling.

"Greta?" Athena took an awkward step forward.

Greta cocked her head.

Athena straightened her scabbard. "I am struck by the thought that we may not see each other again. The thorn that lies between us: it is—is partially due to an untruth."

Greta snorted. "This is an understatement Lord Athen, and hardly the time I think to—"

"Please, hear me out. I did not reject you because I

found you unsuitable. On the contrary, I find you brave, intelligent, and even somewhat clever."

It looked as if someone had hit Greta in the face with a fireplace poker. "Then why—"

"Because." Athena straightened. "Because I was afraid to show you my true self. Athena Boyle. I apologize."

Greta blinked in quick succession. "I'm sorry, did you say?"

She took Greta's hand in her own. "Athena."

Greta's mouth made a very small smile. "Apology accepted." Then her eyes narrowed playfully. "But we shall speak of this again."

Athena smiled in return but then had to steady herself as a weighty cloud lifted from her. She looked down at her calloused hands, her scuffed boots, the sword at her hip. This was not Athen. This was Athena.

There was another silence then, when they knew that they all must go.

Fermat broke it.

"Take care of one another," he said. "That is all."

They turned, and Cram opened the door.

They stepped out into the street, and the heat and scent of rainy summer ambushed them.

Athena pulled the door closed and turned to her friends.

Cram stood there, shoulder to shoulder with Henry.

So did Ruby Teach, and there was wildfire in her eye. "Let's go."

CHAPTER 24

The well-trod road is paved with suckers.
—Aquila Rose, adventurer and ne'er-do-well,
tombstone, 1680–1719

It was half a block to Fox's Stairs, the grand stairway down to UnderTown. Ruby pulled the hood of the cloak down to her eyebrows. The streets were deserted at this hour, but she wanted to take no chances.

The four of them ghosted down the cobblestone street, flitting from shadow to shadow. They had wasted days in Fermat's tower, and she burned with impatience. She found a likely little alley near the top of the stairs, between a dry goods store and a farrier's. There was a sheltered, somewhat clean spot behind a rain barrel, and they circled in. Saying good-bye to Fermat had changed something in her companions, and she could see it in all their faces, shadowed though they were in the moonlight.

Purpose.

Finally. She hungered like wild dog to get to the Swede.

Henry checked his vials. "What is the plan, Ruby? You know this town best."

Her town. Well. "These stairs are the only way to UnderTown for many blocks. If we can make it to the bottom unseen, I can lead us through back alleys to the steps to the water and the yards. Once we get close, we'll just have to see."

Athena and Henry nodded, faces grim. It was a dangerous path, but it was the only one open to them.

"All right then," she said, and moved to go.

"Ferret." Cram put a hand on her forearm and a finger to her lips. He pointed down the stairway.

Four shapes walked up the stairs from below. Even

in the cloudy moonlight, Ruby could pick out their muskets. But they weren't redcoats. They wore ragged breeches and an assortment of mismatched vests and coats. Militia of some sort or volunteers. All wearing bandages around their ears.

They moved carefully up the staircase, heads swiveling.

Looking for someone.

Ruby motioned for her friends to back against the wall. A sliver of a view opened to the street between the corner of the next building and a rain barrel. Just a sliver, and if someone looked their way at just the right moment, there would be questions. Possibly a fight. And then the game would be afoot. Her breathing was way too loud.

One passed by. He was tall and fat, a big man with a tattered beard that he wore like a necklace. He carried his musket propped on one shoulder. An insipid smile played across his lips. Tendrils of black crept up the nape of his neck from underneath his threadbare coat, and they sneaked down his hands as well. Juiced. Ruby shivered in revulsion. A too-small tricorne hat perched atop the bandages that wrapped around his head, caked in place with dried chem.

Someone was talking. It was faint, difficult to pinpoint. Ruby thought it must be another member of the search party, but then the second man passed, and the third.

The last was a short man with squinty eyes and a nose so big you could barely see the rest of his face. He was pigeon-toed, too, and moving a little more slowly than the others, so she got a good earful.

The muttering was coming from *inside* the bandages. It had to be the alchemycal receiver Hearth had shown them. Occasionally the man nodded. Agreeably, as if someone were offering him a cup of tea. When he passed out of the mouth of the alley, Ruby and her friends deflated.

"A chemystral device could be transmitting from anywhere in the city," said Henry.

Cram whistled. "Is it just us against all of Philadelphi?"

No one answered.

Onward.

Aside from the patrol, Fox's Stairs were empty. Even at this time of night there were usually hawkers and wranglers ready to sell skewered rabbit (actually rat) and spiced nuts (actually, well, she didn't want to think about it) to the starving hordes streaming back down from the swing shifts. Now there was nothing but one forlorn cart, abandoned at the foot of the stairs.

The alleys and byways were as dark and shadowed as always, with oily chem pots guttering here and there, but all oddly bereft of the usual crowds.

They made excellent, silent time. Better than Ruby expected, and before she knew it, they were in the part of UnderTown farthest to the east, near the city wall, on the edge of the water. Looming in the distance and wrapped in shadow, rising all the way to the Lid and through it, lay the massive fortress of the Benzene Yards.

The stones dug into Ruby's knees as she knelt atop the city wall. Orange and purple lit the chem-clouded sky as the sun set behind the great forests to the west. It would be dark soon.

Ruby snuck forward on her stomach to look down at the water for the hundredth time. It was the very southeastern tip of the city. To the right, river, all the way down to the ocean. Straight ahead, more river, and the shore just barely visible on the other side. To the left was their goal. If you could survive the sheer five-story drop, you would find yourself in a no-man's-land between the city wall and the even higher and more formidable wall of the fortress factory of the Benzene Yards, home of the Tinkers Guild. The no-man's-land was a steaming sink of strange soil, a pudding more than ground, the results of decades of chem leaching out of the yards.

"Can we walk across that, Henry?" Ruby whispered.

The boy chewed his lip. "You could."

"But?"

"But you might have stumps for feet by the time you got across."

Cram whistled.

Ruby nodded. "All right, scratch that."

On the other side of the no-man's-land, the brick walls of the Benzene Yards rose up almost to the Lid; great smokestacks actually cut through to the other side, popping up out of UpTown like fingers, their tops connected by catwalks and stairways, belching out gouts of smoke and mist. The smoke was horribly beautiful: an array of blues, oranges, and pinks.

Where the building met the river there were a series of docks marching north. In the distance, right near the main gates, the great tinker battleship *Grail* lay at anchor like some iron hippopotamus.

"Say we could get across?" Ruby pointed at the south wall. "Could we bust through the wall with chemystry?"

Henry absentmindedly ran his fingers across his bandolier of reagents. "Possibly. I might be spent after doing it. That brick is thick and probably reinforced against just such an attack." He shook his head ruefully. "But without having seen a plan of the yards, we could be walking into Swedenborg's pantry or a tea party of those husks."

"People," said Cram.

Ruby turned to him. "What?"

"They ain't automatons. They're people. "

"'Course," said Ruby. "But people or not, if we can't get across the field, we'll have to swim."

Henry sighed and started to take off his string of reagent bottles. "Well, these would have been useful, but they won't survive the water." He looked about. "You realize, don't you, that *I* may not survive the water? This is madness. I still can't swim. And neither can you, Athena."

A shape caught Ruby's eye across the water, a shadow really, leaning on a little walkway that she had missed, jutting off the corner of the wall.

Athena clucked her tongue in thought. "Well, what about some sort of viscosity seal for our boots?"

"You mean actually *walk* across the water?" He blinked, shook his head, stared into the distance, then snapped his fingers. "I think I have it." Back to Athena he said, "You know, that wasn't a terrible idea."

"Thank you?" said Athena.

Cram said, "Pardon? Walk on the—"

"Leave it, Cram. Trust me."

"I'll trust you. Just so's I'm not towing you." He patted Henry's belly. "You've gained some weight back since the beaver lodge."

Ruby hadn't stopped looking at the shape. "What's that?" she asked.

"What?" said Athena.

"That." Ruby pointed, sighting along her arm.

They all looked for a moment.

Then Cram said, "That, Ferret, is a reeve. The blacks sort of give it away, I think."

"Well," said Ruby.

"This involves approaching that reeve, doesn't it, Ferret?"

"Yes, Cram."

"Exposed like."

"Yes, Cram."

"On the water."

"Yes, Cram."

Cram sighed. "Well, at least I ain't going to grow old and unhappy."

They scuttled down a set of rickety stairs to a small rusted platform just above the river. As Ruby came off the stairs, the lightly sloshing waves under the platform burned her nose with the smell of acid and chem. Cram blinked tears out of his eyes. "Best not to quench our thirsts, I'm thinkin'."

"Indeed." Henry hunted through the flasks and vials spread out before him on the metal grate.

Even in the deepening twilight. Ruby couldn't keep her gaze from the figure across the water.

Henry rolled up his reagents and stowed them, then moved over to the very edge of the platform, a little tube in one hand and an unstoppered vial in the other. "Who is first?"

Ruby stepped forward. "I am."

Athena grabbed her upper arm. "Ruby. Wait. You must tell us what you're doing before you do it. This is—"

"I think I know that woman, and I think she might help us. Follow my lead. If I get into trouble, storm the compound. Find Swedenborg. Deal with him. Destroy the machine. Get out. What's so difficult about that?" She stuck her foot out to Henry. "Do it."

"When I do this, you need to step on it quickly."

"All right."

Henry held out the tube and sprinkled some powder onto the river. Suddenly it smelled of mud after a thunderstorm.

Ruby trusted Henry. She had to. Just as they had to trust her. She put her foot into the river. Except it didn't go through. It slipped a little, as it might if someone had spilled ale on the deck. But it held her weight. From her shoulder Evie chittered in irritation or fear.

"Good." Henry smiled to himself, relieved. He poured some of the liquid out of the vial, and using a flat stylus, he shaped the water into a kind of wide, curved cup, like a deeper duck foot. Some of the water sloshed over the edge, sneaking in through Ruby's boot, but it held.

"Other foot," said Henry. "Quickly. I'm not certain how long these will last."

Soon Ruby was walking across the water. There was a kind of sliding motion that worked best, she found. Forward and back. You couldn't pick your feet up or you would go into the drink. With her arms out, it was almost like walking a tightrope, a huge, watery, poisonous tightrope. Her pulse thudded in her temples. Over her shoulder, the others had made it onto the river and were following her in a slow, torturous line, like a group of crippled ducklings.

Soon there was only the quiet lapping of the waves and the heaving of her breath. A breeze came up from the opposite shore; it ruffled her hair.

It was almost dark now. The sun had dropped behind

the hanging lip of the Lid to the west; the walls of the Benzene Yards loomed over their little waddling line like the mouth of a whale. The figure still stood on the small balcony jutting just out over the water. It must have been put there for workers to access the back wall. And if workers were meant to be there, that meant there would be a door to the inside.

Ruby's thighs throbbed from the unfamiliar motion of the slippers, but she was almost there. The figure turned its head and started, catching sight of her.

It didn't raise the alarm.

Instead, it placed its meaty elbows on the balcony and waited.

As Ruby sloshed closer, the details she had seen from the wall resolved themselves back out of the darkening shadows. A heavy body, large yet agile. The blacks of a reeve. Pale skin, almost white. A thuggish set to mouth and brow.

"Ward Dove," Ruby called softly.

"Ruby Teach," said the woman, stone faced. "Such a delightful surprise."

Ruby thought to make some sort of clever remark in return. But as she moved closer, the hazy figure of Ward Dove resolved more clearly. The woman in front of her had accompanied Ruby to Fort Scoria, along with the now-dead Ismail Cole. She had raced back to Fort Scoria from the bombings in Boston to rally the reeves, to set them to the winds to empty out the fort. She had also been named on a list of Worshipful Order conspirators that had included Athena's father and Thandie Paine. She was on their side. She was a mole deep in the Reeve, and so far she hadn't raised the alarm. Ruby's heart soared.

And then it fell. In the last light of the sun Dove reached out to Ruby, and the reeve blacks rode up on her forearms, revealing a twisting trail of black tendrils. Her iron hand clamped over Ruby's forearm. A grin plastered across her face, and a strange light shone through the gray streaks twisting in her eyes.

CHAPTER 25

If thy opponent be stronger, make him the object of thy study.
Discover thou his tendencies and his loves.
—Pelham, *Arts Martial and Practice*

The big woman hauled Ruby up over the railing like a bundle of kindling, and Athena's throat tightened at the sudden fear painting Ruby's face. The two spoke to each other, Ruby intently, the woman wearing the strange, plastered grin of the Juiced, but Athena could hear nothing but murmurs.

Athena strained with all she had to speed up, but all it seemed to accomplish was to make her feet slosh more water. The woman was huge. She could flatten Ruby into quince paste before any of them even reached the platform. Sweat trickled down the back of Athena's neck as she drove the cursed galoshes ever faster.

The woman's face hardened at Athena's approach. Athena scrambled to draw the sword Nasira had given her. Aksam. It hissed in the night. The pale reeve was almost within striking range.

"Lavinia Dove, at your service," the reeve said low and quiet.

Athena did not put down her sword. "Move away from Ruby Teach, if you please."

"Athena—"

"Ruby, step back. Are you mad? She's juiced. I can see it from here."

"Wait," said Dove. "I am what you say . . . juiced." She clenched her fist. "But I am still my own woman. You must trust me. You're standing on a—"her blackened lips moved as she searched for the word—"a river. You don't have many options."

Athena cursed to herself. Dove was right. And

Ruby—Ruby was just standing next to her, as if they were fast friends.

"Athen," said Ruby.

Nothing for it but to give over. "Fine," she said, and held out her hand.

Dove hauled Athena up over the railing with no visible effort. Providence, she was strong.

Cram and Henry soon followed, and then they all were squatting or kneeling on the little balcony, inches above the Delaware River, at the very edge of the Benzene Yards, talking to a juiced reeve. Athena's thoughts raced ahead. Why would the Swede juice his own people? What was happening inside?

Ruby leaned forward. "So tell us."

The big woman went still for a moment, her eyes glassy, her mouth slack. "Pardon?"

"They used the machine on you, haven't they? Swedenborg's engine?" said Henry.

She shook her head like a drunken mastiff, and her eyes came back into focus. "Yes. They did. Two days ago the Swede asked for loyal volunteers from the reeve ranks. Yesterday, the volunteers took more of us out of our beds." Athena noticed smaller things she hadn't seen at first glance: the cuts and bruises on Dove's knuckles, the purpling above one eye. Dove turned to Ruby. "I—the Void, Teach. It helps. I held on to . . . part of myself." She ground her teeth through the grin, lips twisted. "It feels so harmless, but something is gone. And there is a compulsion that's taken its place. I must fight it. You are intruders, so I am supposed to sound an alarm and take you, but I won't. I won't. It isn't right." Tears sparkled on her cheeks in the half dark.

Athena's vision wavered for a moment, and she blinked away moisture. The spectacle of this reeve—so strong, part of an elite guard, trained to endure terrible hardship—the sight of her so vulnerable and afraid shot Athena out of herself for a moment. No matter who you were, there was always someone who had suffered deeper wounds, who hurt more. She wanted to fix it, to make it right, and it made her deeply angry that she couldn't. The sword, Aksam, quivered at her side.

Cram's bag rustled, and there was a creak of hinges.

The boy produced a small, squat bottle. He popped it, and a tangy, herbal smell swept the balcony. "Here."

Dove took it. "What is it?"

"Well, the professor over there told me it says 'self-reliance.'"

The big woman sniffed it, then tossed all of it down her throat. She sneezed violently.

Cram's eyes bugged. "All of it. You took all of it. I reckoned maybe a pinch—"

The reeve's shadow straightened. Her breathing came more evenly. "That was— Thank you. I feel clearer. How long will this last?"

"No idea," said Cram.

"Well, we should get on with this then. Before the fog returns." Dove grinned sideways and held up her hand, palm first. "Thought grant us grace."

"Grace protect us all," Athena replied with a start. The words of the Worshipful Order of Grocers. This woman, this reeve, was she an ally? In the bosom of the enemy? Behind her Ruby smiled like an idiot.

The stout little door behind Dove remained closed,

and Athena's neck itched. "I will say that it is very nice to meet you, Ward Dove, and thank you for your assistance. But we're as exposed out here as a horsefly on a Clydesdale's flank. Might you invite us into the parlor? Then perhaps we can talk further about why a reeve of England knows the secret words for a very select order of people?"

Dove looked over her shoulder at the door, then back at the four of them. She shrugged. "I'm a Grocer. You're Athen Boyle, right? I know your father. I—" She blinked, then let out a long breath. "I sent the message that summoned you. To the colonies."

Athena was glad for the railing of the little balcony. The shock might have put her straight into the river. "You?"

Dove nodded. "When the Reeve got wind of Ruby's secret, someone had to tell the order. I—" She looked up at the yards, guilt plain on her face. "I can't help wondering if I hadn't what would have happened."

The shock on Ruby's face matched what Athena felt. Ruby put out a hand. "You saved me, Dove. Because

Athen saved me. If it hadn't had been for him, and these folk, the Reeve would have snapped me up clean, and all it would have done was get us to Juice Town much quicker."

Pride bloomed in Athena's chest. She had flipped Ruby's world upside down, and she had always wondered how Ruby felt about it.

Dove looked at Ruby for a moment, and some deeper tension, some shadow, melted away. "That was a gift you just gave me. More than you know." She shook her head, as if to rid it of cobwebs. "So I will give you as much a gift as I can. You need to know what you're getting into." She pointed back over her shoulder at the door. "It's madness in there."

"Fair enough," Athena said, "but we cannot deal with whatever madness you speak of from this little veranda. Perhaps you should let us judge what—"

Ruby interrupted. "I think what Ward Dove here means is that we ought to get the lay of the land before we go off half-cocked."

Dove raised an eyebrow. "What I mean, Sweetling, is

that you should get your chemyst here to summon you up another pair of river galoshes, and you should quick march right back across that water and down to Virginia or even to England if you can. When I say it is madness in there, I mean that if you go through that door into that fortress, I have no idea how you might find a way back out."

Cram licked his lips in the silence. "I think we should listen further to this fine young lady."

Dove grinned pleasantly. "Shut it, boy."

"Shutting it."

"Can you help us, Dove?" said Ruby.

"Help you do what?"

"Stop the Swede."

"You're mad. How?"

"You let us worry about that."

Dove took a deep breath. "I won't go back in there."

"Can you tell us what to expect at least?" Athena said as gently as she could.

Dove frowned and nodded. "The door behind me leads to the building we call South Wall." She sketched out a rectangle in the muck in front of her. "The whole of the yards is a square. Each of the four buildings, or walls, is built in a rectangle around the main chemystry floor, like the biggest box you've ever seen. Right below the Lid, like the top of the box, there is a latticework of pipes and walkways." She made a circle in the center of the box. The walkways all join at the central tower." She tapped the circle. "That's where Swedenborg's lab is. Stay off the main floor. Crowds of Juiced, and many of them soldiers and reeves. They won't listen to reason, only to those cursed talkers sealed inside their bandages." She ran her hand over her face, a few flecks of her own bandage still stuck there. Dove must have ripped the thing right off her own head.

Athena shuddered and forced a smile. "So, a frontal assault is right out."

"If you want my advice, find a way up through the buildings to the catwalks above. That way you'll see less folk. With all the Juiced working on the floor, most of the laboratories and offices are empty."

Ruby had a queer look. "Ward Dove, will you answer me a question?"

Dove snorted. "Why wouldn't I?"

"Was it you who started the fires in Boston?"

Dove looked at Ruby for a long time.

"You came to Fort Scoria to report that fires had been set by revolutionaries, and the fires drew all the reeves away, distracting them. You were that revolutionary, weren't you?" Ruby swallowed. "Were you trying to smooth the way for me to escape?"

Dove nodded, face drawn with pain. "Don't flatter yourself. You were a part of the picture, not all of it. The fires were meant to stir the unrest, to stoke fear, to drive folk to the idea of independence."

Athena looked at Ruby. Why would she ask that now . . . ah. She turned to the reeve. "Dove, would you do it again? For the order?

"Set Boston on fire? Why would I—"

"Not Boston. Do you know where the juicing shops are in the city?"

The woman went still again, as if someone had snuffed the wick of a lamp. "Yes. Yes, I do."

Ruby hesitated.

"Say no more," said Dove. "It will be done. But I need some things."

Henry opened his coat wide. Dove cocked her head in surprise. She knelt in front of the outstretched folds and ran her finger over the mass of hanging vials and bottles, then made an impressed grunt, much as a fishwife might at a particularly well-stocked stall. She plucked a handful of containers from the selection. "My thanks. The juice they take from folks is stored right there in sparkstones for transfer to the stockpile here. I can use the stones as fuel, but these will work as a starter."

"One moment," said Henry. "Sparkstone stockpile?"

Dove nodded. "In the vault below the chemystry floor."

Henry got a faraway look in his eye. "Stockpile," he muttered.

"Henry?" said Ruby. "Ward Dove's water shoes?"

"Sorry. A moment," he said, knelt at the edge of the platform, and began to craft a pair of water boots for the reeve.

Ruby stepped forward. "Ward Dove, there's one more thing we need from you."

"What is it?"

"Your uniform."

Athena was surprised at how quick and unquestioning the woman was, but in moments she was stripped down to her undergarments, a muslin undershirt and a set of surprisingly frilly bloomers. Henry, eyes averted, offered her one of his belts. She slung it jauntily over her shoulder and hung the containers from its hooks.

"Take care," was all she said, and then she turned and walked onto the river and out of sight.

The waste pipes thundered somewhere in the darkness.

"Time to go," said a voice.

Athena whirled, and Ruby was nowhere to be seen. In her place, under the flickering light of the doorway, in a reeve uniform that looked three sizes too big for her, stood a tall, fierce girl with a cloud of chestnut curls. The one from the bridge. The one from the balcony in Van Huffridge House.

Avid Wake bowed to Athena. "After you."

CHAPTER 26

These tools and chem belong only to Malachi Watson.
DO NOT TOUCH.
This goes Especially for Delilah Toots.
Especially.

—Sign, Benzene Yards, smelting shop #3

Athena didn't move when Ruby bowed. Instead, she said, "Ruby, you know what happened back at Van Huffridge House. Is this safe?"

Safe. She had no idea. A seething, pained rage coursed through Ruby. It was her way into Avid's shape, the part of Avid she knew the best. It shocked Ruby, though, how easy it was for her to unfurl its sails, like an untapped chemystral engine, suddenly blazing to life. She wanted to hit something. She wanted to hit something until it stopped moving. Ruby straightened Avid's shoulders and flexed her fingers into fists. The network of burn scars on her back prickled, puckered skin rubbing against Dove's too-large tunic. "No, it's not safe, Athena. We are infiltrating a nest of reeves, soldiers, gearbeasts, tinkers, most of them juiced." She looked down at the dusky sword at Athena's hip and twisted her lips into Avid's feral smile. "Use your tactical mind. We can't fight all the Benzene Yards. Our only hope is what my friend Ruby might call a sharp."

Henry cleared his throat. "I'm sorry, but it worries me when you refer to you yourself as someone else."

On her shoulder Evie growled low in her throat.

Henry and Cram exchanged a glance, and the tall boy held up his hands in surrender.

Athena shook her head. "This is of what I am speaking. Your control is flawed, and it affects—"

The rage fed her. "You do not get to decide, Athena. I will do as I do, and you can choose to follow or not. You're right, of course. This whole venture is the definition of unsafe. We could die. That is the wager, for all of us."

Memories clattered through her head: Avid's knuckles smashing into her cheek; Ruby tipping Avid onto the rocks; wrestling to keep each other alive in the hot springs; Ruby crumpled on the earth of the orchard, Avid and the other cadets fighting, to defend her, for her life. Avid was a reeve, but in this she and Ruby agreed. She had pledged her life to the protection of the people. "But better to die for an idea than to live for nothing."

Fear and doubt raced across Athena's face, but she nodded. "Very well."

"Then, as your people say, tally-ho." Ruby pulled the heavy little door open, and a blast of sulfur-hot air smacked her in the face. She ducked into the corridor beyond, her team behind her. A low arched brick passageway proceeded into the murk. Small, dim tinker's lamps hung from sconces in the wall, far from one another, creating islands of half-light in the dark. The walls themselves glowed with a slick, opaque sheen.

"Don't touch that," Henry said from behind her.

She looked over her shoulder just in time to see Cram

pulling his hand back from the wall. She gave him a Look. He put his hand in his pocket.

Ruby turned back and glided forward. The clatter and hum of distant machinery, so faint outside, filled the passageway. She could feel it in her feet, in her chest. A kind of constant, very low roar. And above it, just on the edge of hearing—

"What is that?" said Henry.

"Whispers." Athena pressed her lips together. "I think. Many whispers."

They inched forward down the dripping hallway, and every foot they moved forward, Ruby's dread grew. The pit in her stomach twisted tighter and tighter. The passage opened into a deserted laboratory, tools and artifices lying about carelessly where, Ruby assumed, the Juiced had left them. It was a long, high room, the ceiling thirty feet above. A wide, twisting metal stairway sat in its center, rising all the way up through a hole in the ceiling. To the right, two massive doors dominated the wall, each as wide as an oxcart. A smaller door with a leaded glass window was set into one of them. The four of them gathered about the window and looked out into a much larger space beyond.

Dove had been right. They were at the bottom of the biggest box Ruby had ever seen. The main chemystral floor was a vast open hall, hundreds of feet long and at least one hundred wide. The broad, scarred stone floor marched into the distance, scattered with the humps and curves of shuddering engines, pulsing with chemystral purpose. The sides of the box were two long buildings, windows looking down onto the main floor. On the ground level huge archways ran along the bases of both buildings, offering glimpses of a never-ending supply of workshops and smithies and casting shops. A massive brick tower shot up out of the center of the floor, into the "top" of the box, a madly intricate network of metal walks, pipes, and stairways.

The main floor was a hive of activity. Hundreds of people labored along long benches and around cages of scaffolding, hammering and twisting at all manner of metal and chem. In one enclosure, nestled between two clanking engines, a smiling crowd of workers stitched bandages and dipped them into tanks filled with chems, laying them out in shallow baths to keep them ready to wrap the next Juiced, nodding as their own headgear whispered them on.

Every one of them wore the chem-hardened bandages, and they all sported the twisting marks of the Juiced. Clusters of juiced redcoats stood randomly about the hall, grinning and watchful, and reeve blacks lurked in the distance, clustered around the base of the tower.

"How could this happen so quickly?" whispered Henry.

"You ever work in a salt metal mine?" asked Cram.

The chemyst shook his head.

"Well, juicing may rob you of your will and make you look funny, but it makes you feel nice, and at least you ain't get the black lung. Or get your childrens working beside you. Or get your hands cut off."

"But it takes away your life force, possibly your *life*. Don't they know that? Why would anyone just throw that away?"

Cram said, not unkindly, "You ain't hearing me, Professor. The feels nice part, I reckon, is just a portion of it. It's the money. If the choice is get juiced or get fired, or get juiced or lose your house, or get juiced or your wee ones go hungry, tell me: are you thinking too deep about what might happen when you *might* get sucked dry?"

Henry shook his head, jaw tense. "He's stealing their lives, and they're begging him for the privilege. How— Wait, look over there." Henry pointed farther back along the main floor to a collection of humps and hoses half obscured by scaffolding.

"Juicers," said Athena. "They're building more of them."

Ruby ground her teeth. All of the Juiced, every last one of them, was there because of her. Because of her cursed blood. Because she had left the Swede and his machine in Fort Scoria. She could have stopped it then. She had been scared, she had been blind, but she should have tried. Instead, she had run. Her heart raced, pumping the blood that was the cause of all of this. "This has to stop."

It came out so hard and heartfelt that the other three of them stopped moving for a moment.

Ruby stared for a moment longer into the yards. "Well, all right then. Dove was right. As Avid I might make it aways, but if we all even step onto the floor, we're lost."

"Upstairs it is," said Athena. "If anyone asks—"

"You are my prisoners. Cram, do you have some rope?"

"I do, Ferret, right here. What do you want with—"
She looped it about his wrists. "Ah, I see."

Ruby used an old trick of Gwath's to tie them all.
The bonds looked tight, but they were easy to loose if need
be. The others followed her to the carved filigreed base of
the circular stair. "I'll scout ahead. Athena, with me."

The two companions padded up the stairwell. It opened
into a huge workshop. Row upon row of tables covered
with intricate tools sat upon the scarred wooden floor.

At each table sat a bandaged juiced worker, weaving
wire and little chem devices into the chem-soaked cloths
prepared on the main floor.

Ruby froze, her shoulders just clearing the floor.

Several of the workers looked up.

She waved.

They went back to their work.

The room was completely quiet, save for the tick and
whir and clack of tools and the ever-present distant hum
of the yards.

Was it her disguise, even with her swimming in Dove's uniform? Or did they just simply not care? Could she pass through the yards with other people who *didn't* look like reeves? Ruby looked back down the stairwell.

Below her Athena mouthed, "What?"

Ruby hoped the look on Avid's face asked for caution. She motioned for Athena to follow and slowly moved into the room. The noise from the main floor thudded dully through a set of wide leaded glass windows. At either end of the workshop stood a closed large door. A brief thrilling image struck her: a picture of her simply asking one of the workers, "Excuse me, but could you direct me to Dr. Swedenborg?"

But it felt as if a spell had been cast upon the workers, like in *Bastionado*, when the evil chemyst has taken the hearts of the whole village. She blinked. It felt exactly like that. She, however, absolutely did not want to wake the villagers from their work-filled slumber.

Slowly, ever so slowly Ruby moved toward the door on the left. Athena, head swiveling and doing her best to show off her prisoner's bonds, followed her.

Henry was the next up through the hole in the floor, reagents clinking and rattling faintly despite his best efforts.

When he was halfway through, waist level with the floor, a cry of surprise and pain rose up from below.

Cram.

Henry whirled to look back, and then his eyes widened in fear. He cast Athena and Ruby a desperate look before he launched himself back down through the hole in the floor.

Cram yelled again, this time a scream.

The staccato pop of clocklocks filtered up the stairs.

Athena drew her sword, and they ran forward. Down in the lab Henry faced off a group of juiced soldiers, standing over Cram, who lay prone on the floor. That quick glance was all Ruby could get, however, because one of the Juiced—a tinker—chucked a glass bulb at Henry. He dodged it, but it shattered on the stairwell with a flash and a whoosh, and then something was rolling *up* the stairs and consuming them at the same time.

They scrambled back.

The something rose up through the hole in the floor.

It was a shoulder-high cloud of pulsing, molten red. It paused, quivering, at the top of the stairs, as if searching for someone, the edges of the opening blackening and sizzling wider. It quivered, as if it were alive, and then it hurtled toward the two girls, fast as a runaway horse. Ruby barely had time to blink before Athena stepped forward, right into the onrushing cloud of molten chem, raised her sword, and cut downward in a mighty stroke.

The cloud stopped where it hung, bisected by a line of emptiness. The sword had cut it cleanly in half. Through the gap Ruby saw a worker look up, vacantly puzzled. Then the whole monstrosity shivered once, flashed gray, and crumbled to nothing.

They rushed forward to the stairs, but the cloud of chemystry had eaten them up whole. Only sparkling dust remained.

Thirty feet below, Henry Collins faced the juiced tinker and two redcoats while Cram wrestled on the floor with a gearbeast. Red splashed the stones. Henry looked up once, quickly, and their eyes met. "We'll find you," he called, and then turned back to face the oncoming foes.

Ruby grabbed Athena just before she launched herself through the hole. "It's too far. You'll be killed. Or break your leg at the very least," she whispered.

Athena whirled on her, struggling against Avid's granite grip. "What are you talking about? We must! We can't leave them!"

Ruby tried to let Avid's rage burn away the guilt. "We have to keep going. We have to think of the mission." Then Ruby looked behind Athena, and what she saw chilled her to her toes. "Besides, I think we have our own pickle to manage." Several of the juiced workers had cocked their heads. One had her hand to her ear. As one they rose from their tables, grabbed something sharp or heavy, and, still smiling pleasantly, began walking toward Athena and Ruby.

CHAPTER 27

Treat them feet like your beloved childrens. You never know when you might need to ask 'em to help you out of a tight spot, and you want them dogs to still like you when you do.
— Jimmy Two Hands, hunter extraordinaire

Somewhere an alarm bell was clanging. That was the least of Athena Boyle's worries, however, as she faced down an ambling, amiable, juiced crowd, each waving the sharpest or heaviest thing from the worktable.

Without taking her eyes off the crowd, she said "Ruby—"

Behind her a door creaked open. "This way."

Athena lashed out with her blade at the lead worker,

whose gray skin seemed even paler under her black-as-night hair. The woman blinked and took a step back, as if a cat had just batted at her. She paused, puzzled.

Athena spun.

Ruby stood in the open doorway. "Run."

They tore down a dilapidated hallway; it was only moments before a hundred feet hammered the floor behind them. Athena cast a look over her shoulder; the juiced workers were pursuing them as one. And they were not stopping. Door after door sped by, and Ruby led them seemingly at random. A left, a right, two lefts, skip four hallways, ever deeper into the structure. Every time they came to a gasping, heaving halt, finally having lost their pursuers, a juiced worker would stick a bandaged head out of a doorway, mumble a call that the others somehow heard, and off they went again.

Up and in, in and up they went. Dove had said the Swede's lab was in the walkways connected to the Lid, and Ruby took every staircase they came across.

As they ran, the surroundings got richer. The floors began to acquire rugs. The paint stopped chipping. The furniture grew upholstery. Athena hoped desperately that they were on the right path. Ruby pulled up for breath in a smoking salon. "I—" She started to speak. But Athena never found out what she might have said because her eyes widened at something above them. Athena looked up.

There, peering out of a hole in the ceiling, was another Avid Wake.

The real Avid.

In a blur the girl above leaped at Athena. The air next to her ear whispered as Ruby launched herself at her twin. The real Avid twisted, almost too quick to see, and Ruby slammed into the wall.

The reeve girl's blows suddenly rained down on Athena. A knee to the stomach, folding her over; doubled fists smashing her back, driving her down to the rug. Mold and pipe smoke warred in her nose. She slammed her elbow into Avid's chest, driving her back. Athena reached for Aksam's hilt, but a foot slammed it back into place before it cleared an inch. Then an iron hook of an arm was around her throat, and a knee in her back, and

Athena was bent back and helpless, staring at Ruby just getting to her feet, shaking the cobwebs from her head.

"Who are you?" said the voice at Athena's ear.

"Just . . . passing through," Athena managed to say.

"Shut up. I'm talking to—to me. Who are you?" The arm tightened, and the edges of Athena's vision began to darken.

Ruby rolled her eyes. "Let her go. It's me, Avid. I— It's Ruby."

The arm flexed. All went dark.

Athena woke with a sharp pain in her head and seeing double. In an otherwise dark, close space a line of light shining up through the floor painted the faces of two Avids crouched on their knees, staring downward. One of them looked up, noticed Athena, and put her finger to her lips. The other one eased the panel closed.

Darkness.

One of the Avids whispered into her ear, "We're safe for now."

"What happened?" murmured Athena.

A voice on her other side said, "You tried to fight a reeve."

"Oh, Brilliant. I adore reeve humor."

"Avid agreed to parley."

Athena straightened and then immediately regretted it. Lances of pain shot through her head. "How long have I been out?"

"Only a few moments. Juiced were coming down the hall, and we got you up here."

"Ah. Well, then."

"Enough chatter. What are you doing here, Sweetling?"

Ruby blew out her breath. "We came to stop the Swede. You let us go at Van Huffridge House. You're hiding in the walls. I think you might want to stop him, too."

Avid hesitated. "The doctor . . . he—he forced Levi and Ever, Gideon to take the treatment."

A grim curse came from Athena's other side. "Ward Corson, too?"

"She . . . volunteered. They—Corson and the others—

guard Swedenborg now, night and day. I escaped. I found these crawlways. I—" Her voice dripped with shame. "I have been up here for two days. I sneak down for food and water."

Athena cut in. "Do you know where the Swede is?"

"His laboratory, on the top of the central spire. Where he keeps his kennel."

Kennel. Of what? Athena shuddered to think.

"Can you show us where it is?" said Ruby.

"Do you have a death wish, Sweetling? Did I not just tell you—"

"Avid. I *know* you. You—" Ruby cut off her whisper as the thump of feet trotted by below. Athena's heart was in her mouth. When the footsteps finally receded, Ruby began again. "Look at you. You've been hiding in this place for days. Days when you might have sneaked out."

"I can't leave! This is my only family!"

"Exactly. You are here because you are too brave." The voice smiled in the dark. "And too stubborn. Help us."

Athena's hand drifted to her hilt. This girl was ferocious. If she refused . . .

"Help you to do what?"

"Stop him. Shut it all down."

Avid's hair rustled as she nodded. "But first, you need to follow me."

Athena moved her fingers away from her sword. "Where?"

"I think I know someone who can help."

CHAPTER 28

When we tap the Source, we employ the energy of our souls. But it is the Will that directs it, that allows us to break the very bonds of the world. I shudder to think what might happen if that will was somehow stolen.
—Robert Boyle, *Principia Chymia*

Henry kept his eyes glued on the three men in front of him.

"Flasks down. Now," the tinker said. His yellow buckteeth poked out of his gray, black-webbed smile. He had a crystal vial aimed straight at Henry, a small hammer poised above the neck, ready to strike. A curly mop of hair peeked up out of his bandages. The two soldiers beside him leisurely reloaded their muskets. The screaming pain in Henry's shoulder told him that at least one had hit his mark. At Henry's feet the clanging and the frenzied, sobbing breathing had slowed. Cram had finally done in the gearbeast that had turned his back into a cascade of red ribbons.

"Flasks down, I say." The man's eyes flicked between Henry's hands, where the two flasks—one glass, one clay—were held. The muskets came up.

Henry chewed his lip. Battles were not his strong suit. Of the last two he had been part of, one had resulted in Alaia Calderon's almost choking him to death with her knees, and the other? Well, the other had burned down the greater portion of the forests west of the Susquehanna River.

The tinker's snaggle-toothed smile widened. "Kill them."

CLANG CLANG CLANG CLANG CLANG.

The alarm sounded from just above their heads. The men's eyes clocked upward, only for a moment.

Henry threw himself to the side. The shots tore the air where he had been. The tinker's hammer hurtled down and smashed open the neck of the vial. Jets of emerald foam twisted through the air at Henry and washed over him, in his ears, in his mouth, in his nose. He fell to the ground encased in a cake of green.

But not before he had indeed put his flasks down. Right at the feet of their opponents.

His throws were true. The last thing he saw before the acidic foam surged over his eyes was both the clay flask and the glass exploding into shards at the tinker's feet. He fired his Source as the green acid began to tingle and then to burn. His face lit up with pain.

But even through the swirling foam the gaseous *phaaaah* of the stone floor vaporizing under their feet rang in his ears, followed by the yells of the three men falling through the superheated vapor of what used to be floor. Far away Cram cried out.

The acid hurt. Oh, it hurt. He hoped they had given Ruby and Athena enough time.

The green crust burst away, and light poured in: light and Cram's face. "Professor!" he said.

Base. He needed a base. "M-m-milk?" He forced the word through his sizzling lips.

Cram disappeared.

And then white, a blinding amount of white.

A fountain of cool, cool whiteness poured down onto his face, down his back, across his skin. More and more of the stuff, a never-ending rain that covered him and washed away the chunks of solid acid, even down to his toes.

Henry levered himself up onto his aching shoulder. He blinked. He could still see. He looked down at his hands and arms. Terrible scars crept down his forearms just below the burned and pocked remains of his jacket.

They didn't hurt, though. He flexed his hands, felt at his neck and face. Nothing hurt. Somehow he had been saved.

Where the three men had stood, there was only a wide, oval hole. He pulled himself over and looked down. Twenty feet below, in some kind of cellar, three shapes lay crumpled and still.

"Nice work, Professor." Cram knelt next to him. The spice box lay thrown open on the ground behind him. He held a tiny white pitcher, a broken wax seal around its lip.

The edge of some lettering peeked from the side.

"Cram, could you turn that about?"

The boy did. The letters were written very clearly, in a precise hand.

Henry chuckled.

"What's it say, Professor?"

"Cram, old son, it says 'heavy cream.'"

Cram grinned. He tipped the pitcher up for a moment, and still more threatened to spill out. "Good old Nasira. What I want to know is how she got that much cream into that wee pitcher."

But he couldn't have read the label. He couldn't read. "How did you know?"

Cram's eyes were wide. "Didn't." He held up the little pitcher. "Didn't have time to dither, with you sizzling and such. I guessed this was the closest to milk. Had to take a chance and hope it was what you needed."

The alarms kept ringing. They were exposed here. Beyond the doors on the main floor someone would eventually go looking for those three guards. Henry tentatively got to his feet. His clothes were in tatters, and there were a few holes burned in his boots; but otherwise, he seemed whole. A careful probe at the musket wound revealed it tender but healed. The ball had gone straight through. He silently thanked Nasira and her box of goodies.

Cram tried to push himself up from his knees but gave a small moan and flopped back down to the floor like a newborn foal. He looked up at Henry. For the first time Henry got a good look at the boy's back. It was a ruin of red.

"Oh, Science."

"It—it hurts, Professor. Bad, is it?"

Henry's heart was in his throat. He told the truth. "I—I think it is."

He rushed over to Nasira's box, cursing himself that he hadn't taken the time to fully look through it earlier. Next to the compartment labeled "Heavy cream. For chem burns," he found a little pot of salve labeled "Stanchweed paste. Superconcentrated yarrow. Clotting, pain. NOT TOO MUCH." Right next to it lay a sealed paper envelope with "Napkins. Also for bandaging.

Keep clean." He tore it open and popped the seal on the yarrow pot. Something spicy filled the air, like rosemary and oregano mixed together. How much was not too much? Cram's shirt was oozing red, and he lay on his side, grunting rhythmically. Henry wrapped a napkin around three fingers, scooped the whole patch out, and coated it thick on another bandage.

He knelt behind his friend and put his hand on the boy's shoulder. He was shaking. "I need to do this quickly. There will be some pain."

"Do it."

He lifted the shirt. Henry tried not to think about what he saw. As carefully as he could he placed the poultice over the deep wounds running down the boy's back. Cram twisted and whimpered. Another torn bandage tied it in place. And then it was done.

"Cram, do you think you can stand?"

The boy shifted up to his knees and grimaced. "Less pain now. If you help me, I can."

"I don't think we can take your bag."

Cram looked at him owlishly and held out his hand.

Henry swallowed and nodded. He stowed the box in the pack and then pulled it over. Cram fastened his hand onto it with a death grip.

"You saved my life, you know," said Henry. "With the cream."

Cram forced a smile. "Nah. Just offering a cool beverage." He made a show of smelling the herbs. "Someone making dinner?" He looked up at the hole in the ceiling where the stairs had been. "Following them is right out. Where to?"

Henry looked about. Cram was right. No way they could make it up the stairs. And the main floor was suicide. But they couldn't stay here. With the alarms the Juiced would be on them at any moment. "We can't go up. Or forward."

"What about down?" Cram had hobbled over to the hole Henry had torn in the floor.

Henry followed him over, and his heart leapt in hope. Just past the three men—the bodies—lay the unmistakable outline of a passage. "Down it is."

They moved as fast as they could. As Henry lay flat

on the floor, it took all of his strength and all of his length, using the pack as a kind of harness, to lower Cram down to the top of a stout bookcase in the cellar, and then he followed. From there they moved to the floor. Cram leaned against the door, breathing shallowly, sweat glistening on his face. His pack lay on the floor, its strap clutched in his hand.

"One moment," said Henry. He pulled a brick of sandstone from the remains of his coat, unwrapped it, and tapped into his Source. He crumpled the stone into powder and blew on it. The dust whirled upward and bonded to the sides of the hole. As it bonded, he fired his Source, and quite quickly he had filled in the opening.

In the dark Cram said, "That was quite the trick, Professor. Do you think you could have lit a lamp *before* you did it, though?"

The tunnel led into a long series of corridors in the bowels of the great building. They twisted and turned at random, shuffling as fast as they could, brine and crumbling mortar warring for pride of place in the brick passages. Eventually dust lay deep and untouched beneath their feet.

They were lost.

"Alas, alack, alay."

"Cram?"

"Yes, Professor?"

"How are you feeling?"

"Well, scrabbling fire beetles are not trying to eat their way out my back, so."

"All right."

They stood for a moment at a crossroads. The passages ahead and to the sides seemed utterly identical. The distant ringing of the alarums had faded, as loud only as the constant dripping of water. Henry racked his brain. Cram's breathing had gotten more shallow, and he was holding less of his weight on his own feet. Ruby and Athena were up above somewhere, running or fighting for their lives. He tried to stay cool, like Athena, confident that the world would provide the answer to his troubles if he just pushed on far enough. But the friend on his arm was fading. It was a simple mathematical equation. Time in the yards was equal to an ever-diminishing chance of survival. It was—

Foomp.

"Did you hear that, Cram?"

"What?"

"Listen."

They stood there in the dim, both leaning forward, straining to hear the slightest something, anything.

Silence.

Henry sighed. Now he was hallucinating. Like seeing a mirage in the desert or—

Foomp.

"That, Professor, was a *foomp*."

A tiny flame flickered in Henry's breast. "Indeed, it was Cram. From the forward passage?"

"That was my thought, too."

"Onward!"

They crept forward as slowly as they might. There was no consistent interval. They were irregular, but the *foomp*s just kept on coming. Two more turns, and they were at a partially open wooden door, with just a sliver of light coming through.

Foomp.

It was a little bit louder now.

They eased through the doorway, the corner of a storeroom of sorts. The soft blue glow of older tinker's lamps kept it half lit. The ceiling rose twenty feet or more, and tightly packed, segmented rows of black stones stacked twice as high as their heads marched off into the distance, filling the whole chamber.

"Cram, do you know what these are?" Henry whispered.

"No, Professor."

"They're sparkstones."

"What, all of them?"

Henry nodded. A wave of dizziness passed over him. It was too big. It was too much. This much Source—it could power a city. Or a god. "I think this is where the Swede keeps his energy."

Foomp.

They moved as quickly and as quietly as they could down the aisle between the outside sparkstone towers and the wall. The room seemed empty, except that as they approached the other end, a few other sounds emerged. One was the crackling of parchment. Another was the scratching of a pen.

A third sound was a voice.

"Elfreth's Alley, UpTown: broken wheel on sparkstone wagon. Group twenty-two to the smithy." It was like a whisper, but as if you had freeze-dried a whisper and then cracked it with a hammer. Dry. Like desert soil. "All citizens in the yard report to the upper floors. Intruders likely headed to the Apex Laboratory. Subdue intruders, citizens. Subdue, if possible. If not, terminate. No cost is too high for your freedom."

Scratching followed, then another *foomp.*

"That's Ferret and Lady Athena!" Cram whispered. "They're still free!"

Henry and Cram craned their heads around the corner of a column of stones.

At the far end of the room a circular brick wall bulged out. On it hung a riot of pipes, like a church organ mated with a school of squids. The pipes ran into the room through the walls from all sides, even out of the ceiling, twenty of them at least, and they all twisted about one another to come to rest in a bank of circular slots, arrayed above the desk.

Foomp.

The person at the desk, all in reeve blacks, reached to open a slot and pulled out a capsule, from which they removed a piece of parchment. They read it, then turned to grab a horn hanging from a long tube that passed up through the ceiling. Into the horn they said, "Cancel shipment of cochlear apparatus. West doors. Focus on location of targets." They scratched another note and then put it into a different slot, which closed with a hiss and another *foomp.*

Cram and Henry looked at each other.

Henry made a motion as if to grab someone and wrap them up.

Cram made a motion toward his legs as if to say, "Good luck with that, fine sir."

Henry nodded. He carefully lowered Cram to sitting on the ground. He rushed forward, grabbed the occupant of the chair, circled his arms with one hand, and got his other over the mouth.

It was like grabbing straw. The boy (it was a boy) was skin and bone. He did not struggle.

Henry turned the boy about on the stool. It was the worst juicing he had seen yet. The grayshot olive eyes were almost completely clouded through, and the black veins formed almost a cobweb effect over every visible inch of his skin.

The boy offered no resistance, only stared up at Henry, mouth open. His tongue was made of metal.

A terrible juicing, an artificial extension to a withered tongue. Henry pulled his hand away. "You're Evram Hale, aren't you?"

The boy nodded.

"Ruby sent me."

A wide smile split the boy's face.

Foomp.

CHAPTER 29

Cry me, old river
Sit with me and weep
For the Company drowned me
Full nine fathoms deep
          —Benzene Yards work song

The pipe running along the crawl space thrummed next to her, and Ruby imagined its innards—some strange chem or gas or whatnot—speeding along to who knows where. Avid led them, and Ruby had no choice but to trust her. The young reeve had said they should follow the pipe, and so that was what they were doing.

Being near Avid helped Ruby stay changed. And it wasn't just that it was impossible to lose yourself in your disguise because your subject was crawling through an air shaft three feet in front of you. No, it was something about her fire. Avid did not doubt. She didn't struggle with demons. She had pledged herself to the service of her country, and that was that. Ruby had no illusions. Avid would turn on them in a heartbeat if she thought it would be better for England. Didn't Ruby have her own priorities? She tried to focus on the other girl's purity of purpose and drive away the fear for Henry and Cram that ate at her belly.

Avid froze. Underneath them came the now familiar tread of a juiced patrol. Avid waited until the sound faded, and then she fiddled with a latch on the "floor" of the crawl space, opened it, and stuck her head down through.

After a moment she hauled her head back up. "This is it," she whispered. "All clear."

They dropped down into the passageway. As they had kept climbing upward, the yards had gotten even more posh. Gone were the peeling wallpaper and knotholed wood of the manufactory rooms. They were at the end of a hall, in front of a stained glass window. Prosperous scenes of chemystral discovery and human progress filled its panes, stark against the night outside. The plush, expensive rugs masked the sound of their passage.

The corridor was empty and quiet, save for the far-off ever-present hum of the yards.

Avid motioned them over to the last door on the right. It was deep mahogany and boasted a vivid carving of a dolphin soaring through the air above the water.

They gathered around it.

Avid knocked softly.

"Enter," came a muffled reply.

Avid opened the door and ushered Ruby and Athena in, then followed them and closed the heavy door with a *thunk*.

The room was completely paneled in walnut. On the mantel above the empty fireplace hung a painting of a pack of hunting hounds, coursing down a stag. The stag was at bay, but two of the hounds were down and bleeding. A fresh breeze wandered in, fluttering the lace curtains of a window looking down on some square or another. A porcelain tea set sat unused on the sideboard.

An overstuffed chair faced the fire.

In it sat Wisdom Rool.

He was battered and bruised, his thick haystack of hair splayed out at all angles. He wore the remains of his reeve uniform, though it, like him, looked as if it had been dragged for miles along the sooty cobblestones of UnderTown. Heavy antimony chains bound his chafed wrists and arms into the thick wall behind the chair, as did a stout collar about his neck. Just out of reach, as if to mock him, sat a bowl of beautiful stone fruits.

Rool looked up, and the scarred skin around his desolate eyes crinkled, unmarred by any sign of juicing. "Well. Two Avid Wakes." He looked over at Athena. "That must have been confusing for you, Evallina Puddledump, of the Virginia Puddledumps."

Athena smiled grimly. "What can I say? I have been broadening my tactical reach. Perhaps you should think about brushing up, too? It cannot have been part of your intricate game to have been chained up and put on the shelf. You seem to have lost control of your people, your city, and your colonies."

Rool looked down at his chains. "It does seem that

way, doesn't it?" He peered at Avid and Ruby. "Though apparently one of the prayers I threw into the wind has come back to me in the nick."

Ruby permitted herself a small smile. She nodded over at Avid. "Are you calling her a prayer, sir?"

Rool's eyebrows rose. "Well, whichever one of you is Ruby Teach. Though finding an Avid in my back pocket is a pleasant surprise as well. Whose uniform is that? A giant's?"

"Ward Dove's," said Ruby.

"I hope she gave it to you willingly."

"Oh, indeed."

"Well, my friends, have you come to view my discomfort or to free me?"

"That depends. Will you help us?"

Rool smiled emptily. "Of course. Dr. Swedenborg has exceeded the authority granted to him. He has refused direct orders from the crown, forcibly taken the will of reeve, soldier, and citizen, and truly has just been entirely unpleasant. He must be put down. I would hope that we could postpone our own assorted disagreements until a date where we have dealt with this threat most dire."

Ruby summoned her finger picks, and she unlocked Rool's manacles.

Rool straightened his filthy uniform, glanced about, then tore off the chair's hardwood armrest. He tested the heft of his newfound club. "Very well," he said.

Athena hid a smile.

Ruby found herself grinning. For once she wholeheartedly trusted the man.

He grabbed a stone fruit from the table and bit into it, his eyes flicking to the ottermaton on Ruby's shoulder. "Let's be off. I assume you didn't come to see me for a stone fruit." He took another bite. "Though, please, help yourself. They are quite delicious."

Avid led Athena, Ruby, and Rool up one more flight of stairs and then through a trapdoor onto the roof. The great mass of the Lid loomed above, and below to the west lay block after block of UnderTown. A blast of hot air brushed Ruby's neck, and she turned toward the center of the box, to the heart of the matter.

"Science," muttered Athena, and Ruby could not

but agree. Like a great sea coral, like something living, a wall of twisting pipes, tubes, passages, and walkways lay before them, blocking their path. She fingered the hilt of her sword. "In there?"

"It's the only way. This labyrinth roofs the entire main floor and twists even up into the Lid." Avid was breathing heavily, her eyes wide. "He's in there, at the center."

Evie chittered in Ruby's ear. *Is she all right?*

Ruby had seen the other girl like this once before, in the Swede's lab back at Fort Scoria. "Avid, what happened at the fort? With you and the Swede?"

Avid set her jaw. "He was experimenting on folk long before you arrived, Sweetling. Let's leave it at that."

"Ladies," said Wisdom Rool, "if you could stop forgetting we are on the same side, might I draw your attention to something?"

"What is it?" said Athena.

Rool put his finger in the air, as if he were testing the wind. "Listen."

"What?" said Ruby. The yards had gone quiet; no sound of works or machinery echoed through the air.

Then she heard it: a wave of shuffling feet and hoarse breathing coming upon them from the rear.

A hand popped out of the trapdoor, black tendrils twisting about a thickly muscled forearm. Then another hand, then the thick, soot-stained head of a grinning juiced blacksmith. The four of them moved as one, sprinting back to the opening, forcing the man back down into the hole.

But there was nowhere to force him *to*.

The hallway below was filled with the Juiced, shoulder to shoulder so they could barely move. One of them, a thick woman with blackened teeth, climbed up the blacksmith's back and grabbed Ruby's wrist with a grip of iron. The woman yanked so hard it felt as if Ruby's arm were coming off, and she fell forward.

"Ruby!" yelled Athena, her face frozen in fear, a bespectacled Juiced hanging from her neck.

Wisdom Rool wrapped his great arm around Ruby's waist and pulled, and she screamed now in earnest as he hauled not only her but also three more Juiced who had grabbed her arm onto the roof.

They were everywhere, swarming out of the trap every which way, and every second there were more of them, twisting, tearing, grabbing, pulling the five of them back toward the trapdoor.

The woman with the teeth hadn't let go, and Wisdom Rool had ten juiced workers hanging from him. For every one he shook off, two took its place. The woman had Ruby by one ankle and then the smith grabbed her other and together they dragged her remorselessly along the roof back toward the door. Evie had wrapped herself onto the smith's massive forearm and was tearing it ragged with her teeth and claws, but he paid her no mind. Ruby struggled. She kicked. She cursed, but nothing worked.

The trapdoor was now so full of juiced workers that they couldn't get out of it. Just a twisting mass of reaching hands and grinning faces, reaching out toward her.

Then they stopped.

They let go. They cocked their heads.

And just like that across the rooftop they turned their backs on Ruby and her friends and silently filed away, without even a final glance.

Evie planted herself in front of Ruby and chittered triumphantly as one by one the Juiced calmly disappeared down the hole.

Ruby's arms and legs burned. Her breath came in great gouts. She felt as if she had just towed the *Thrift* into port by swimming.

Next to her Athena pulled herself to her knees. "I suppose we have some friend to thank for that."

Rool spit out something onto the slate roof. Ruby didn't want to know what it was.

Avid was back staring at the walkways. "In," she said. "Before he gets control of them again."

Ruby couldn't argue with that.

Foomp.

Cram pulled the speaking horn a bit closer and tried to sound as raspy as he could. "I repeat. All workers, and soldiers, and reeves, and anybody else, leave the intrudies and, well, just go your ways. Leave the yards. And when you're out, cut your bandages off, and help your neighbor do that, too, and take this voice outa your ears. Er, signing off, and you know, be good, be free, and Van Huffridge for queen!" He turned to Evram. "You think that's enough?"

Evram watched him as if he were a mildly interesting beetle.

Cram shifted onto his other elbow and dug it into the big desk till it hurt a little. It took his mind off the things that he couldn't feel: his legs, his back. "Professor, the intruders Evram was speaking of, that's milady and the Ferret we're thinking?"

"And us, Cram. Though it doesn't sound as if the Swede knows we're down here."

Cram tried not to glance guiltily at the speaking horn. "I think he might now. But can we get *to* milady and the Ferret? Can't be of much use stuck down here with all these sparkstones."

They looked at each other for a moment.

"Evram?" they said together.

The juiced boy stared, kicking his feet idly.

Henry cleared his throat. "Er, could you tell us how to get to the Apex Laboratory?"

Evram pointed.

Bolted to the brick wall among the tubes and traveling straight as an arrow up through a hole in the ceiling far above was a metal ladder.

Cram sighed.

He looked down at his legs.

Foomp.

Henry looked at him.

"I don't think I can, Professor." He moved his legs around. They were sluggish; he could barely feel them. The bandages squished at his back. More blood. He didn't tell Henry, but he reckoned that if the yarrow wasn't there, he might be hardly moving at all. Or in so much pain he couldn't think to move.

It was hard to look at the professor's face. "Cram, I won't leave you."

Suddenly the full weight of the thing hit him. He was a bloody pile of bones on the floor in the middle of tinker country. Far, far from safety. And he was slowing the professor down. He put on his best confidence face, the one he used for stealing pies. "You have to keep moving,

Professor. They need you, I bet. I think I can make it out the way we came if I start real soon." It was a lie, for certain, but no use telling Henry that.

The other boy shook his head fiercely. "Cram, no."

He changed the subject. "Professor. Henry. I been thinking. You know what you gave the reeve out there by the water? When she was going to set fires and have a go at the juice shops, using the sparkstones as kindling?"

Henry looked at him. Then he looked behind him at the thousands upon thousands of sparkstones. "Yes, Cram. Yes, I do."

"And do you think you could rig something up so that could happen here?"

"Yes. I could. But someone would need to spark it. To set it off."

Cram waited. Sometimes it was better to let folk work through something they didn't want to hear.

Henry got it.

Before he could say anything, Cram said, "You know it needs to happen. We need to wipe this place off the map. No matter what happens when you get up that ladder, this can't be going on anymore." His eyes strayed to Evram, sitting at his desk staring into space. "*That* can't be going on anymore."

Henry nodded. He held the tears back, which was really good, 'cause Cram didn't need to be starting any waterworks himself.

The professor laid all his remaining bottles and such out in front of him.

He began.

Foomp.

Athena tried to keep her sense of direction, but two minutes into the labyrinth she was completely lost. They twisted and turned, up stairways and through crawl spaces, down ramps, and under clusters of tubes, following Avid ever deeper into the dark web of pipes and walkways that hung from the Lid. It thrummed with some kind of vibrating pulse up through her feet. And occasionally, just at the edge of her vision, she thought she saw things . . . moving. She shook her head to clear it. She was going mad. Oh, for a bloodless tea party or to be bored out of her mind at a harvest ball.

Adventuring was starting to get to her.

For example, Athena tried desperately to keep her mind off the fact that occasionally, through the grating of a particularly low-hanging walkway, she could see that they were hanging in space, far, far above the main floor of the yards.

So she put her attention to other things, things that had been eating at her.

"Ruby," she muttered.

Her friend ducked under a crossbeam and then glanced at her with Avid's eyes. "Yes, Athena?"

"You are Ruby, right?"

Avid's eyes rolled in a particularly Ruby way. "Barnacles, Athena—"

"All right, good." She lowered her voice even further. "I'm worried about our other companion."

"You mean me?" Wisdom Rool rumbled from behind her.

"No, not you. Though someone should put a bell on you, you move so bedamned quiet."

"Thank you."

"I mean—"

Avid stopped in the middle of the passageway and turned about. "I can hear you, you know."

Athena sighed. "The whole reeve superhearing thing is just not fair."

Rool chuckled.

"That goes for you, too, Lord Captain. And yes, I am worried, Avid. I am worried that you might be losing your grip."

"My grip?"

"Ever since we have entered this labyrinth you have been, well, twitchier."

Just at the edge of her vision, just beyond a hedge of pipes, something was moving. Stalking them. "You haven't said two words out loud, but you are mumbling to yourself all the time, and you must admit you and Ruby do not have the best history. I need to know what your intentions are."

"What my intentions are?"

It moved again, closer this time. Athena fought the

urge to pull her sword from its sheath. *Play it out*, she told herself. *Wait for it. Let it think you are arguing.*

Ruby cleared Avid's throat. "Is this really the time, Athena?"

"We are going into battle, Ruby! It is exactly the time."

Avid swallowed what looked like a healthy chunk of rage. "After I saved you, after I showed you the lord captain, you question my—"

It struck.

With a hiss of escaping chem, a worm lanced in from between a set of tubes. It was as wide as Athena's waist, its metal underskeleton covered in viscous goo, and it moved as if it had been shot from a cannon.

Aksam cut it in half.

It fell to the walkway floor, quivering and hissing.

"Neat trick," said Rool.

Athena smiled. "Thank—"

The other one struck.

From above, so quickly, before she could bring her blade back up, and it slammed onto her face, strong oily flaps whipping around the back of her head. She couldn't get it off. She dropped her sword and wrapped her hands around it, and something was crawling on her arm; but the worm wouldn't come off her face and—

—she took a deep breath

—and she knew as soon as she did it that she was lost, as the worm breathed sweet beautiful calming vapor down into her and it started to take all the fear and anger and shame away.

Athena smiled.

There was a yip and a tear and a chattering, and caustic chemystral air rolled down her throat so she was choking.

And then she could see again. Wisdom Rool stood before her, the twitching remains of the worm quivering in his massive hands, Evie, the ottermaton, still tearing at one side of it, the bodies of four other worms littered about the passage.

One of the Avids knelt in front of her. Athena realized she was sitting.

"Are you all right?" Ruby asked, eyes wide. It was Ruby, she knew it. And Athena wiped the stuff from her face, and she saw there, around her wrist, the faintest trace of a gray tendril. It sang to her, to just lie down. To stop. She fought it with all she had.

"Athena. I am Athena."

"Well, of course you are."

She had to say her name over and over again, because that thing wanted her to give it all up. The fight, the fear, the anger. Everything that made her . . . her.

And to her horror she understood what she had not, about all the folks who had been juiced. It would have been so much nicer to just let everything go, to let someone else worry about it all.

Nevertheless, she persisted.

She stood up, and her companions stepped back at the look upon her face.

"I'm all right. But first I have an idea."

"It's ready," said Henry. He held out the improvised artifice to Cram and pretended he didn't see the boy wince when he reached for it. The poultice on Cram's back was dripping now, soaked through, with blood pooling on the floor around him, and he kept blinking, as if he were trying to stay awake. The thing itself was nothing more than a squat ceramic vial with a wax seal on the top. From the seal sprouted the tail of a long silken thread.

"Flick this seal, and the catalyzer will wander down—"

"Wander?"

"It's a technical term. It will wander down the thread. It should take approximately three minutes to reach the igniter and the sparkstone stack."

"And when it does?"

Henry blinked.

Foomp.

"Right," said Cram. "When should I do it?"

Parchment rustled.

Evram pulled down the horn. Henry leaped up and pulled it gently away, covering it with his hand. Evram spoke into his fist as if nothing had happened. "All yard citizens. Forgo any previous orders. Terminate the intruders. Protect your freedom to juice."

Henry let go of the horn and sighed. "I don't know

when, Cram. I don't know how long it will take me to get up that ladder. If anyone comes, you should do it. If it feels like the right time, you should do it. I— Trust your gut."

Cram tapped his temple. "Strategery." The boy twisted to get a better seat against the leg of the desk, and his eyes lost focus. He was looking far into the distance. Henry chewed his lip. This wasn't right. This wasn't fair. "Cram—"

Cram smiled, but it turned into a gasping, bubbly cough. "You know it's the right thing, Henry."

"I know, but Evram here, and—"

"You have to go. I'll be fine." He looked over at Evram. "We'll be fine. I'll flick the switch and then get Evram here to help me scarper out. Or you know what? Send me a *foomp* when you all get Swedenborg's goat and we'll all meet for tea in the river."

That's when Henry realized. Cram wasn't consoling himself. He was consoling Henry. The dice were thrown. The sparkstone trove couldn't be allowed to exist. The juicer machines couldn't be allowed to exist. Whoever controlled them couldn't be trusted.

They locked eyes. Cram smiled. "All right, Professor. Get up that ladder. You got things to do." He swallowed. "Take my pack, will ye? There's important things in there."

He took Cram's pack. Because Cram didn't think he would be needing it.

And when Henry took it, the taking somehow tore away a piece of him, too. A space, a hole he feared would never be filled again. Tears came. He couldn't see.

What do you do?

How do you leave a friend?

Henry hugged Cram.

He said, "You are the best man I know."

He climbed the ladder.

As he passed through the ceiling, he heard Cram say, "Now, Evram, you ever play whist? An old friend of mine, Winnie Black, taught me to play."

Ruby followed her friends out of the dark onto a wide stone circle, like a great clearing in the middle of the metal and chem forest. It was the top of the central pillar. About fifty feet away, at the center of the clearing, squatting like a spider with walkways and twisting passages traveling up into the Lid, sat a wide platform, strewn with the worktables and glittering glass of a chemyst's laboratory. A squad of black-clad reeves waited there. Among them a flash of fire red hair. The laboratory floor rested on a foundation of cages. Fifty at least. Each one held a comfy chair, and in each chair sat folk from all walks of life, some in the rags of the Shambles, others in finery that looked as if they had just found their way over from Van Huffridge House. This must be what Avid had called the Swede's kennel.

They all wore masks, and the tubes from the masks wound into a braid above the cages that passed through the floor and into a clockwork chair.

In that chair sat Emmanuel Swedenborg.

He waved.

"Hellooooo!" His high, lovely voice rang out across the distance. "I do so wish we could talk, but I am *so* busy."

A clear, pure rage took Ruby, as if she were waking from a dream.

"My people, please show them out! Forcibly, if you please," drawled the Swede.

The reeves surged forward.

And so did Ruby and her friends. The four of them pounded across the stone. Evie ran with them, coursing between the two Avids.

The lord captain of the king's Reeve leaped ahead of them with a great bound and called out, "Edwina! My companion! Reeves! You go against your oath! Your duty is to the crown, not to this man!"

None of the grinning reeves answered as they ran or even seemed to have heard. Ruby saw clouds of gas swirling about their heads. The Swede had somehow improved on his bandages.

"They are mine, Wisdom!" called Swedenborg. "And I so value your sense of honor. I will be absolutely tickled when it belongs to me as well!"

Rool slowed his approach and, smiling mirthlessly, rejoined the companions.

The reeves fanned out in a flying wedge, Ever and Levi Curtsie, Gideon Stump, Edwina Corson at their head.

Any one of the newly promoted cadets was a threat, and Corson herself was a match for Wisdom Rool. Avid would hold her own. But Ruby had never been the top of her class, and Athena—

There was a ripping sound from above. Just by instinct Ruby threw herself to the side. Something slammed into the platform with a scream of tortured iron and wood. A catwalk, torn loose from its housings in the Lid, reared up again like the talon of some steel insect. Another, and then another, tore loose from the catwalks above.

On his chair the Swede moved his hands like the conductor of some orchestra from hell, slicing down, and one of the catwalk tentacles swooped in to wrap itself around Athena's waist.

He moved his hand as if he were plucking a flower, and it lifted Ruby's friend up like a child's toy.

Athena stabbed it.

With a shriek of spasming gears the catwalk flew apart, and she landed heavily on the platform.

But she stood. She twirled Aksam and closed ranks with her friends. The Swede laughed, and then the true storm began. The catwalks stabbed down again and again. Balls of strange chemystry came streaming toward them. But Athena and her sword spun a web of cancelation, stopping the chemystry in its tracks over and over as slowly they moved forward.

Then the wave of reeves came down upon them.

Wisdom Rool roared like thunder and Edwina Corson growled like a hurricane and they came together so hard Ruby thought they might split the very pillar apart. They used no weapons, only their hands and feet, Rool ever questing to subdue his former lieutenant and Edwina Corson ever countering, stabbing with her jade-fingered hand over and over to tear the life from him.

For Avid, Ruby, and Evie, it came down to protecting Athena. Gideon Stump and the Curtsies were a never-ending storm of punching hands and kicking feet, flying around Athena to try to pry her sword from her grasp. But Ruby and Avid were a matchless team. They could have truly been the same person, anticipating each other's moves and coming to each other's aid. With Evie biting seemingly every ankle and clawing at just the right moment, they crept forward.

"Enough!" At the Swede's call the reeves fell back.

Heaving and ready to drop, the friends stood at the foot of the Swede's platform. The space about them echoed with menace; the next attack might come from anywhere. Ruby dug her toes into the stone of the pillar and cast her attention wide. This was no time for triumph. She braced herself against the coming storm.

Evram's hand sat kind of limply in Cram's, but it made Cram feel a little bit better.

It was quiet. The room was cool, and that was a blessing.

Winnie Black had been right.

Cram would have chuckled, but he didn't want to set off another coughing fit.

The woodswoman had named it true, back in that clearing by the gorge. "People like us, Evram." Cram gave Evram's hand a little squeeze. "People like us. In times like these people like us get smashed up on that forge." Saying the words opened up a kind of river in his chest. Sadness rushed out of it, so hard and fast it scared him. But he wouldn't take back no part of what he'd done, even if he could. He hoped Miss Winnie, and Cubbins, and Peaches were safe somewhere deep in some fern grove, dappled with sun. Remembering him. Well, it kept him warm a little. And slowed the sad river down a mite, too.

He reached up with his other hand and took the horn again. He cleared his throat, and then he repeated. "All city-zens in the yards, if you have not, pretty please proceed out of the yards. All city-zens stay away from the juicing shops. Keep going. Out the door. Leave the intruders alone." After a moment he added, "All city-zens should also take a goodly walk. And perhaps find themselves a nice piece of cheese."

Surely that was enough time for Henry to reach the labratory?

Surely he had said it enough times to get the folks to safety?

It had been a ripping yarn, it had. He had met true pirates. He had fought wild beasts. He had tasted that vanilly spice. He had mastered the wilderness. He had seen the city of the Algonkin. He had fought evil.

He had found courage.

He had helped his friends.

Mam would be proud.

He let go of the tube and put his hand back on the vial in his lap.

Covered in sweat, Athena gripped Aksam. Her spirit burned. It had been the fight of her life, and she had mastered it. A few yards away the reeves, battered and bruised, waited in a loose oval. "Four against five, Doctor. You can't blame them for failing." At her sides, the twin Avids readied themselves.

Swedenborg laughed. The mesh at his throat jangled wetly.

"Oh, dear. Ohh, dear, that is amusing." The Swede brushed his hair out of his eyes. "I don't think we've met."

"Athena Boyle."

"Charmed. Masterful blade work, by the by, and that is a truly impressive weapon. I am Dr. Emmanuel

Swedenborg. And I surmise that because of the changeable qualities inherent in one of my former collaborator's blood, one of these Avid Wakes is actually the tenacious Ruby Teach."

Neither Avid responded. Not the one on Athena's left, swimming in Dove's uniform, or the one on Athena's right, taut with purpose.

"My dear friend Ruby has always suffered from a kind of disability, however. A flaw in her character." His eyes skittered to Athena's right. "Isn't that correct, Avid?"

Avid's hand struck Athena's wrist like a hammer. Aksam fell to the ground, and Avid kicked it skittering across the platform.

Heart sinking, Athena leaped after it.

Behind her the other Avid yelled, "No!"

Athena never reached her blade. A walkway darted down from above and yanked her into the air, where she hung, motionless, iron bands crushing her chest. The Swede waved his hand, and a blast of pure chemystral energy flung Wisdom Rool up, slamming him into the

Lid. With another flick of the Swede's hands, the stone had melted and re-formed about Rool until only his head and shoulders were visible. Another walkway pulled the second Avid into the air next to Athena.

The Swede giggled. "Ruby Teach, you see, believes with the deepest of fires that who she is actually *means* something. That friendship actually *means* something."

The trapped Avid yelled wordlessly, limbs wriggling back and forth in Dove's baggy uniform.

"Avid, however, is loyal to a fault. She is a good reeve, aren't you, Avid?"

Athena yelled in frustration, struggling against the merciless bonds. The girl looked blankly at Athena as she stalked away, pausing a moment to pick up Aksam and examine it. The reeves parted wordlessly as the tall girl passed through them and crossed the yards to stand next to the Swede on his throne.

The Swede patted her on the hand. "Ah, Avid, my little poison seed sent into the wilderness to bear fruit." He looked up at the two clutched in the claws of iron. "Once we heard you had come to say hello, I thought it would be intriguing to see just how close you could get."

Metal screamed as he pulled the trapped girls closer, to hang helplessly in front of him. He leaned forward, as if to share a particularly juicy piece of gossip. His eyes did not glint with madness. There were no flecks of spittle on his cheek. And that terrified Athena the most. "We are on the brink of a new age. The people have chosen to give me their energy. It makes them feel good. They make a good living. This"—he waved his hand at the carnage around them—"is their will. You *never* could have stopped it. You underestimate their power, and mine, by geometric proportions. If I wished, the fuel in the kennels below me would allow me to tear Philadephi apart stone by stone and to re-form it in the sky, it would allow me to pull fiery rock from the earth and build a tower to Science a mile high, it would allow me to—"

Thunk.

Aksam's hilt crunched into the base of Swedenborg's skull.

"It would never, however, have allowed you to shut up," said Ruby Teach, back in her true form.

And then in both hands she took Aksam and buried it in the heart of the Swede's machine. It sputtered, quivered, and went silent.

Athena grinned down at the Swede's motionless form. "They switched uniforms. You self-satisfied gasbag."

Ruby grinned.

"Now could someone get me down from here?" said Avid, rapping her knuckles on the catwalk claw.

Corson and the juiced reeve rushed forward, the vapor around their heads dissipating with their speed.

"Stop!" yelled Ruby.

The reeves stopped, deathly still.

"Jump on one leg!" yelled Ruby.

They jumped on one leg.

"Sweetling!" yelled Avid.

"Sorry. Stand down. Friends."

And astonishingly they did.

A few feet away a trapdoor slammed open in the floor of the laboratory near the back wall.

Henry Collins, drenched in sweat, heaved himself out of the hole and then hauled Cram's bag up after him.

"Henry!" cheered Athena. "You're late! We've finished! I hope you don't expect applause!"

Henry ignored them all, taking in the platform like a spooked deer. After a moment he burst into action, sprinting over to a corner of the Swede's desk dominated by an upthrust pipe. He looked about wildly, as if their fates depended on it, and yelled, "For the love of Science, someone get me a pencil!"

Cram lodged his thumb under the wax seal at the top of the vial.

Foomp.

Rustle.

Evram's scratchy voice read, "Don't do it. We're safe."

Cram blinked. He very carefully moved his thumb away. He sighed. "Well now, cutting it a bit close, don't you think, Professor?" He sat up. "He better not forget my bag."

CHAPTER 30

FARNSWORTH: *My lady. Look in the sack. It's a baby.*
CATHERINE: *A baby? Please, Farnsworth. We are victorious.*
We are triumphant. But still there is the Mad
Baron to deal with. And Evil Cousin Jervis.
And that cursed pudding plague. Whatever
shall I do with a baby?
FARNSWORTH: *It is a baby tiger, my lady.*
CATHERINE: *Ooh, give him here at once! He is ever so cute!*
I shall name him Thunderfatch.
FARNSWORTH: *... must you, Lady Catherine?*
CATHERINE: *Thunderfatch!*
  —Marion Coatesworth-Hay, *A Most Tenacious Flame*, Act V, Sc. xiv

The sun peeked up over the horizon, bathing the Benzene Yards in the fresh light of morning.

Ruby rested her elbows on the makeshift prow, Evie curled about her shoulders, the warmth of the ottermaton's stomach fighting off the diminishing chill. With the help of a few liberated sparkstones,

Henry had crafted a chemystral skiff once the lot of them had escaped to the little dock, including the half-juiced reeves—biddable now that their chemystral ear devices had been removed. They had sculled on makeshift paddles past the city wall and out into the open water.

Cram was laid out, sleeping, in the bow of the skiff. It had been a near thing, but with the remainder of Nasira's herb box and a mighty Work of Spirit courtesy of one Wisdom Rool, he would be all right. Next to him sprawled the unmoving form of Emmanuel Swedenborg, unconscious, drugged to the gills, and trussed up with a bag over his head.

She would not kill him. Not yet.

A heavy cat of a man with a haystack of hair made his way through the crowd of passengers to crouch down next to her.

He nodded back toward Philadelphi. Fires dotted the cityscape glowing up out of the mouth of UnderTown and shining from UpTown like birthday candles.

"That your doing?" he said.

Ruby smiled. "Lavinia Dove."

Rool whistled in appreciation. "You know, I never would have thought it was Ward Dove."

Ruby frowned slightly. "She was a traitor to you."

He shrugged and sighed. "Stopping this . . . event washes away all manner of sins, I think."

Ruby nodded. "Is this the end of the war, do you think? Or just the Swede?"

"I wager that the carnage in the city will stop the crown's lust for war, at least for a while. Who can say if the French will follow their lead?"

They watched the fires for a while.

Ruby straightened. It was time, she thought. "Henry?"

"Yes, Ruby?" Henry called back from the front of the skiff.

"Are we far enough away?"

"I think so."

Given a bit more time and the Swede's laboratory, Henry had crafted a better version of his fuse, one that they could set off from far away. It had a button. Ruby pushed it.

The Benzene Yards erupted in light. The walls turned white, then to ash. The gray flecks drifted neatly down into the hole cut into the docks, as if the whole thing had never been.

Rool cleared his throat. "You have a talent for this sort of thing, young man."

Henry blushed. "It's really only the few hundred tons of sparkstones."

"Ruby!" Athena called from the prow. She was pointing at something, coming at them out of the mist.

It was a figurehead.

Fat Maggie.

The *Thrift*.

The refugees were taken aboard a strange jabberwock of the *Thrift*, half its old burned-out self, half a steaming, modern mechanism of gears and chem. At the rails, battered and torn, stood Wayland Teach and Gwath, and they lifted Ruby into their arms.

She searched the deck behind them. So many familiar faces, but one was missing.

Ruby looked back at Wayland, the first father she had known. "Is she—"

He nodded, stricken. "She held a mountain of earth and stone at bay until we could escape."

Gwath's eyes glimmered. "She burned herself out for us."

And then, right there, Ruby cried. She cried harder and deeper than she would have ever thought possible for her mother, great racking sobs that shook her like a doll. They lasted a long time.

Until, in fact, a voice echoed across the deck.

"I am delighted to see you all safe and sound, and I do not wish to spoil a family reunion," called Petra alla Ferra as she stalked across the deck, "but we fought our way out of those ruins and followed these men to a pirate haven at great personal cost, so I will ask you only one time, where is my *money*?"

The waves splashed against the side.

Cram cleared his throat. "Er, Miss Captain, we spoke with Thandie Paine, but—"

"She is imprisoned on the *Grail*," said Wisdom Rool.

"Yep, she's in the hoosegow," said Cram, "but she did give us this little vial necklace, and—"

Petra alla Ferra's eyes narrowed, glittering like a hunting hawk's. "Sam," she said.

"Um, really, mum, it's Cram."

"Cram, could you open that vial, please?"

He did.

Out of the little vial into his hand flowed a thin brown liquid that resolved itself into a very official-looking document. Henry took it, read it, and his eyes widened. "This is a letter of credit for twice your asking price," he said. "I hope it will suffice."

It did.

The *Thrift,* moving faster and quieter than ever before under First Mate Skillet's deft hand, headed south to deliver Rool and the reeves at a smuggler's cove not far from the mouth of the ocean. The reeves had slowly recovered most of their faculties, and Never and Levi and Gideon were shy, but Avid said they were grateful. Evram rode about on Gideon's shoulders. He had spoken only a few words; but he smiled at Ruby, and his eyes shone with wonder at Evie.

Edwina Corson smiled and gave Ruby a bow. "Well, Teach, you may not have made a reeve, but I am grateful to you for what you are."

Avid clasped Ruby's forearm in reeve fashion and then shocked Ruby to the core by wrapping her up in a fierce hug and whispering in her ear, "Call on me whenever you have need."

As the others were loading into the longboat, Wisdom Rool found Ruby sitting on Fat Maggie's shoulder.

"Teach."

"Rool."

"This is where I first saw you."

Ruby nodded, but she didn't smile. "In pigtails, playing the terrified waif."

He chuckled. "Not the waif now, for certain." His empty eyes flashed. "What are you, do you think?"

"You said it yourself. I am a fire in the field. Chaos follows me wherever I go."

He waited.

"It's true, you know. I won't run from it. And I'll use it for these people."

Rool smiled. "I know."

"So what will you do, Lord Captain?"

"Well." He counted off on his fingers. "There are cities to rebuild. Wars to defuse. Nations to build. I shall start there. And then, perhaps, have lunch." He looked at her a moment. "And what will you do, Ruby Teach?"

She smiled. "I think that knowledge is not for you."

He bowed. "The crown thanks you for your help in this matter."

Ruby laughed in shock. "For what? For all the chaos and terror that have come to pass?"

"Indeed." He winked. "We shall see each other again, Ruby Teach."

And then he was gone.

The moon shone full in a cloudless sky above the new *Thrift* that night, and a crisp breeze cooled the summer heat.

Skillet whistled a tune at the great new wheel, a masterpiece of sculpted cobalt and seven years' oak. As if by some agreement they gathered on the foredeck: the captain and Gwath, the crew, and Los Jabalís. Petra alla Ferra had pledged part of their enormous payment for the *Thrift* to take them back to Europe. There would be a vote among the crew in the morning. But for now they talked and joked. They sang. And then one by one they drifted away, down to their hammocks and holds. Gwath and the captain were the last to go, each with a hug and a kiss for their girl, until all who were left were Cram, Henry, Athena, and Ruby, sitting shoulder to shoulder, their bare feet over the side, with only the wind and waves for company.

Finally Cram broke the silence. "What now?" he said.

Athena sighed. "Eventually I will sail away to England, I think. The Worshipful Order may need a steadier hand. Cram, will you join me?"

"If we can first make a wee quick crown delivery?" At her smiling nod he said, "Then I will join you, milady. I hear there is good eating across the water."

"Indeed. Indeed, there is." She gently nudged Henry in the ribs. "And what of our great chemyst?"

"I have to go back, I think. To Fermat and Nasira. It's

home. And someone needs to figure out how to *un*juice all those people. It's a thrilling problem. Absolutely thrilling." Henry stared into the distance and chewed his lip, gears whirling. He caught Ruby staring, though. He smiled and pulled himself back to the present. "And Ruby? What lies ahead for you?"

Ruby stretched her arms above her head. "Well, Grocer or Un-juicer both sound brilliant, but so does pirating up and down the Spanish Main in a first-class chem ship. Of course there is still a mad chemyst trussed up in our hold. We'll have to find something to do with him. I'll have to decide at some point. But not just yet." They all laughed, and the talk finally petered out, and they lay there on the deck, the stars spinning, in easy silence.

She *would* have to decide, tomorrow or the next day, but just then Ruby looked about at her friends, there in the light of the moon and stars, and part of her simply wished that this one night would never end.

She scratched Evie under her golden chin.

The moon went down, and the *Thrift* sailed on.

Acknowledgments

Stories never really end. It's just that we stop watching for a time.

It's equally as impossible to mark where they begin. I sat down to trace back through the events and people that helped give Ruby and her crew breath, and I couldn't actually find a clear place to point at and say, "that's where it started." I don't think ideas—or people— are like that.

So. Thank you.

To my three parents: mom, dad, and books. To my brother, Tony, and sister, Julie, I owe my independence and my understanding that good things don't come easy. To the creative community at Penn that first lit the flames: Stu, Soren, Katie, Jeff, Colin, Yaz, Seth, Kenly, and legions more. To Moey, Karl, Erin, Josh, Carey, Wilder, Naomi, Mike, Kiersten, and all the other UCSD folks who helped me understand that if you break the right rules, you can summon something holy right in front of someone. To Fump and Matt and the Troubies, who taught me that true comedy is both physical and wise. To Finkel and Bennett and Brian who got this chemtrain running. To Molly, for conspiracy and space. To Janet, Kiri, Sharon, Maurene, Sandy, and Michelle. To Chris, for an understanding of True Science, and True Epic-icity. And to my improv and gaming families in Bozeman, Montana, where I have found joy and sanity year after year. To Sylvie, Tim, Virginia, Gina, and the miracle workers at Greenwillow Books.

To Valerie, for belief.

To Susanna, my champion.

To Martha, my sage.

To Anna. For my life.

And to you, who reads. We made this story together.